Venter has written a successful and movir
novel bursting with energy. – *Trouw (Hol*

South African cuisine, as well as the langua
country, all converge in a single stream of c   .... ~u~iu moments are
intermingled with utter confusion. At the end of the book the reader 'loses his life'
with Konstant Wasserman. *Ik Stamel Ik Sterf* is written in a masterly way.
– Murat Aydemir, *Het Parool (Holland)*

Ambiguity is present at every level of the novel. The religious symbolism of guilt
and penance permeates the entire novel. – Ludo Teeuwen, *De Standaard der
Letteren (Flanders)*

It is the kind of text that attracts me: dense, lyrical, moving. It is a book written
with integrity and careful craftsmanship. Although set mostly in Australia, it
confronts local readers with it's raw but also delightful reality. – Rachelle Greeff,
Rapport

The precision and perfection of Venter's rendering of the experience of return to
a village where one is well known, and the obligations and expectations of the
community and family are both suffocating and overwhelming. – Jane Rosenthal,
Mail & Guardian

Chillingly skilful. – Herman Wasserman, *Die Burger*

The psychological insight into individuals and their vulnerability reinforces the
humanity of the characters. The lush, virtuoso manipulation of the language is
more gripping than the relatively simple story, which nevertheless draws to a
moving close. Seldom in a narrative text has such a high level of tension been
sustained. *Ek Stamel Ek Sterwe* is an exceptional literary achievement. – Lucas
Malan, *Rapport*

My Beautiful Death

EBEN VENTER

translated by Luke Stubbs

Tafelberg

Copyright © by Eben Venter
Translation © by Luke Stubbs
Originally published in Afrikaans by Queillerie, 1996

Tafelberg Publishers,
a division of NB Publishers (Pty) Limited
40 Heerengracht, Cape Town, 8000

Cover photograph by Leigh-Ann Thomas
Cover design by Michiel Botha
Page design by Chérie Colins
Set in 10.5 on 15 pt Stempel Garamond
Printed and bound by Paarl Print,
Oosterlandstreet, Paarl, South Africa

ISBN-10: 0-624-04425-4
ISBN-13: 978-0-624-04425-3

FOR MY PARENTS

TO GET THE HELL out of here and make a life of my own somewhere else. That's what I decide in the Red Store, the corrugated-
iron monstrosity on the hill above the dorp. It's an old red, the
colour of blood, painted once and left to fade.

I arrive at the loading area behind the Red Store and pull the
bakkie up close against the buffers. A young farmer waits for his
order to be loaded. He nods in my direction, picking his teeth with
the corner of his receipt. I've never seen him before.

It's past two already, and the midday break when everyone goes
off to eat and have a little lie-down is over. The Red Store's iron
walls burn like hotplates. The roof crackles in the heat.

The store is laid out like a dorp: there's a main road that runs
straight into a mountain of lucerne bales. Side roads lead to a tower
of feeding pellets, a stack of lime, a pile of mealies. Black men push
loaded trolleys through a haze of lucerne vapour and a fog of fine
flour.

I must place my order with the clerk in the office to the left, just
off the entrance. It's suffocating in here.

Afternoon, Tannie . . . Ummm . . .

My goodness, Konstant, is that you? Just a moment, let me get out from behind here. I simply must get a proper look at you . . . Heavens above, it's been a long time. She starts moving.

No, okay fine, Tannie.

The rubber plant in her office is sickly, as if, like her, it's also wheezing in the floury air. And the fan on her desk is worse than useless. Her upper lip is sweaty. She's wearing pumps; no, they're slippers. Old bunny-foot approaches. The office door slips opens a bit then clicks back shut again. Looks like bleached magnolias on her dress: faded green material with a low-cut neckline. And a matching belt to give her waist some definition. Does she still want to be sexy? Even at this age? I suppose all women do – till the day they die. They really are something else. Ha! Caught her out: the belt loop on her left side is unravelling. Is that a Cyma on her milky wrist? She's still lactating, even though the children left home centuries ago. Here she comes. She's going for my lips. Determined to invade my space. There's a whiff of the Red Store with a tinge of rose about her. Shame.

My goodness, Konstant; no, it can't be. You don't look a day older than the last time I saw you. Her moustache whisks across my cheek.

If she's noticed me flinching, she doesn't show it. She's a real old flatterer. I shouldn't be so obnoxious – the old bag's only trying to be nice.

Now when was that, good heavens, man, what are you up to these days? I must say: you Wassermans, all of you, carry your age so well. Look at that mother of yours. Do you know, it was only the other day I was saying to Oom Giep when I saw your mommy going up for communion, I said to him: Giep, never in all my life would I have said that Mirjam has raised five children. Oh my, she always looks so stunning. And then your pappie, working so hard.

I'm telling you, boetman, that Raster Wasserman is one of the old sort. Real go-getter, that father of yours. Really hot in here, isn't it? Ah well, you get used to it after a while. But I must say: it's quite something today.

Tannie Thingy, hell, what's her name? Hasn't seen me in years. Won't ever forget *my* name. Obviously it's easier in a small town. She means well. I can't believe she's still working here. Suppose she can't find anything better. And she's probably dead satisfied here.

Where's the order? In my pocket. My khakis feel nice and rough. I make sure I wear the same as everybody else: bushveld hat, the lot. Blend in, fade away. Lie low and you won't be bothered. Pa's co-op number: 25311. In that Valbazen pocketbook. I wrote it all down – I'd remember bugger all if I didn't. Boarding school, a year in the army, three years at varsity: you forget what it's all about here.

Ureum tops the list. That's piss to make the cattle eat more. Could humans also drink their own piss to improve the appetite? Drink piss, get fat.

Tannie Thingy doesn't have to do much: just enter the order on her computer and wait for the printer to spit out a receipt in triplicate. Then she'll slide it across the counter and under the window for me to sign for Pa's account. And then I give the green form to one of the trolley men.

I wonder if any of them still remember me: kleinbaas Konnie, hey, but the kleinbaas, he's getting big man now, come, let me lick the kleinbaas's arse. What were their names again? I was never all that interested when I was small. They were no more than faces: the old ones wrinkled, the young ones still smooth and black. Nothing more than overgrown boys, the lot of them, Oupa Konstant used to say. Even though they remained nameless, they never looked the same to me. Not like the Chinese. Of course, they say we whites smell like corpses. The thing is: whiteys don't really bother about darkies' names. The trolley men should have their names pinned on their overalls, but most of them work topless. So where would the name tags go?

I must keep the white form for Pa and check that they load everything. Haven't brought a pen to tick off the list. Who gets the pink form? Mustn't forget to close the bakkie's tailgate properly. God help me if the thing fucks up on the way home. Can't even begin to imagine it: milk powder like snow on the dirt road all the way to the farm. The guy who's loading should get a tip. I bet no one ever tips here. The trolley men may as well whistle in the dark for it. The problem is: sometimes five work on a single load. So who gets the tip? Talk about over-employment!

Ma moaned when she saw me going to town in this shirt. Oh, Konstant, please no. When will you lot ever learn? It makes me squirm just looking at the trolley men. Though an old top like this is handy for a sweaty forehead.

Oh, Tannie Thingy has stopped nattering at last. I blurted out: no, I'm fine, even before she asked how I am. Bloody idiot! Why's she staring at me through the window like that?

So, Konstant, just say the word. What does your pappie want today? She shuffles back to her office and takes up her position at the computer. It's a blessing for her: less paperwork to flutter around.

Ureum, vitamilk powder . . .

What do you know about me, old Milkywrists? You're so washed out, I wouldn't be surprised if you evaporated in this heat. And your ears are so bunged up that you can't even hear me properly. Tannie should have heard me years ago, Tannie. Those days in the Free State Youth Choir; my voice was like drinking chocolate, Tannie. Hell, what balls I'm talking.

Look how busy she's pretending to be at that computer of hers.

Her back is turned on me, she's waiting for the printout. By the time she looks round I'll be gone. No more chit-chat – I've already reached the mealie-bags.

There's not a single rat in sight today. And this place has monsters. That I remember. You can scare yourself silly. You'll be going around a corner when suddenly you bump into one – right in front of you! Sometimes they sit bolt upright on those licking blocks. Delicious, salty licking blocks. Cattle really love them. It makes them guzzle everything in sight, only to get fat and be slaughtered – and then one Sunday after church the tongue's on the table, soft and pink next to a dollop of mustard.

Look out! Wherever you find a rat, the viper's brood is sure to be, Oupa Konstant always teased us. What do the snakes eat, Oupa? Albert wanted to know. Mice of course, Allie, dumbo! We often went to the Red Store with Oupa Konstant. Very often. Me on the left, Albert at his right hand. Or the other way round; makes no difference. Once we got inside he'd let us run free, up and down the aisles. The Red Store was heaven for a kid. Hey, Allie, you know what a dead man's hand looks like? Come, I'll show you: rub it over the cement bag, see, like this. The dust on the bag makes it grey. Here he comes Allie, mind the dead man's hand, mind the dead man . . . I'm telling oupa now, Konnie, right now. You're not allowed to play like that. Hey, Allie, check out this hole in the powdered milk bag, it's where a snake's been munching away.

Here're your papers, Konstant, Tannie Thingy calls from her office.

Where is the old bag's voice coming from? I can hardly see her through the clouds of mites. The thick air muffles her voice. Don't want to go anywhere near her again. I'll grab the order form and get going. Where's the man who takes the form from me? Where's the . . . Oom Piet Broeksak? No, Oom Piet Pockets, how could I ever forget oom's name? Oom's lame hand is always tucked away in oom's left pocket, the little albino hand that no one's ever seen.

Here comes Oom Piet Broeksak. Year in and year out, shuffling along between bags of crushed mealies. Oom Piet, the foreman, hand in pocket, eyes downcast, on the lookout for the enemy: man, those rats wreak havoc with my stock. Hope the Red Store bosses give oom a gold watch for oom's loyal service.

How's it going, Boetman?

No, also fine, Oom. And so on.

And: here's oom's green form, neatly into oom's only hand. I'd give anything to see oom take that other hand out of oom's pocket.

Youngboy, you old shyster, Oom Piet Broeksak commands with forced indulgence, come take the kleinbaas's order here.

Youngboy approaches and holds out his hand; Oom Piet Broeksak passes the form with his right hand then places it in Youngboy's.

Ugh! The place stinks of fish. Must be the fishmeal. To be transformed into disgusting chicken meat. Ma swears she'll never touch that sort of chicken. Now, let's inspect these mealies behind me here. That way I'll save Oom Piet Broeksak the burden of having to make small talk with me. He'll be amazed at how interested Konstant Wasserman has become in his stock today. Who you trying to fool, Konstant?

It's nice to rub my bum lightly against the sacks of mealies, gently, bump-bump, ah! luxurious bum. They're sowing-mealies, these: NOT FOR HUMAN OR ANIMAL CONSUMPTION. Each kernel has been rinsed in poison. Yellow death to any blue crane that pecks around on the fields. When we were small the fields were sometimes blue with cranes; today the poor things are almost extinct. Pa always fired warning shots over their heads to scare them away. He had a soft spot for them. Actually, for all his animals.

Still does. Old softy, old big heart . . . and what about his family?

Jeez, I wonder what it is with this dorp's old women, forever wanting to kiss you. I guess it's some diversion for the old girl here in the Red Store, a taste of my bachelor's lips. It really *is* dreary here. And of course, she means well. Like the boertjie outside there, greeting me without really knowing me. The women always wanting to kiss you! Men obviously just shake hands, that's all. If you're still a boy you can sit on your pa's lap. Then the day comes when that too passes. Just as well really: your bum gets too big anyway. Ah! But the rugby boys, the rugger men, they're allowed to throw their arms around one another's necks for the media shots: we're mates, after all.

If Tannie Thingy starts interrogating me again . . . I swear, I'll slap her. I swear. These people better leave me alone. I could hang around this pile of mealies – or go back to her office and talk another load of crap. Shouldn't be too rude, either.

Oh yes! Tannie Trainkie, no, Trynie. That's it. Tannie Trynie of Oom Giep van Straat. Strange how some names come back to you after you've been here a while, and others fade away. What was that army guy's name again, the one next to me . . .? I can see him as clear as daylight. A pale mug, always talking about how he shags his girl. I never believed him. Arsehole. Trevor? Some feeble English name like that. I can still see him pulling on his army boots. He had a flabby white belly, never firmed up, not even after all those sit-ups.

Wait, let's go closer, otherwise I'll never get away. Let's make Tannie Milktrain accountable for the Red Store's service.

Youngboy, in his string vest, walks alongside of me to the office and stops a short distance from it. He rests his elbow comfortably on a bale of empty hessian sacks and waves the green receipt at the white woman behind the window.

The days of arse licking are over. Youngboy sets his sights right past me on Tannie Trynie behind the glass partition, he's not interested in me at all.

Mies, he shouts, playing dumb, that ureum, he's finished, one bag there only.

Is that how we taught him to talk?

How can that be? Tannie Trynie sighs. Why does the computer say we're still in stock? Wait; let's have another look. She abruptly stops what she's doing.

In the safe haven of her office Tannie Trynie reaches for her glass of water, drips some sort of tonic into it and swallows greedily. Then she sinks again onto the piece of foam rubber on the chair at the computer and tick-ticks away, the epitome of efficiency. With as little effort as possible, she turns towards Youngboy. Only her left shoulder moves slightly backwards, and her head and neck even less, so that her left eye, surely out of focus, barely rests on Youngboy.

Twenty-four bags of ureum, she reads out: twenty-four, Youngboy. There should be twenty-four. Are you people seeing things in halves again?

Youngboy, still leaning on his elbow against the hessian bags, ignores her.

Well, she says, give the kleinbaas what there is. Then she turns around to me fully, so that only her right arm stays on the desk.

And I recognise the collusive look: oh, fellow citizen of the race, you have to agree that *they* are simply beyond redemption. They're born idle, and they'll die idle, every one of them.

Listen Konstant, man, I'm really sorry. You'll just have to tell your pappie that we don't have enough ureum in stock right now. I don't understand it. She struggles up: bring that form here and I'll change it for you.

Skin folds around her elbow as she rests it on the counter. Will mine also become loose like that one day? Tired-out old skin all puckered up around her funny bone. I swear she's read my mind. One mustn't underestimate her.

And tell me Konstant, have you come back to farm? Come to help your pappie out a bit? You know, honestly: he deserves a bit of a break.

Where's she coming from now?

You know, that man has worked himself to the bone for you lot. Keeping you going at varsity and all. I've thought that about your father for a long time now. No, really, it's your turn to give him a bit of a breather now. The Lord hear me. And she shoves the receipt across the counter, her eye fixing mine.

She doesn't stop. She simply *will* not stop. Oh really, Tannie Trynie, what are you on about now? What the hell did you say there? You don't know me. I can feel it. I can feel it coming. A blaze of fire burning my forehead, a violent heat overwhelming me.

Dear heavens, Konstant, you look like my turkey . . .

I see my own earlobes glowing, my neck too. My beard stubble stands erect. Prickly pear thorns. I can't see you any more, Trynie, you're floating behind glass on vapours of flour. Can you hear my gasps, Trynie?

Bu . . . bu . . . you won't do anything silly, will you . . . Konstant?

I will, Trynie, I will! See my hands pressing against your window? See your sagging cheeks tremble! No, your office door is not locked. A creature of habit, you always lock it. Not today, though. Thought you could trust me with your life in the hands of the Dear . . .

I can't look at her any more. At that straggly, wispy hair. Look down, down: no need to look her in the eye. Down, still lower, the counter's grain is worn down, smooth to the touch.

And what the hell has it got to do with you, T-T-Trynie Fuck-ing-van-Straat, I finally manage to get it out. Wish I didn't stutter. Gives me away every time. Where's my receipt?

Good one! Green gob on her step. She can be grateful it wasn't against her window. Should I go? I, I, truly: I must do it. Must get away from here. It's high time. Now or never. Away from this part of the world, this country. For good. The time has come. I must decide. Just give me a another moment. Hanging around is the thief of time.

Have to get back to the loading area; my stuff is probably there already. I've got the receipt. My body is sopping – slippery cus-tomer. I grab the receipt and go.

Who's this now? It's Oom Dirk, Oom Dirk Plaasdam's pulled into the loading area. Oom Dirk who's always complaining about the state of his farm dam.

I can't talk to oom today, sorry, oom, I know oom's eyes are pure compassion. Known us since childhood.

Hello, Konstant, dear heavens, can't I give you a hand there, Konnie, looks to me you're in a state.

Probably, Oom, probably just a fever or something. Bye, Oom.

Shove off, Oom Dirk. My keys? Okay. No, I know the ureum is finished, I say to one of the guys loading. Okay, everything in, tailgate closed.

I must go, Oom Dirk.

Well, give my regards to old Raster – he's my old mate, that pa of yours. And to your beautiful mother. And drive carefully.

Drive carefully my arse. I'm driving like the devil today. Sorry about the dust, oom, my screw's loose, oom. I'll give oom a ring tonight and apologise, oom's not a bad oom, oom.

What's got into him now? He shakes his fist at me in the rear-view mirror. Ag, you go to hell, Oom Dirk Droppings. Just because

I'm younger you expect a yes-oom, no-oom business from me. That's asking too much. Remember, it's you old guys who taught your sons to become as angry as you are. And in any case, why did that bloody Trynie have to mess with me? I don't care what I said: I don't give a damn about any of it – not now, not ever. These people must learn to think before they speak. Trynie got on my nerves, and I came unhinged. What's it got to do with her whether I come farming, whether I ever farm in my whole life, whether I come to help my pa and all that shit? What the fuck has it got to do with her? That's what I want to know. Who gives her the right to interrogate me: your pappie's worked hard for you lot . . . Jeez, she's lucky I didn't slap her.

Open the windows, I'm still smouldering. Where're my cigarettes? I don't give a damn. Today I'm using the ashtray in Pa's bakkie. He can also go to . . . sorry, Oom Dirk, I've got nothing against you, but you must realise that all people are not always the same. I must get away from here. Really and truly. I don't belong here. They're not my people, these. Away? Five bags of ureum, four bags of feed, fucking hell! What am I still *doing* here? Your pappie has worked hard for you . . . Pappie, of all things. I ask you: whose pappie? She can go fuck herself, man. This is the last straw. Tonight. I'm going tonight. All my life I've wanted to get away from here. I'm telling them tonight that I'm off. I've made up my mind. Tomorrow I'll catch the train, bag and baggage and all, and be gone for good. They won't believe their ears.

It'll be hard to tell them about my decision. When? At supper? But then the meal goes to pot for everyone, man, for me too. Your food sticks in your gullet. Maybe after supper. Albert will also be shocked. I know he's got some or other scheme planned for the two of us. Wasserman Bros. and Co. And Ma? I hope she doesn't cry. She probably will. A bladder behind her eyes, not so, Oupa Konstant? You knew. Ma will just have to deal with it. Tonight or never. It's my life after all. Can't stay here a day longer: honestly, there'll be nothing left of me.

We're having braised meat for supper. Lamb chops, browned on the stove and then left to simmer with a dash of water until tender and smooth like marrow. Braised meat with white rice, boiled potatoes for Pa. And a cucumber salad with pepper and grape vinegar.

I'm hungry. I'll wait until everyone's taken a toothpick from that silver goblet. It's not on the table. Who gave it to Ma? Can't remember. Anyway, who gives a damn what idiot trundled along here with the thing? I'll wait until after supper, or the food will be spoilt for everyone. Until after supper, then I'll say: I'm leaving this farm like the rotten shit I am.

Can't get rid of my thirst: it's all that sweating this afternoon. I'm onto my third beer, tonight no one's saying a word about it – Albert and I usually only drink two in the evening, at most three on a Saturday when we're braaiing and we've got visitors. Not counting the one or two you quietly pinch from the pantry when you fetch more. That's reward for your labour, Albert reckons. Clever dick.

I get up to fetch my fourth beer, and my father says: At this rate you'll drink me dry tonight. Is this *really* necessary, Konnie? You guys will have to think about contributing to the kitty yourselves if you want to drink so much.

I don't look at him, but at my mother. She's stopped eating without finishing her meal. She scrapes the remains from her Queen's Green plate into a pudding bowl and asks Tilla to pass the gravy boat. Ever so slowly she drips the meaty gravy over the cat's supper. The lamp sheds a glow over her smoothly combed hair, the French roll Pa likes so much. And under the table I feel Ketjoerts's luxurious fur electrically charging the hair on my calves. He's impatient for his share of stew and gravy. There are still people about outside. They're seeing to the milk buckets. The curtains, made from thick material to give a heavy drop, dampen most of the sounds.

I know my mother only too well. Even though there's still food on her plate, she has stopped eating. She knows something is in the air. It's highly unlikely that old Trynie admitted to my mother, when she phoned late this afternoon, just how much *she* had pestered *me*: No, Mirjam, I can't imagine what went wrong with that son of yours. Apparently the old bitch couldn't even bring herself to mention my name. I have become unmentionable.

Trynie complained to Ma that she had to steady herself with a tot of brandy when she got home. And you know yourself how appallingly hot it's been today, Mirjam. No, I've never seen your son behave like that before. Always seemed such a lovely boy to me, so polite, and that's the way I've come to know all your children, Mirjam. Something suddenly snapped, it seemed, and he let fly at me, oh, so very horribly. No respect at all. Believe it or not, Mirjam, he even called me by my name, just like that. I know that's not how you and Raster raised him – though your old man *does* get all fired up sometimes, I've seen him angry once or twice myself, hope you don't mind my saying so . . .

So what went wrong? Ma's been on at me for an explanation the whole time.

I haven't said. I know that's the way people are here: they twist a story to suit themselves. Ma's obviously noticed something's up. Yes, I *am* sorry for her, but I refuse to brood over it now. Otherwise I'll never get round to telling them what I've decided – let alone actually ever getting away. And Pa? If only he could provide some comfort in my present state, but all I get from him is: Why is the bakkie's ashtray so filthy, and why are you drinking like a fish tonight, and when on earth are you going to get married, there're such lovely girls around here – so that we Wassermans can plant our seed, hell, life doesn't stand still, you know. Remember, our family comes a long way and we've always been richly blessed. No chance! I want to get as far away from him as possible.

I say what I need to say. A sentence that has grown stale in my mouth from repeated silent practice. Shit scared, but utterly determined I say: Well, Pa and Ma, I just want to say that I'm leaving tomorrow. By train. I've thought about it very carefully. I want to go and see what the big wide world looks like out there. I'll be trying to get a residence permit for Australia.

Well, well. The big wide world. Really? No matter how hard I try, I can't get rid of the tremor in my voice. The problem is: one gets so few opportunities to say this kind of thing. Maybe I'll become more adept once I'm living across there somewhere.

Well then, Konstant, you must do whatever makes you happy – and my father moves his chair back and gets up. Remember, if you leave here like this, you go without your father's blessing, and then he looks at Ma and has the gall to speak for her too: you also leave without your mother's blessing.

And her tears start flowing.

Everyone is present on the station platform, each prepared with a last word of wisdom for me which they hold back until I board the train and lean out of the window. Only Tilla and Mirjampie chatter away and race around and exhaust themselves bumping into suitcases and boxes of things and blankets rolled up with belts, belonging mostly to the black passengers. Behind the peppercorn tree at the disused milkcan depot they play hide-and-seek.

Konstant! The peppercorn! says Albert pointing to its delicate pink and poor-man's-green. He's remembered it's my favourite tree.

And adds: what the heck, I suppose you'll see them again – somewhere in Australia.

My father puts my box of padkos down, looks at it lying on the tar platform, pushes the thing with the tip of his velskoen, one of his fancier kudu-leather pairs, picks it up again, balances it in his hand for a moment and holds it out to me. I'm not ready to accept it yet, and he moves back a step without taking his eyes off me. I don't look directly at him. He fiddles with his white hanky. It's always an almighty affair, this nose-blowing of his, though today it's a sniffle in the wind, and that's that.

So is this first class, then? my mother wants to know. They say the pillowcases and sheets in second class are filthy – black curlies wherever you look and lie.

Even Pa insisted that I buy first class:

No. Definitely not. Decent folk don't go second class these days. Yet he wouldn't contribute a cent to the train ticket nor to an overseas flight.

It's not that I don't care about you, he reassured me, but when a man holds out such great prospects for himself, he'd best make his own way. Oom Dirk told me exactly how rude you were when you left the Red Store. Here, take *this* along, he said last night when he walked past my and Albert's room where I was packing – and he stuffed a packet of razor blades into my hand.

Ma holds my hand through the train window, flattens my fingers out on hers, tries to say something she can't, pulls me closer towards her and stands on tiptoe to embrace me with all her heart, then lets me go again and looks down the platform: Hester, call those sisters of yours so they can say goodbye to their brother, the train's leaving now, it'll be gone before you know it! Have you got everything, Konnie? And have a happy birthday tomorrow. Oh, Ma's heart is so very sore that you won't even be with us on your birthday. And let us know how things go with the visa and the overseas ticket, and write to us, don't go off and forget about us completely.

We're still your father and mother, you know, Konstant, doesn't matter what happens, and happy birthday for tomorrow, and my father stuffs his hanky back in his pocket. He doesn't expect a reply. The window next to mine is closed, and its springbok emblem is clearly visible.

Why's this train taking so long to move? I must get away, clear out, beat it, *now*. Pa could've contributed something towards my tickets. He really could have. I hope I've still got enough money left over. Oh well, I'll be okay – if he'd wanted to, he could have paid for both my tickets. He's got more than enough money. Beat it! It's like voertsek. I'm leaving this place like a dog. To dig my own hole. Maybe it's just as well.

Do you have any idea where you'll stay in that big city? my mother asks. I'm only aware of her voice. The parting is so awful that my other senses have switched to automatic go-slow.

And Pa: a slum, that whole bloody city. Sodom, if you ask me. Even if you paid me, I'd never go anywhere near the place.

Will he *ever* bloody stop? I'm glad he hasn't paid for anything. Honestly, it's much better this way: at least I stay independent. As soon as money comes into the picture you have to be accountable to them. You can't give without something being expected in return. Which is totally contrary to the . . . What the hell, drop it. I don't have the energy to think about it. I'll torment my soul for no good reason. I wish this bloody train would get a move on now. Where are Tilla – and Mirjampie? They can't even be bothered to come and say goodbye.

Has Hester gone to look for Tilla and Mirjampie? I ask.

Excuse me, sir, I just need to come past, a woman says behind my bum.

Pa stands on tiptoe to peer down the narrow passage and into my compartment.

Are there lots of coloureds here in first class? he wants to know.

What difference does it make, Pa?

I'm only asking, for heaven's sake. There's no need to bite my head off like that. Tell me Konstant, when will you get a chance to talk to me again? Just tell me that?

See! That's exactly what the people here do. Any baboon knows *they* are the ones being ridiculous, but say a word and they turn the whole thing around and make out as if *you're* the one who's crossed the boundaries, *you're* the one who's suddenly all wrong. You can't defend yourself against people like that. Best just shut up. Oh, I know these people. No one knows them better than I do. As soon as this train moves, I'll take my seat across the way and scrape every last piece of dust from my soles. I swear.

From the moment my foreskin was cut, Pa's been messing me around. I'm finished with it. That'll be the day, sonny – I knew he'd say it. Well: now I'm telling you, Pa – the moment this train moves, I'm out from under your wings for good. Besides, lots of things are beyond your control these days. They take photos of our daughters these days – naked, right in front of the Voortrekker Monument! Did you know that, Pa? And anything could happen on this train tonight. There's no more stopping, just like my decision, no more stopping, no more stopping now. This train is taking me away. Bugger off, traitor. Go to hell.

Somewhere ahead, invisible to the circle of my family on the platform, the conductor blows his whistle and the sound ricochets back to us.

Albert. Dear old Albert. See how he hugs himself. It's a tragedy, he kept saying last night. A tragedy.

I don't even know where I'll stay in Johannesburg. That's the biggest tragedy.

Konstant, Albert calls out, Konnie.

Hester's yellow polka-dot dress rushes up between the people on the platform. Our two crazy little sisters are still nowhere to be seen. Konnie, she screeches, wait for me . . . I want to give you a hug.

Trains don't wait for anyone, says Pa. He stretches out his hand and shakes mine through the window. And all he's able to give me is: Don't forget what you've learnt here, son, and don't turn your back on us. I hope you'll drop all this nonsense of yours on the other side and come back one day. Come back like the Konstant Wasserman we all know.

Be careful, Hester. Please! Ma shouts.

The train starts rolling and Hester swings from my neck like a yellow finch on a reed, her saltiness wiped all over my cheek.

Hester, come away from there, accidents happen before you know it, you don't play around with trains, my mother screams again. She's getting very anxious. Whiffs of the perfume on her skin linger at my window.

As the train moves past the peppercorn, Tilla and Mirjampie storm out from behind its trunk, and I couldn't have hoped for a better farewell. Konnie, it's us, Tilla shrieks as she runs alongside the train holding out a branch from the tree, laden with red berries. Konnie, Tilla and Mirjampie shriek together, goodbye, stay well, and they wave kisses at me, their teeth shiny with spit. Konnieee they yodel until the train takes the turn around the bend.

Tilla, Mirjampie, I cry, my mouth as wet as my eyes.

At the bridge over the spruit I get a view back across the dorp. The late afternoon sky opens up ahead of me. Two crows, squawking and triumphant all at once, circle up in free flight against the apricot clouds and the translucent blue of the sky.

I can still smell traces of Ma, or is it Hester? What does she wear again? She told me to bring her some Chanel lipstick when I come back. So it wasn't too bad after all, the departure. I'd expected Pa to behave the way he did. So what? I've survived many farewells before. All in the past and done with now – and not worth raking up ever again.

Except the one time Pa's eyes got all teary, the time I went to the army. Maybe he was sozzled? First all the usual stuff: Take care of yourself, Konstant, and so on and so on. Then: This is your big chance, man, make the most of it, the army will make a man of you. Oh! For fuck's sake, Pa, what do you know about me? Without a shirt upon my back, at least I'm on my happy track – and free from your sjambok. What's old Konnie up to now? Who knows? Only Ma and me. She looked so sad. Her children: that's all she lives for, not for Pa. Oh well, I suppose she lives for him too. She certainly listens to him. Dances to his tune. And Albert. It was really sad saying goodbye to him; but then he's also totally in cahoots with that family. Never says what he really thinks. Real two-faced bastard. That's what makes me so the hell in with him. And if I ever confront him about it, all he says is: I know who I am, and I know what I think. Yet he never spells it out. Poor bugger – he can't really help it: doesn't want to bite the hand that feeds him. I'm the only one who ever opens my mouth. Sometimes. And Pa, I must give him credit where it's due, he says exactly what he feels, whenever and however he likes. Consistently. And that's not necessarily altogether noble. If Adolf had been a little *less* consistent, fewer of Abel's offspring would have landed in hellfire. Man, he doesn't even want to keep a sliver of hope alive for me. That's what makes me so . . . Wonder whether he could ever squeeze out any feeling at all? Suppose he could, but doesn't know how. The only thing he values about me is my prick. He needs it to keep the family – I mean the family tree – going.

Multiply and fill the earth. Actually, he means more than that. It's a question of two birds with one stone. Somewhere at the back of his head there's also an outnumbering, an out-whiting of the blacks. Surely he must realise it's hopelessly naive. Still, I guess it's one of his unexpressed hopes, like the one that night I eavesdropped on them.

I know it wasn't exactly right, and I'll never do it again, because it's better if everything is said, done and messed up openly. What's more, the eavesdropping left me confused: Pa and Ma were sitting outside on the stoep. It was quite late already. Ma said, no, I must go in; the mosquitoes are driving me crazy. Then he said: Sit a while longer; I want to tell you about my most heartfelt wish. I'll sit on this stoep one day when I'm grey and look out towards the big poplars and see all my children and grandchildren frolicking between the tree trunks. Mirjampie would be there, perhaps pregnant with her first, and maybe Hester's oldest giving Tilla's baby a piggyback. But the stunner would be Konnie's firstborn. A beautiful brown-eyed boy. And his name? Raster Wasserman, of course. Everyone would call him Rassie. And then there'd also be Albert's bat-eared sons, cavorting madly in the bushes, and every now and then one of them would come rushing past the stoep here: Watch this one, Oupa.

I wake in my bunk, one of the two top ones in the compartment, like a child who has wet his bed. It's the small hours of the night. My one hand has got pins and needles. I pick it up from the pillow, all blue and bloodless, and lay it next to me to bring it back to life. The rectangle between my bed and the ceiling presses down on me. Despite the stuffiness of the compartment, a chill passes over my body, damp with night sweat. I rest my thumb and forefinger on my eyelids.

It's claustrophobic in here. The railway blanket is too thick. Only good for winter nights on the Trans-Karoo. I must get it off me. This train is taking me away, taking me away. I've surrendered myself, and it's my own free choice. If anything goes wrong, I'll have only myself to blame. Could you please help with a few cents, Pa? How much do you need, Konstant? You can't buy yourself anything decent with a few cents, you know? You're going to have to learn to ask for what you need, son. Ma, I need socks, and I won't say no to another warm shirt. And why is it easier for mommy's boy to ask his mother for something? Lord hear me, Konstant, from now on you'll have to have balls. Remember, it's all over: you can't run to your father every time you need a few cents any more. I don't care, I swear. It will be a pleasure to buy my own socks.

The compartment smells of men's feet and beery farts. All of them fast asleep. On the farm too. Will I ever see them again? Of course, my boy, you're not going to throw out your mommy and pappie, are you now? What's got into you? Sick, my heart is sick, too much beer too soon after the tennis. I have to hide my nausea, it's shameful. Nothing helps. And Ma's already noticed it. I must get to the men's changing room, behind the clubhouse. I need to vomit my brains out. The men's changing room is full of ooms, and a few younger guys, old classmates. They're all changing, washing away tennis sweat.

Fools! You thought I'd left already, wiped my mouth, flushed the toilet and buggered off. But I heard you. Hung around for a while behind the low wall, and heard every damn word. Oom Jassie from Donkerpoort: Has he at least got a dick? Oom, I don't think the question is whether he *has* one. It's that English farmer, the one who farms behind the dam. Dunkeld, I think, stupid name.

The question is whether he can get it up, he says, laughing.

I hear you. I smell your rubber soles, your Deep Heat. A man answers Dunkeld, I can't place his voice: No, no, no, you're all talking crap; the real question is: can he get it in? Another voice pipes up, more laughing, the spieuttt of a match lighting a cigarette. In what? asks the voice. Into *what*? I ask you that.

I run away, unseen. No one saw me. And never again. This train is taking me away, taking me away. From now on I'll be buying my own socks, and it will be a bloody pleasure.

I sit up, knock my head against the low ceiling of the compartment, double my body over and find the nightlight with the sleepy-dead hand that has come around again. From behind its dull glass the light casts a faded yellow glow in the compartment. A snorer on the bottom bunk turns over in his sleep, and a bluish-white foot protrudes from his sheets. I drag four nails over the hollow of my back and inspect my find: a sweaty railway-grey crust stuck beneath my fingernails.

Enough to give you the creeps. Nothing like a train to give you palpitations. You can hug yourself, wrap your arms around your naked body, nothing helps. I've left now, once and for all, gone into the unknown, may the Lord preserve me.

My anxiety is something deep-seated. And icy. It ploughs me under so very easily. I won't allow it . . . Where's my padkos? Up top. Here it is: sandwiches neatly folded in wax paper. Tomorrow I'll enjoy all Ma's different combinations. Cucumber and cheese, biltong and tomato. Peaches. Here's one of Pa's peaches. A juicy Oom Sarel. Pa's doing: this morning he went into the kitchen, took the basket from the rack, stepped out through the screen door to the orchard and returned with the extravagant but well-intentioned quantity of twelve ripe, yellow-cling peaches as a contribution to my padkos. Thank you, dear Pa: your peaches are sweet.

I REMEMBER THE EXACT dish I served Deloris Williamson the day I met her: snoek frikkadels in a lightly-herbed cream sauce. When I placed her meal before her we both stared at the two undersized fish cakes plonked inelegantly in a pool of sauce on the large white plate, and burst out laughing.

With my best Wasserman foot forward, I managed to grab a job at a restaurant. Just like that: remember, my child, if you dress properly and behave like your father and your mother taught you to, nothing can ever stand in your way.

My stay in Johannesburg is lasting longer than I expected, though with Deloris and her orange BMW coupé it's becoming worthwhile. I realise I've always wanted someone like her.

Will Australia take me, Deloris? I fish for sympathy. I applied for a visa at the Australian Consulate, had myself examined by the district surgeon at the Braamfontein Civic Centre, and now I'm waiting for the result, plagued by doubt.

You're white, you're educated, you're healthy and you're still young. I don't know why you're so shit-scared, Konstant.

Deloris's BMW is one of the older, smaller models, unobtainable at the moment. And her big fat bum fills the bucket seat behind the steering wheel.

The strange thing is that after a while I don't notice her big bottom any more. The Wassermans, of course, require a small backside. Or you'll hear them talking. Not openly, oh no: a facade of decency must always be maintained. Meanwhile: My goodness hasn't she got the most horribly big backside, poor thing, can't she do something about it? Only now, here in Johannesburg, do I realise how this family actually operates.

That must be Deloris now, hooting away just to wind my land-lord and -lady up. I can hear her perfectly well, even in my outside room behind their house. It's the *girl's* room, Pa and Ma – at least it's in a garden. With lavender bushes, not cannas or marigolds at the front door. My landlord is frightfully posh.

I was only too happy to arrive safely back at this very girl's room the afternoon I returned from the Australian Consulate. The city centre was grimy and full of papers and there was a taxi war in full fray and not a policeman or police dog in sight. And even if they had been there in huge numbers, it would still not have provided any life assurance. The opposite, actually. Streets near my bus terminus had been blockaded by taxis. The situation was volatile, and I was terrified. What a tragedy if I died just after applying for emigration. I felt very small. Small fry Kay Double U. I could have been a dead mossie by now. It was truly blissful returning here. Back rooms are a refuge for many in this city.

Deloris always arrives raring to go. With her raunchy fully developed bosom.

Whose party are we going to *this* time? I ask as she walks in.

Who cares? Someone's. Deloris gets to hear about all the parties in the northern suburbs, and we make sure we go to all of them.

What do I see in the woman? My dear Ma, I'm blinded by her massive bum, and besides, she's the one who introduced me to dope. The army-green leaf. I must say: at first I refused to take even a puff of her special ciggies. Then – well: moderation never harmed anyone.

Crush a few pips between your teeth, hell, Konstant, where did you get such perfect teeth?

Lime water, sister, the limey water of the Karoo.

Let's throw the rest of the pips out of the window, like this, and one of these days the babies will pop up, too cute.

Jeez, Deloris, you can't, man, what about my landlord!

Now let me show you: grind the green heads finely between your hands, have you got a magazine, Konstant? "Esquire"! Oh, no, I can't believe you read that pretentious shit. A bit of tobacco, mix it together well, chuck away the sticks, roll the Rizla-paper nice and firmly. Can I tear this page? Look: you take a piece of stiff paper, roll it into a spiral for your filter, voilà!

You're the one I've been waiting for, Deloris. You are my salvation. I won't tell you that right now – but one day, maybe. You're such a loudmouth, and everyone falls in love with you. Me included.

When exactly did I start smoking? Oh, I can't remember that first skyf now, my dearest Ma, all I know is that one day I took a puff. Oh, nothing to worry about, Ma, absolutely nothing; we're not talking drugs and things here. No more than the chewing tobacco old Anna always had on the farm.

Still remember old Anna, Ma? What on earth's become of that old soul? Always did the washing so faithfully. Wonder what went through her head as her hands washed the shit tracks from my underpants? So clean and pure they looked, as if they'd been sanctified, when she hung them up on the washing line. You were already a grandmother over and over again and I should have called you Granny Anna, respectfully – but white children are taught to treat blacks like sh . . . No: I shouldn't pass the buck. I'm the one who'll eventually pay for it. My great thrashing is already recorded in the Big Brown Book of Shit-Stirring.

And tell me, Mister Konstant, do you see this woman sitting here beside me?

Dear Lord, it can't be old Anna. Chewing her juicy tobacco ever so happily, and – can you believe it – on her throne.

Then? Explain to us, Mister, why you spoke so disrespectfully to Queen Anna? Someone much older, and much wiser than you? Queen Anna: will you please tell us how many of this white arse's shitpants you had to wash with your own hands?

Yes, sure, it's all true enough. I didn't know any better. I was just a tiny tot then.

Too late, Konstant, too late: from generation to generation . . .

Wasn't it the only way for old Anna to get to where she is now? See how those diamonds sparkle on the cracked skin of her neck. Take Mandela, for example. He *had* to sit in jail for twenty-seven years: that was the only way to knead the philosophy of reconciliation into him.

You're too clever, too late, Konstant. Too late.

And off we go. Where to tonight, Deloris? Fuckit, you're driving fast, Deloris!

True. You know why, Konstant? She never calls me Konnie.

You know why, Konstant? You don't understand this city yet, do you? You don't know how things have changed here. I drive like a bat out of hell, that way there's less chance of being hijacked. And *if* I stop at traffic lights, I turn my music up as loud as possible, and sometimes I even scream above the sound as well. Need to hear it to believe me? Frightens the skollies away.

At the Ontdekkers Avenue traffic lights, Deloris pulls up next to a full-bearded motorbiker. She hangs her goods over her window, left hand resting on the steering wheel, the music audible eight cars back. This is a chick who knows how to make things happen.

Like your bike, she strokes his ego.

The lights turn green. The guy gives her a look. Roars off: we think his bike is about to rear backwards over.

Fucking whore, he screams at Deloris.

Was that *really* necessary, is all she says.

Only then do we see ANGELS FOR CHRIST written in shiny rivets on the back of his leather jacket.

Anything is possible for Deloris, especially after a few skyfs. That's when she walks her fingertips all around the base of my nipple. Round and round, first this one, then the other, having a real field day.

How does she manage to give me such pleasure just there? Must be the dope. And I usually begin to stimulate her nipples as well – and *that* she loves. I can't go being all frigid with her. And she tolerates me, even my decorous shudders.

Later I take a good look at myself in my cleanly wiped mirror: well-formed pinkish-brown areolas with proud centres. Fecund little tits, and that on a man. You ought to be ashamed, Konstant. I won't. I left my shame behind on the farm: don't take yourself for a ride, my dear man.

Wonder how they're doing on the farm. What's going on there?

No one believes it when they see Deloris and me together, and yet our contact goes no further than nipple flirting. On weekday mornings when I'm off we also have a standing arrangement to drink champagne together in my back room.

How do you manage to keep your place so clean, Konstant? she wants to know.

I had a wet dream again yesterday, I say out of the blue.

Me too, I swear, she says.

I can't believe that of a woman.

What do you know, Konstant, you've only ever been with that student pussy of yours and even that sounds a bit half-baked to me, except for the open-wide part. Remember: anyone can do it, but that's only the beginning. You're hardly able to call these things by name yet. Come on: say *cunt*, come.

Don't be idiotic Deloris, why should I? You're only blurting it out now because I caught you out the other day when *you* refused to say it. Are you forgetting that I was in the army? You should hear how the boys talk there. What they *do* there. Sunday afternoons in that camp at Rundu everyone, the corporals, the lot, dragged their mattresses out on the sand and lay stark naked in the sun. I saw a guy sweating so much you could wring his mattress out like a towel afterwards. You should have seen all the things they got up to there.

What? What did they get up to?

Never mind. I admit, though . . . at university they always kept their knees together. Why do you want me to say *cunt* for you now, as if it's my ticket to eating the fruit of paradise. Can I tell you what, Deloris? It's time you also got away from here.

Are *you* rolling this one? is her only response.

And off we go to the next party. Deloris always dressed as if she's on her way to a mediaeval fair: black silk stockings with ladders, black lace gloves.

I may look fantastic to *you*, Konstant, she always says. But don't you notice how people stare at me.

I see, and I don't see.

Deloris never looks tarted up, unlike me in my clover-green pants and red shirt hanging out, 50's-style. These days I'm able to walk into any place dressed like this and feel dead at ease. For the first time in my life. Oh, I'm still tender meat. I've got a lot more bones to chew. Chops, please! It's been a long time since I last enjoyed lamb chops. So nice with the wind in our hair in Deloris's BMW. Whose party tonight?

Such a clear Highveld night, isn't it, Deloris. The sunset looks like blood and mustard over Soweto. No one could ever catch us at this speed. I dig the peanuts and whiskey flask from the cubbyhole.

When do you buy your provisions – I never see you stopping at a café or anywhere else.

That's the secret, Konstant, make sure you stay on the move, or do you want to feel a 9 mm pistol against your temple?

Suppose you pinch the stuff from your mother. I guess you

Williamsons are mighty rich, old money, hey Deloris?

Why don't you ever talk about *your* family, Konstant?

There's nothing to say, Deloris.

Scapegoat.

What do you mean by scapegoat, Deloris?

It's one of the Ten Commandments: thou shalt not make thy family into a scapegoat.

And what might you happen to know about scapegoats, Deloris? What's got into her? She's not one to go on at me. In fact, that's precisely why I'm here with her, driving along in her orange BMW. Where are we heading tonight?

Well, if the Israelites commit a terrible sin they build a stone altar up on a mountain, catch a goat and roast it for Yahweh. The smoke curls up to heaven, and if God senses true penitence in their hearts, everything is forgiven.

Where on earth do you get that? You Catholics don't read the Bible.

Give me another shot of whiskey.

Zulus also sacrifice goats. It can't be a sheep. After a whole life of sheepishness, sheep die without hope, and without a sound. A goat screams terribly, like a child, so it must be a goat.

Hold it for a minute, Konstant – you're not answering my question.

I've told you already.

As soon as it comes to your father . . . What's his name, again?

Raster.

. . . you go dead quiet. I suspect something's bothering you, there's some or other resentment deep inside you.

You've bloody well said it.

I suspect a cancer; a big green tumour growing inside you. If you're not careful it'll burst open one day.

Jeez, Deloris, if you knew me any better you wouldn't have spurred me on like that, not on that lovely evening of ours, bedevilled by many shots of whiskey and a couple of skyfs. I couldn't help myself. I shouldn't really have . . . No, I *had* to. You, you were shocked shitless. If your hand hadn't been so firmly on the wheel we'd have landed up in a ditch – and let me admit right away: you're a damn good driver of that BMW of yours. Your face went into spasm, white as a sheet. And me? How did I look to you? I know how my head was about to burst any moment from all the blood that had pumped into it. To prove how important blood really is to me. No, you don't know me, Deloris. You'd have kept your trap shut if you did. I really shouldn't have hit you. We could have been dead, right there at that bend at the Wilds. Roast me, Deloris; sacrifice me on a stone altar. What on earth should I do now?

I must start by eating something. The whole day I've been feeling sick in the pit of my stomach. Fill it with guava juice. It's nutritional, but it won't soothe me, not until I bring you my offering, Deloris, in return for a kiss. How long has it been? Two whole days without any contact between us. You avoid me, drive past me to how many parties have we missed in the meanwhile, or rather: have *I* missed? I can't survive without you. I bet you – you could have dropped me off anywhere in the city that night, prey for the men-of-the-small-hours. You must still have a bit of mercy somewhere, otherwise you'd never have brought me all the way to my back room. Or you'd never have let my hand lead you right to my bathroom cabinet, nor have turned your cheek to me so that I could smear it with Zambuck. An absurd cure for a wounded cheek. I wish it could draw the humour out again, and return things to the days before the slap.

This time roses won't do. So I'm drawing you a bouquet now. Fax it with flowers, directly to your home. Hope you find it more amusing than the genuine article. I'm getting pissed off with the whole thing. If you don't want me like this, then at least believe that our friendship is worth more than a single slap.

The fax with the bunch of roses melts her iciness. Deloris laughs with abandon at the whole affair, even takes the blame for provoking me beyond the limit of my self-control. She has two personalised stickers printed: OUR LOVE MEANS MORE THAN A SLAP, one for her BMW's back window, and one for me.

We celebrate peace with champagne, and I, ravenously hungry, choke on the charred crust of toast that I scavenge from my kitchen table. From the Portuguese's smallholding nearby we get a ripe watermelon. And carefully cut into squares the tray of cannabis cakes slyly baked in her parents' kitchen, then wrap them in foil and hide them in her BMW's cubbyhole.

Off to the Magaliesberg where we frolic in mountain pools, and chuck watermelon peels to the baboons. Deloris sunbathes stark naked on the smooth belly of a rock. On her left bun a gigantic raspberry grins onto which I rub factor 15 sunscreen. I accept her buttocks for what they are: like her bosom, they too are abundant and generous. Deloris Williamson is my kind of girl.

As for me: I readily drop trousers and shirt, but cling self-consciously to my last piece of prim clothing. Until the green cookies bring on the death throes of decency and I stretch out on a mountain rock without a trace of shame. Baboons, whoever, are free to look.

Lying there on the rock under the blue sky, don't know why, I beg Deloris to forgive me for the slap I'd given her weeks ago. Her rock is an arm's length too far from mine, or this time, she'd slap me.

I don't hold it against you, arsehole.

Deloris, I'm sorry, man, why did you have to use the one word I can't handle?

I've forgiven you, ages ago, Konstant; I've forgotten the whole thing, man.

It's worth my while to make a mental note of Deloris's attitude towards her debtors. Every day there are new lessons to learn. Laughing and screaming do not necessarily end in tears, and we arrive at my outside room dead tired. At ten o'clock Deloris collects me for another party, this time at a bunch of hippies who live on nothing on a smallholding somewhere near Fourways with chickens and ducks, a goat and a brown pony.

En route I say nothing about looking forward to Sydney. I wonder if it'll be more fun there, is all I say.

Whenever I speak of Sydney Deloris gets upset. It happens again. As we arrive at the goat people, admittedly a little out of it already, she pulls up under a thorn tree in a cloud of red dust, slams the door and kicks the front right-hand hubcap so that the chrome cracks in three places.

I don't want to go on about it: my time here is getting shorter, and yet I'm happy with life as it is. I'm blessed with a retard's sense of awe: I can't stop drooling, and when I think of all the day's shenanigans I have to swallow once more. I can't wait to get to bed and can't wait to get up in the morning. I'm not mad, but madly alert and alive. At parties they say I'm radiant. Bambi at Fourways even asks how I keep the whites of my eyes so bright. I laugh from ear to ear. With newfound knowledge, cocky questions, and witty repartee, Deloris and I dare to engage with anyone at any party, in any bar, anywhere. And time and again we come away triumphantly.

Jack and his wife Lorry, a couple doing really well by cleverly copying fashions from overseas magazines for the local market, are having a gala dinner. It's on the rooftop of a block of flats behind the reservoir in Yeoville. Such extravagance is becoming pretty rare in Johannesburg. Security arrangements at the party meet the highest standards: there are two armed bouncers at both ground-level entrances. What's more, they're in mobile phone contact with two more pistol-carrying guards at the entrance on the rooftop. The display immediately puts the guests at ease, and everyone can't wait for the evening to start. Jack and Lorry are lauded: This must have cost an absolute fortune, I overhear more than once.

Up on the roof top the lights quiver in the distance. We feel far away and safe from the city centre and the ghetto of Hillbrow's dilapidated skyscrapers. A few double shots at home have worked up our thirst, and Deloris and I gulp down everything on offer. It's a wind-free evening, the only time when even the southern suburbs appear friendly.

So have you taken a careful look at your father's personal effects? Deloris asks me.

Why this pestering tonight? Innocent banter? Like bloody hell. By now I know that Deloris means what she asks. When it comes to me, she's lost her innocence.

Where he keeps his razor, the drawer with his folded socks, the stuff he rubs under his arms, his toothbrush, you know exactly what I mean, Konstant, all the things you leave behind when you die, when people say: oh yes, these are his personal effects. This is the razor he used for years, and this is how he always kept his comb – neatly placed in his brush.

Why *this* question, Deloris? What's it got to do with tonight?

Deloris laughs it off, and all I get in response is a hug. Nothing, really, she says.

Another beer, a few more cocktails irresistibly dolled up with pineapple wedges, fresh cherries, umbrellas, and sugar-coated rims; a few more glasses of champagne; a skyf, and then another; a chaser of witblits before the starters, and finally dry white wine with the meal.

Deloris stares at me with a prawn hovering at her lips. She knows what's coming: I'm forced to excuse myself to go and puke in a corner.

I can't believe what's happening to me. Ggga! My hand's covered in cotch and there's nothing to wipe it with except the big white napkin on the table. I should have kept it with me, but it was too sudden. Jack and Lorry went to so much trouble: what will they think of me? Japie that one, better off chasing springhares on the farm, poor thing. I should also have dressed smarter, why didn't Deloris warn me? Look at her tonight. I'm really pathetic – been ages since I've felt like this. How do I get back to the table without drawing everyone's attention? The city lights keep shimmering, no matter how tightly I screw my eyes shut. What's that stink? Me? It's coming from below; must be squatters nearby. Their boiled sheep-offal. Or my own mess. On my shirt. Stained myself. How will I ever get it clean? A little spit on the tip of Ma's church hanky: come along Konnie, here we are, let Mommy wipe your mouth, how on earth did you manage to get yourself so filthy?

The table is laden with silver dishes of seafood, drink, dripping candelabras. Anyone not invited to tonight's grande bouffe is a no-body. I don't belong here.

Deloris walks across to me. She comes right up and holds me tight, and I realise from her gesture that *her* breasts also play a role in my life. So I start to laugh. I wipe the slime from my mouth with the man's hanky she always carries, and repeat what I always say to her when she rubs rose salve on the peculiar fungi-like spots on my back: one day you'll make the best mother ever.

In a Rosebank pizza café I hear a soprano voice, steady as ever, coming from behind me: "jou Martie, jou liefie, die son sak weg."

Martie is thrilled to bits to have bumped into me, and we grab a bite together. We decide on one medium pizza with salami, capers, tomato and mozzarella.

She has outgrown all her zits and blossomed into a pretty woman, petite and highly strung. A nugget glitters on her engagement finger. While eating our pizza, she talks about the night we performed together in the NG Church Youth Choir in her home town.

How indescribably well we sang that night, didn't we just, Konstant? And everyone was there. From all over. I can't think of a single chorister whose parents didn't drive over to Wepener that night. It was so special for everyone. So very, very special . . . Do you remember: Weber's "Hunters' Chorus" was everyone's favourite. And Prof Maatjie Viljee was so excited about his organ playing. I can still hear him talking about it afterwards at our pool: Man, I really blew the cobwebs and bats out of your organ tonight. And he *did* play well. I've never heard anyone play like that ever again. Do you remember the reception at Saamstaan, Konstant? I remember it as if it happened yesterday.

Martie glows at the memories. She beckons a waiter: she'd like a Babycham. I order espresso. Martie smiles and settles down for a cosy chat.

She's modelled her self-confidence on that of her parents, successful farmers, dutiful and so very proud. What she actually wants to talk about is the reception her parents, Gertjie and Krissie de Bruin, threw for all the choristers and their families on Saamstaan.

After all, it's that event that binds us together, even after all these years, isn't it Konstant?

Binds us together? Hell, Martie, you live on a farm. A paradise for boeremeisies to bake and brew to their hearts' content. Don't you realise, what happened at school was a meaningless fling? A go-getter like you can't possibly cherish it as a failed romance.

Oh, Konstant, you know exactly what I mean, she giggles girlishly. Then snaps back into the young lady with the tightly-sprayed head of curls, round as a beach ball. She tick-ticks away at the tablecloth with her car keys. Martie has come to the limits of her risk level, but wants to edge over anyway. She's determined to get my pants off. I excuse myself and go to the toilet.

I'm irritated that after all these years she still wants to talk about the incident that night at Saamstaan. It should have been consigned to oblivion. What does her life consist of if she still wants to coo about her carefree schooldays? Deloris will laugh herself silly if she gets to hear about this: Konstant runs into the delightful Martie de Bruin, an unexpected pleasure. Diamond ring and all, who does she think she is? Dolled-up little bitch. Would do her the world of good to hear that: everything isn't all moonshine and fannies. Just as well she's engaged, wouldn't surprise me in the least if she still wanted to do it with me.

Behind me in the men's toilet two guys in tailored suites resume their conversation after shaking off.

What time tonight? asks the one with the carefully combed bald patch. Age? I don't want older than sixt . . . then notices that I might be listening, puts his hand on the other's shoulder and steers him away from me. Their conversation becomes inaudible.

I take a seat. Must be the coffee, I went this morning as well. Martie will simply have to wait. That'll teach her. It's nice and clean here. Lots of paper. Stylish place, this. Oom Dikkie and Tannie Pienkie from Smithfield paid for their tone deaf Dolfietjie to be in the choir. Poor child! And Tannie Skat and Berrie Vermaak from Bloemfontein were also there – on the way home Pa kept talking about old Blurrie. One thing about Pa, though, no matter how pissed he was, he always kept to the road. Who else was there that night? Old Lalie de Beer and her fiancé, Rinkhals, who talked about golf till it came out of your ears. Jeez it . . . Foeee! Hope those two guys have left, I didn't hear them go. Can't be the pizza already. What else could I have eaten?

Mr Koevoet Cronjé, head of Grey College, and his wife, Bolla, were there that night too, and the mayoral couple of Wepener, Boytjie and Gannie Buys, dolled up in her glittering necklace, an heirloom, apparently. And old man Fichardt and his grey better half, Fienie, both in wheelchairs, poor dears. And the great mealie farmer from Kroonstad, Dampies Calitz and his wife, Sissie, who suffered endlessly because he was so miserly. At boarding school the Calitz children never had any slippers. I get depressed just thinking about it. And don't forget advocate Buksie and his wife, Smirna Tromp. Apparently a virtuoso pianist in her day. And the sturdy widow Tollie Smuts who carried on her husband's cattle farming somewhere near Dewetsdorp long after his death. I must finish off here, poor old Martie. Hope she's ordered herself another Babycham.

The De Bruins couldn't have hoped for a better evening for an outdoor function that night. Everyone expected the worthy old dame Fienie to hand over the silver trophies – but no, Tannie Krissie de Bruin, in her purple dress with elegant points down to her ankles, refused to surrender the honour to anyone else. The trophies were intended for the longest-serving and best choir members. The matric exams were just a week away, and I knew in my gut that one of the trophies would come my way. It must be the pizza; can your tummy juices digest food this fast?

Let me admit it today: I *was* proud of my trophy. Especially because Pa and Ma were there. Of course, I know what their unexpressed hopes were. Bloody expensive keeping me at boarding school, and one or two achievements would be the least reward I could give them in return. My academic record was pathetic. As for sport . . . Hell, I couldn't even hit a tennis ball against a wall properly. Poor Pa and Ma.

Konstant Wasserman, Tannie Krissie de Bruin called out from their fancy fan-shaped steps. I shot up, utterly delighted, and bowed in all directions at the clapping, and let me tell you, they *were* clapping! I swear, the rest of the choir whistled for me more than for anyone else. They all adored me. Don't ask me why. I wanted to take my trophy and hand it straight over to Pa and Ma. How stupid can you get! As I climbed the steps to receive the trophy, I turned around: Pa and Ma, are you somewhere in the audience? Gone without a trace! Can't be. They had to be there. They drove all this way, specially. I can't see you, can't see you. Where are you? In the de Bruins' house enjoying a quick drink, or in Oom Gertjie's museum of precious stones?

I've got an arse . . . I was making an arsehole of myself. I didn't want to burst into tears. So I crawled off like a whipped mongrel to the back of the garden, under a tree. Don't look at me. Leave me alone. Fucking trophy.

Strange thing to wipe one's own arse, isn't it?

Martie, hell, she's not too bad. A little blighter. Right there under that very tree – wild olive or something, they grow so well in the Free State – she got me. I looked up and Miss de Bruin was standing next to me, while tears rolled down my cheeks. She knew exactly why I was blubbering away like that. This was her chance to snog me, she even lapped up my tears, crushed my breath out and sucked my Adam's apple, my ears, thumbs, everything. No one would know.

She pressed her thingy, a steaming little pudding, tight against me and started panting horribly. I could have creamed her right then and there – but that was the last thing on my mind. That's the point, you see, she'd come along to pay me back for all the years I'd refused to have anything to do with her. Well, her excesses certainly surprised me. Pa and Ma found me much, much later that night. Ha! Too much beer for a schoolboy. They treated me like a child. Went on at me for boozing too much, and Ma even had the audacity to crack a joke in Mr Koevoet's presence about my hair being a bit too long for school standards. So it wasn't Martie's embraces . . . I must get back. She's been waiting for ages, poor thing.

Well now, Konstant, is all she says when I take my place opposite her.

So sorry, Martie, man, upset tummy or something, man.

She waves away my excuse. I suspect she finds the mention of tummy trouble distasteful, especially at table, though I speculate no further and order another beer. Martie starts talking rather unconvincingly about the virtues of knitting. She plans to use it to stamp out the idleness of the black women on her prospective husband's farm. We're unable to converse freely again.

She's seen through me: I once was, but am no longer, her sort. And I also underestimated her level of sensitivity. Martie de Bruin. She *does* have a good heart, maybe we should . . . Oh, hell, can you imagine? She'd clam up terribly, of course, I'll never really know for sure.

Martie insists on paying the whole bill herself.

Oh, Martie, I protest, that's really not necessary.

We take leave of one another at her car, which she unlocks from a distance. She kisses me lightly on both cheeks. Smells of lanolin, of rabbit fur.

Martie, I say, I hope you marry happily, man. I don't manage to look at her for long. Once she's in the car, she touches my shoulder lightly, almost unintentionally.

Me too, Konstant. And I hope you're successful in Australia.

Write me something now and then if you have the time. Or the inclination.

I turn to walk towards the bus stop. My eye catches a Portuguese guy who was in the army with me. I pretend not to see him and look the other way.

Towards the end of spring I receive a letter from the Australian Consulate. My hands tremble in a paroxysm of doubt and faith: I read greedily and then wish I could still cry. YES. Take one heaped silver spoon of everything. Wear your very best shirt tonight. Comb your hair perfectly. Polish your teeth till they're extra bright. YES. When last did I celebrate my joy with tears? Both fade away as the years go by.

How fitting that my landlord and -lady have chosen tonight to invite me to a little get-together, as they put it. It'll most probably take place in their sitting-room, a long, perfectly appointed space that spans the whole front of the house. Their good taste makes me jealous.

I wear my Hawaiian shirt and a pair of freshly ironed, tight jeans. My hair is so long now that I can comb it all to the back. The style suits me. I brush the few hairs that stick in my comb off into my rubbish bin, an empty instant coffee tin. And stand my comb upright in my nailbrush. I splash on a bit more Blue Jeans aftershave.

Don't overdo it. Once you've put on too much, you never get rid of the stuff. I brush my palms over my face and smell them. Too-too. Water *must* help. How many times can you rinse your face? That'll have to do. Then it's just my skyf. I need a big one tonight: what's a man without a zol?

I finish my smoke and walk around the house to the front door.

Very welcome, Konstant, sorry we've never really had you around before, man, too busy, you know, nothing personal.

Mister landlord probably smells the excess on the dandy. Should I crack a joke about it?

Just then two coquettes, bouffanted and high-heeled are dropped off by a chauffeur and let in at the security gate. Tick-pick-tick, swinging hips, up the freshly hosed garden pathway.

Squashed feet will be their lot. By sixty, their little toes will have crept over their big ones. They'll be crying bitterly from arthritis. Who gives a damn now? Sir is clearly more interested in *them* than in me. Don't blame him in the least.

I wish Deloris could be here tonight, but it's one of those by-invitation-only affairs. Perhaps I can phone her a little later. No one need know she's a gatecrasher. She's an asset anywhere and the two of us make a formidable couple.

I step inside, am immediately served, and lean against a faux pillar. Two baldies complete with earrings walk by. Not too bad. The one on the left's skull looks like an egg, though. Did he regret it, or was he pleased when he discovered he had an egghead *after* all his hair was shaved off? I've never seen a pinhead, except in that book of freaks. Needlehead. Must be horrible. The only way to guarantee social acceptability if you are one, is to wear a cap all the time. Or else migrate to the land of pinheads.

A short distance away I notice a person sitting alone on a white sofa. Next to the sofa, a kidney-shaped glass table top mounted on sandstone holds a glass of white wine. I watch the person. The wine on the table remains untouched, as if the person wants to prove that even a sip of wine is an unnecessary crutch for such perfect isolation in the midst of the feasting and babbling.

How long can you watch someone without being noticed? It's a matter of time. Before such a presence, I can't last long. Oh, damn it, man. When Deloris and I met over a snoek cake it was completely different, and by the time I came to my senses I was being treated to peanuts and whiskey in her BMW. Now *this* one.

I must confess, my heart is melting.

In the most perfectly modulated voice I have ever heard, the name Jude is mentioned to me. Jude is wearing a black knee-length monk's habit. The dress consists of only two panels and is made of heavy cotton. There's an embossed V-motif on the crotch, with the V pointing downwards. A long wide tongue of the same material, also V-shaped, hangs from the chest to more or less just above the spot where the bellybutton ought to be. Jude wears a lot of rings: wide silver bands and gold ones set with striking stones. The shoes on the person's feet have a handmade look: dark brown with black cowhide inlays.

Allow me to observe you uninterruptedly and shamelessly, or is that in fact what you expect? It doesn't surprise you, and it's certainly no challenge for you – rather a condition, not so? Otherwise I'd be excommunicated. But tell me now: have you ever met anyone with such perfectly smiling teeth? Thank you, Deloris: tonight I've passed your final test, I'm loud-mouthed and mature enough to be kicked out of your nest.

I'm unable to read Jude's look. Raisin eyes, with hard little pips, no wonder no one's sat down next to you yet. I'll soon be asking you about all those rings of yours. And what, if I may ask, is your gender, exactly? It's impossible to decide: doublegender, heartbender... so it's Djude, then?

We start talking. On the soft white sofa Jude and I can't get enough of each other. We don't talk as if we're old friends, rather as if we suspect a shared vocation. Jude's attitude implies: choose me or be off and leave me alone with the peace I live with anyway.

I have chosen.

I'm on my way to Australia, I announce with the greatest possible satisfaction. I couldn't wait to say it. And now Albert's theory about me and my silver spoon in my mouth, worth its weight in gold, is proved: Jude's been living in Sydney for the past three years.

Although Jude has been pretty formal up to this point, I sense unambiguous enthusiasm when it registers that Sydney will be our shared home.

Jude definitely likes me.

And from that moment on we knock back countless glasses of wine together. When the host comes by with a bottle of cold Hem-el-en-Aarde, I thank him from the bottom of my heart for inviting me to their get-together: one of the nicest I've ever been to!

Ha! I express my joy at the evening. I've offered myself on a platter to my landlord. There he is, filling the high heels' glasses again, I doubt he gives a damn. But to have said it in front of Jude! My words have undone me; my game's up. Do with me what you will, Jude. I've sold myself for peanuts. And yet, I *am* being true to the candour with which Deloris and I express our emotions.

In any case, Jude reveals nothing apart from gazing at me and the guests with an all-knowing smile. Every now and then Jude gets up to refill our glasses at the bar, a heavy industrial metal table with shatterproof glass, purposely cracked for effect. The way Jude moves between the guests is something to behold: like the neck of a giraffe above the trees.

Now *this* I appreciate about Jude: during our uninterrupted conversation saliva sometimes flies, literally. Then an Indonesian silk cloth appears from Jude's leather bag – a roomy, old-fashioned doctor's case with a classic copper clasp – to mop up the blobs of saliva.

What do you do to keep body and soul together, where do you come from, where do you live, where did you go to school, did you go to university, what about the army – we do the well-known national identity parade. Do you know so and so? No, he was that one's brother; not too bad, that one? Yes, man, and didn't so-and-so sleep with so-and-so, and so on.

Jude's always the one to suggest a new topic of conversation. Once it is exhausted, his boredom soon becomes apparent and a new topic is hurriedly proposed.

Most of the time I surrender myself to listening. I've already exposed myself with too many words, and don't want to let slip that my listening borders on awe. I am amused – that's for sure. Especially by the person's formality. Almost as if approaching a subject formally comes spontaneously to Jude.

It must be well past midnight by now. Jude excused himself a while ago. How long have I been sitting on this bench all alone and sweaty-bummed? I was too generous in expressing my emotions; perhaps that's the problem? Did Jude say he'd come back? I can't even remember now, just took it for granted. A glass of wine will help. It's stuffy in here with so many guests. They've all been in this room far too long. The teak blinds are spattered with red wine, oyster shells have been trampled to grit on the floor. My landlord and host is in no state to care any more. I must get out for a breather.

There are scores of late-nighters on the stoep. They all smell, and are all drunk, me too, I suppose. A tomcat has pissed here. Who's that kneeling under the bottlebrush there: surely not one of those high-heelers snogging away? Who is it?

Haven't seen you here before, hi, I'm Chris du Plessis, a man introduces himself. You look as if you're enjoying yourself. There's cigar smoke in his voice.

Under normal circumstances I'd happily have chatted to him, but right now I have no appetite for small talk. All eyes are on my monk. Chris won't even notice if I walk away. Too drunk. Anyway, it's normal to come and go as you please at parties. Maybe he's noticed how I keep looking around behind his back. I don't care what Jude thinks of me any more – I'm not a dog on a chain. I follow my own heart. My quest has begun.

Looks like you've lost your lay for the night, he says.

I laugh, smoke a cigarette with him and move off. The guests in the reception room are dancing to jazz. Jude isn't amongst them, nor in any of the bathrooms. The kitchen is crowded.

Why everyone always gathers *here* at parties! The Russians would know – they sleep on their stoves.

The dew has crisped the kikuyu, and it's fresh in the back garden. A group of bass voices sit in a circle: indunas sharing a skyf – no tits welcome here.

I unlock my back room to refresh my glowing face with cupped hands of cold water. Recomb my hair that has held up well so far. What's up with this bloody Jude? Clearly I'm approved of. Was it a one-off meeting? And what about Sydney? I can't believe how that bloody aftershave still smells. Jude dropped one of those discreet remarks about it. Dammit! The fact is: I'm already wanting a certain response from this Jude person. Why haven't I been invited along for the rest of the evening, for the rest of my life, ha! Jude doesn't know me well enough yet. Is it because I messed that stuff all over me? A skunk is more than its stink, after all. Must keep a cool head.

My place smells mouldy, I should leave a window open. Where is Jude? Hey Jude, don't make me so fuckin' sad. Ridiculous. Let's roll a quick little something. Why not? Or try to score from the big chiefs outside? Pass me that skyf please, guys. I'm not manly enough. Mister Hawaii only couples with men in his head.

I slip past the dagga smokers and through the kitchen, down

the passage to my host's phone, despite my noble intentions not to abuse his hospitality.

Look here, boykie: at this stage your landlord doesn't give a damn who talks to whom on his telephone, even if you spend an hour talking to the man on the moon. What's the time now? Deloris won't be asleep yet, a real snorer that one.

There's no answer. Deloris, my mainstay, where're you cruising tonight? I must get hold of you: I want to tell you everything. I absolutely have to – a woman is a man's cook, cunt, and shoulder to cry on. Shame on you, Konstant.

Two gentle hands take hold of my hips. Ringed, brown hands with flat, manicured nails. Sensual fingers slip from behind into the front pockets of my jeans. I gasp and sigh and feel how my toes squirm in my shoes and the heavenly itch of my sex, until now curled up in my white underpants.

Konstant, Deloris eventually answers the phone, hoarse from sleep.

Too dozy, Miss Williamson, or my tone of voice would have betrayed my situation to you. At this very moment my – mine, already? Okay then, *this* – this newly rediscovered Jude's warm crotch is rubbing against my bum. And, generous-hearted Deloris, if you knew that, you'd end our conversation right now. On the other hand, if you knew that I now regretted having called you in the first place, you would definitely *not* put the phone down. So there you are, stretching out your hand to where you last left your extra-milds. Of course, you know that it could only be me phoning so late at night. Suddenly I wish you'd go back to sleep on the top floor of your parents' thatched house in leafy Northcliff, but I can hear that your never-ending desire for nightlife is arousing you. And now you're shaking your cannabis sativa carefully onto zol paper.

Konstant, I'll be there right away, she cries out enthusiastically.

You don't understand where I'm at, Deloris, and a drop of sweat that's formed on my earlobe is noticed and licked away by Jude.

And why are you only ringing me now to say you're at such a wonderful party, darling Konstant?

Oh, Deloris. I can hear it's on the tip of her tongue to rebuke me for flouting our standing arrangement.

Meanwhile Jude, respectful of the privacy of the telephone conversation, removes both hands from my hips and conveys the message, in perfectly-mouthed words that I am expected back on the white sofa.

Deloris, you don't understand, you're the last person I want to see right now. Can't just dump you, can I now? I'll never leave you. Deloris?

She's put it down, impatient to get here. I still wanted to let her know that I've met someone very interesting here, which means I won't be able to give her the usual attention: hell, Konstant, I know her well enough – once I get there, do you think I'll mind, I'm shocked to think that you know me so badly. Then she'd laugh like crazy and put the phone down.

How will Jude respond to Deloris? Jude must surely have the capacity to accommodate anyone, despite all the formality. The flying saliva is proof that Jude is also open-minded.

Walking back to the white sofa, I have to negotiate Jude's stare again, a still-waters-run-deep kind of look. Could look the other away. But the dope has deadened my senses. I'm glad I'm sozzled.

As I take my place beside Jude, I receive an elegantly rolled skyf in the jaws of a split golden key. Then Jude embraces me and kisses me.

My best ever. My bundle of codes of conduct is fraying at the edges. Who could resist such a kiss? Just like that, in full view of everyone. And it was no ordinary kiss either. Is Jude also freer now? The monk's habit has come undone. Did anyone see us? It's the way Jude kissed me. Rather too intimately for a public place like this.

I sink back into the sofa and *this* time it's me who wants to hug Jude. As my hand nestles under the root of Jude's long, thick plait, Deloris walks in from the stoep.

Old rogue, that one, she immediately notices my bright shirt in the packed room: rara avis next to you, Konstant! It's as easy as pie for her to read my feelings from the look on my mug as I glide along in seventh heaven at a quarter to four in the morning.

In a flurry of rosewater and a recently smoked skyf she flutters down upon us. So gorgeously that I don't care what Jude might think of her any more. No one could resist a being like this: a Calcutta-pink sari and gigantic golden earrings set with dark green stones. She's worn the earrings before, but that sari! And the canary-yellow brocade shawl with gold fringes. She kisses me with great big pink lips. I have no doubt that Jude is also transfixed by this flamboyance, and introduce them right away. Jude masterfully camouflages whatever he really thinks of Deloris by immediately starting up a conversation with her.

The best sari-seller is down near the market, he begins. I go off to prepare a tequila for Deloris. When I return, they're still chatting away. I place myself so that Deloris sits between Jude and me. However, when she turns to say something to me, without turning her back to Jude – she's deliberately sunk back into the sofa precisely to avoid that – Jude leaves our company.

I half get up from the sofa. The party has nearly come to an end, it's now or never: When do we see each other again, Jude?

He looks at me playfully, and a visiting card appears from an inner pocket.

Phone me in the evenings, between six and seven.

That's all. What about Sydney? All the beaches a bus-ride out of town? Will we see each other again?

I was too open with my feelings, I confess hopelessly to Deloris, far too extravagant.

Deloris laughs: Just listen to my loverboy.

See the way Jude walks, Deloris.

She's not impressed, and snatches the visiting card from my hand. A curly Victorian typeset on faded paper. Jude, and a telephone number. Printed in pitch-black ink.

Anywhere, it doesn't matter at all, I say to Jude over the phone.

It does matter to Jude, and I thought it might. When can we meet again? And where? I can't help myself, any time, anywhere – just as long as we meet again.

And I'm dead certain the foreplay has begun when I'm phoned at the restaurant, and so on and so on, until I end the lease on my back room to begin my life in the immediate proximity of Jude.

My suspicions are confirmed: Jude is blessed with an abundance of everything. He never allows our topics of conversation to dry up; our wine glasses are never empty for long. Sometimes we spend passionate nights together, right through to daybreak, on spotlessly white sheets. I learn new positions, new extraordinarily sensitive ways to stimulate genitals, new techniques to delay the final ecstasy. Sometimes, in sheer uncontainable expectation, I scream out loud with Jude's encouragement.

Although I'd like to, I can't spend much time with Deloris any more. Just to pick up the translucent soap on the fluted silver dish or to discover fine traces of the soap's fragrance on Jude's skin later, provides enough reason to enclose myself freely, and forever, in Jude's flat.

It all happened faster than soft-boiling an egg. I don't think Deloris could quite keep up with it. I have to admit: I've been feeling awkward here in Jude's flat – apartment as he calls it – I've only seen Deloris once since the party. My love for her is indisputable, and she ought to know it.

What about the fax I sent her? She's the one who hasn't responded. And I *do* phone her regularly. A call a day. No, that's a lie, Konstant: you're far too busy with your newfound night bloom for that.

Jude becomes prickly: The schoolgirlish way Deloris wants to possess you is quite ludicrous. Jude notices that his words offend me. It's the first sign of his impatience since we've been living together. Off he goes with this parting shot: Here's a chance to sort out your personal business and to make a decision if there're decisions to be made. I'll be back at a quarter to six.

Deloris is no adolescent, especially when it comes to handling her emotions. She's just experiencing a huge absence; and I can understand it. I phone her. She tries to reassure me: I'm learning to sublimate it with a skyf or two a day. In any case, it's an opportunity for me to prepare in advance for your departure, which is going to happen anyway.

At our last breakfast together Deloris says: I anticipated the intensity of your relationship with Jude.

The remark I made that evening at the party about Jude's way of walking was a definite indication to Deloris that my power of observation, usually so sharp, had been temporarily coloured by my obsession with Jude.

I understand, Konstant. You're obsessed. He is so contrived, you know.

There's no hint of obsession, I hit back. Why are you being so bitchy? I don't know you like this.

I'm not a bitch, and you know it. I'm just trying to bring you to your senses.

My senses? My senses are mine, I know them . . . Things are spinning out of control here, Deloris.

Deloris is silent.

Say something, please, Deloris, I beg.

I'm checking up on my selfishness, Konstant. It's your destiny to continue the relationship with Jude. I'd be exceeding my bounds if I tried to stop you.

Deloris throws the bones. I've lost her, won Jude, betrayed myself. Or have I? I shrivelled up like this when I had to choose before: the farm, or leave. It's no choice for mere mortals. I wish Deloris would hold me one last time like a puppy.

What do you mean by contrived? I prod her. She refuses to elaborate. Our eggs get cold. The last bite sits rancidly in my cheek.

Was it the way Jude walked? I ask again. I never let anything go, to my bitter and eternal regret.

In contrast with her usual chattiness and the frankness of our relationship, she refuses to say another word. Her bosom heaves. Over a third and last coffee the two of us – the once formidable couple – collapse in shivers.

Deloris, it doesn't have to be like this.

In the silence we both realise that our relationship has finally changed: I know she knows I know. Deloris gets so upset at this turn of events that she starts choking, and even refuses to let me slap her on her back.

She flies out of her chair and tries to rein herself in: That old boil of yours is flaring up again and something horrible is oozing out. You can guess what: your obsession with Jude. You've chosen with your balls. And something else, Konstant, you've always spoken about your closeness to your brother, Albert, and left it there, all just to avoid confronting yourself. You know, you've no idea what your face looked like that day you hit me. Fucked up like hell, and blood red. If you want to become socially acceptable . . . She swallows her words.

Where on earth is all *this* coming from? The coffee is cold and bitter as gall. I don't even have the energy to get angry. It's tragic.

Deloris, all this is totally irrelevant.

In the first place, I'm in no condition right now . . . She starts crying.

In the second place, she can't help herself, moves round the table and holds me tightly. Sincere heart and bosom, that's Deloris for you.

She rubs her hand over my new, very short crew-cut, and minutes later her orange BMW races past my table with its windows closed. I allow myself the luxury of calling a taxi, and when I arrive at the apartment I go straight to sleep, hoping to rid myself of the rusty aftertaste of the life-changing choice I've made.

When I awake, Jude makes us each a vodka and guava juice and comes along with two heavy glasses, talking about how it's the first time there's been enough money to come back here, and to pack up and ship the furniture. He's glad I've been able to see the place like this one last time, arranged in the way that's always given him so much pleasure.

Later Jude dusts down the wardrobes, unpacks, sews things together, mends, makes piles, rolls bundles, folds up, irons, presses, hangs in folds, packs away. It goes on for hours.

It's mostly just the two of us here. We dine expansively, always on the fine, pure white German plates, and linger over every meal. Jude is a first-rate cook. He explains how important it is to have a critical attitude to all the culinary horrors committed in South Africa.

Although some traditional dishes, like good boerekos recipes, must never be chucked out. On the other hand, some of it needs spicing up. So during those thrilling last days he prepares many traditional South African meals, always with a twist: pumpkin fritters for breakfast with maple syrup, lamb chops with red Spanish onions and tamarind sauce, spaghetti in sweet boiled milk with a glass of Cape sherry.

When I do leave for work, the minimalist furnishing of Jude's place brings me a healing serenity on my return, despite the traffic noise outside. It's the most stylish living space I've ever known. Polished wooden floors with a low-gloss varnish throughout. A heavy club-style lounge suite in the sitting room, voluptuously covered in peacock blue material. Quite a few South African artists are represented on the cream-white walls. Jude also points out a small Chagall pen-and-ink drawing to me, so matter-of-factly that it's quite impossible for me to imagine he's boasting. There are African masks everywhere, each one grinning like the next, all the way into the bathroom. I've yet to develop a taste for them.

Jude teaches me to give up all selfish questioning after he's been away – sometimes for a whole day or night. He always returns seductive as ever, especially if there's something new to narrate, always with that same irresistible honey quality in his voice.

Though not everything is quite as smooth as that. I'm just too agitated waiting around for Jude. I get so upset when he goes AWOL, it's as if I don't even know myself any more. What's Jude up to? And where? Aren't I big enough yet, why can't I know, and what can't I know, why can't I question him, aren't I big enough? Am I only getting to know myself now?

I toss and turn at night, can't fall asleep alone like before. I turn waiting into a game. I often take myself in hand. Not much consolation in it – it's just not the real thing. Usually I can then recall every movement of our last night of passion, or that wordless time in the kitchen, or the position on the unravelling – apparently irreplaceable – Persian rug.

Abuse. Is that the word? Stop: I must stop the self-gratification. It's not really at the root of my discomfort. I've been doing it since schooldays: small, white chrysanthemums on the soapy-grey bath water. I never felt uneasy then, dead satisfied in fact, and dozy-headed on the enamel bath rim right away. No, it's more than just a physical disease, this.

I never eat much when Jude is away. I grieve so much that I'm losing weight, and only drink water. The bottle in the fridge is nearly empty. I'm forced to go out for more. The mere thought of seeing other people in the street, of being seen: Can you spare me a rand, sir? Water won't cool me down. Maybe I should take a shower.

I've been abandoned to my own devices. How far will I be fucked over? Why are the long stayaways never explained? My patience is running out. We're together, aren't we? Is all this distress just worms in the belly and snakes in the head? I'm ashamed of myself.

I sit in one of the spacious blue easy chairs, take the white writing pad from the table next to me and, with great difficulty, start a letter to Albert.

I pause. Yet again. Learn to play the waiting game. I start by snooping through Jude's personal belongings. Why not? Cupboards and drawers and suitcases, all exquisite leatherwork. In the wardrobe: first the long rows of trousers – cotton, wool or linen – clipped leg-first into clip hangers, then the wide-shouldered hangers for the monk's habits, kilts with each pleat perfectly pressed, a merino wool winter coat, small drawers with sections of bleached underwear, ironed and folded as if just taken out of shop cellophane, bundles of socks and silk stockings in parallel rows, pure white hankies, each and every one folded into a tiny square, a drawer full of exotic shawls and scarves, a shelf of folded jerseys, co-ordinated so that two of the same colour are never stacked together, rows of shoes, sandals and boots, each kept in shape by its own wooden shoe tree inside. The cupboard exudes an aroma of old-fashioned farm soap and rosemary.

I refuse to breathe it in: will not abandon myself to it. Everything makes me sick. I light a cigarette, only after ensuring that Jude's wardrobe is tightly closed against the smoke. Then open my own cupboard, a gift from Jude. Ready to wear, my new set of long-sleeved, button-down shirts: old gold, faded blue, white, white, white – gifts from Jude. I stroke the material.

I return home, weary after work, the inside security lock must be on, I can't open the door. I'm about to hammer angrily when Jude, naked except for a kikoi, opens. He kisses me, and without a word of explanation announces there's a visitor in the apartment. With a turn of his head he gestures towards the kitchen and goes there himself. I smell percolating coffee and get undressed in our room. It's humid, an exceptionally hot day. Then I walk towards the bathroom, as always, to wash away the food smells of the restaurant. I push the bathroom door open. There's a man at the basin, also naked, goatish, washing himself down. My white knuckles clasping the door handle become even whiter, I'm aware of my heart in my shoes, of not much saliva to swallow down. It *is* exceptionally hot today. I say nothing, retire to the bedroom, and only then notice the intruder's pile of clothes on the floor: jeans, a jacket, T-shirt emblazoned with the new flag, Tiger walking shoes and brightly striped socks. Ill at ease, I turn around and flee to the sitting room, don't feel at home there either, and remove myself. Nor do I find any peace in the study. My palms leave wet marks on the surface of the table.

Who stripped his underpants? Careful, don't mess with food. Peel away a handful of crown leaves from the cob – and peep in to see if the head is ripe for the picking. Who undressed him for Jude – Jude or the guy himself? It sickens me – Jude's fingers on his skin, I'll go crazy. Horribile dictu. How *could* Jude? I can't believe I missed his clothes the first time. Where are my eyes – blind head – in my pants? Who is he? Picked up from the pavement, flat on his bum guzzling fish and chips from a funnel of newspaper when good fortune fell upon him: like to feed in my pastures? How does Jude manage it? With honey?

After an eternity that I hope against hope will last forever, as I want to preserve myself from Jude's merciless silences, I hear voices at the front door. It opens, then closes. I go to shower.

My ears are still glowing, even after my shower. I sprinkle Eau Savage on them. Alcohol only cools temporarily. The lid is loose. The bastard, he's used some: there are traces of fish and chips on the bottle. Everything's possible, I don't trust my peace. It's Jude who makes me want to question him. I don't possess a monk's detachment, I talk my heart out.

I spend ages brushing my teeth and let the water cascade over the edge of the rinsing glass. What should I do? How long can you dawdle in a bathroom? My sister Hester, yes sure, she dawdles until the water becomes lukewarm; and when the door eventually opens, the scent of strawberries and cream lingers on her skin. Can't believe anyone on that farm ever thinks of me – I'm lying so low. Hope I never have to come out of here. I'll phone Deloris. Come and fetch me, drive me to the Magaliesberg, hand me peanuts and a mouth full of whiskey. How I miss what I no longer have. Does this mean the end of our relationship, and what about living together in Australia? Must clear my head now.

I discharge myself from the bathroom and get dressed in the bedroom. I find that the bed has been made up army-style and all traces of Jude and the man's sex have been removed. Incense smoulders in the basket on the head of the small Zimbabwean woodcarving on the bedside table.

Jude stands at the sitting room window in a loose-fitting Indian outfit. He turns around: I can't believe you didn't even have the decency to knock before bursting into the bathroom.

I can't look at Jude. All I manage is to rub my aching head with my hands. I hate sobbing so unrestrainedly, so bloody uncontrollably. I don't cry, after all – when last did I? And like *this*?

Jude comes closer and cradles me, holds me tight, takes out a hanky and dries my tears. Until dark we sit like that. I'm embarrassed by my outburst and angered by my embarrassment. My body twitches; there's nothing more to hide.

Couldn't he have closed the bloody door – or are there no doors where he comes from? He sickened me, that guy in the bathroom. The thought of him and you together sickens me. I trusted you, Jude, believed in you so much, but now . . .

Then I become silent, vulnerable and remain moody, especially because I express myself so awkwardly. How little I've changed, after all, and yet, Deloris, that last morning, stunned: Can't believe what's become of you, and so quickly.

Jude talks on without ever raising his voice, without letting go of me. He declares that his feelings for me are pure. He promises, again and again, that he'll never dump me. Until I'm able to weigh the truth of the words, until, reassured, I am able to sit apart from Jude and accept a glass of whiskey and a cigarette. Jude settles my future situation: If I don't take such exception to the sight of him and someone else together, I'll save myself a lot of pain. It's my aversion that tortures me, and the pain is doubled by my fear of being abandoned.

All watered down. Disgust. Suffering ahead. I'm tired. Have to protect myself to survive. Must cut myself off from Jude. My muscles feel weak. My fuse is smouldering, my ears only half-listening. Hell, I've slaved away all day at that restaurant for pinstripes with cell phones. They use waiters like whores: There's a drop of soup on the rim of my plate, waiter. Portion's too small for our bellies, waiter. Keep the steak blue, open the wine at the table, more bread rolls, more butter balls, coffee now and later. There's a message from your wife, sir: don't return home unexpectedly, and please note: you've mispissed the urinal, sir. Curious thing for a pig to be so choosey about his Sauterne, sir. My pores reek of their sour breath, their filthy farts, their pathetic small talk.

Jude ignores my exhaustion. He doesn't want to postpone this opportunity to enlighten me, and talks on. He'd like to bring home to me that I'm holding onto a static concept of a relationship – actually I'm clinging onto it – and that means I have certain expectations of him. He cannot and does not, ever, want to meet those expectations of mine. He is a free spirit and will not allow himself to be the object of my suspicions.

Don't let my feeling for you become conflicted by my sex life, says Jude, that's my own business, and I won't allow anyone to meddle with it. Nothing I do, or shall do, will ever affect my feelings towards you.

Why reveal all this only now? That's what I can't bear. Why did you allow me to come this far with you, and only now you tell me you'll be sharing your bed with me, with many. Do you hear me, Jude?

Jude's done with talking. If these are the only questions and reactions I'm able to come up with after everything he's explained, it's a clear sign that we must stop right here and now. He's long past where I'm at.

Jude touches me, and when we're finished, I feel strengthened by the conviction that I've won something of Jude back for myself.

I brood over the incident for days. Sometimes, when I return from work, the flat is quiet and pitch dark. Arranged formally and all air-tight, it smells different then. Especially after Jude's cabbage-soup farts.

Our life drags on, there's little to say to one another, still less intimacy. Jude comes and goes, as always. He doesn't seek reconciliation, doesn't even try to explain things any further. I stand in front of the mirror and floss my teeth the way I've learnt from Jude. The mint-flavoured string between my closed lips pulls my cheeks flat until I'm grinning at myself.

How could I have been so naive about Jude staying away all those nights, all those days. I've been a sheep. Should have guessed someone like Jude has a busy extra-mural life. I could phone my old shoulder to cry on, Deloris – but that would aggravate her prejudices against Jude. Martie, then. Where's her number? She'll take the simplistic view: Why not come around here, Konstant, my door is always open for you, without any ulterior motives. Remember I'm getting married soon. Sounds as if you've made a bad choice, Konstant, you're still young. Go back to the farm – the days are peaceful there, the nights long.

Perhaps I should try to finish Albert's letter: My dearest brother, here I am blurting my life out to you so you in turn can go and blurt it all out to Ma. To demand your silence is asking too much. The temptation is too great – for Jude, too. If I had a body like Jude's, a voice like Jude's, if only I could caress the way he caresses, I'd be able to steal any heart. Oh, Albert, if only you knew how Jude really tastes, that thing, you know. You must understand that you can never experience what I'm saying here until you've tasted Jude yourself, and that, of course is possible because everything's possible. Albert, if you did that, I'd obviously never be able to forgive you, and apparently you wouldn't do it anyway – you're just too damned prim and proper. So I'll make do with feeble sentences. I'm happy, Albert. I will be happy. Just watch me. I must accept the urge to protect myself; otherwise there'd be no one to look after me. That's my chief consideration. Which is why I can't tell you about these things. What I still can't understand is why Jude wants to feed in other pastures. My Jude, your stolen pleasures are surely slight in relation to the lifetime ahead of us.

The fact is, my relationship is my own. What's more, speaking freely about Jude would be digging my own grave – Jude who explains everything patiently so I can appreciate how it all fits together. So, Albert, when you're sitting on top of that ridge where the dassies build their stony nests, where the blue-bush smells dusty and the sun rises over Valskop, where there's no trace of me any more, please, Albert, think of me. Even if you no longer know how.

Then, after a week of mutual stiffness, pinched goodbye kisses and uneasy nights in the same bed, I pull myself together. From now on I'll ward off shock by preparing myself for the worst whenever I return home. I have my hair shaved off again, crew-cut style, the way Jude likes it, especially between his splayed thighs.

What I couldn't prepare myself for is the visit to the city by my father and Dominee Pietie, his minister friend.

Well, I do in fact try to prepare myself for it: I cook a delicious lamb stew. I roll a skyf. I add pepper to the pot and skim off some fat.

In my opinion, there's nothing to be gained by a meeting between Jude and my father. Jude thinks differently. At the same time, he wants to leave nothing to chance. So he'll pop in for a quick glass of water between twelve and a quarter past twelve, and then leave. Wear one of your white shirts – it's always safe, Jude suggests.

What for?

Perfect planning minimalises embarrassment.

The lamb I seek out for Pa is the best cut. Perhaps a little heavy for lunch – but so what. I should have prepared something lighter. Where's Jude straying now? Nothing can be salvaged any more. Just don't get the purpose of Pa's visit to the city. Are my eyes red? No, they look alright. I'll draw the curtain a bit. Cooler like this. That's the second time the cat's miaowed at the door. Should I have a beer? In broad daylight? Pa will kill me. Dead give-away. Of what? My nerves are shattered. What am I trying to avoid? Our place is clean, we're decent people – nothing to be ashamed of. If only Jude were returning after they're gone. But he's decided differently, and that's that. Must be them now. The cat better stay outside.

Hello, Pa, Pa's looking well. Dominee Pietie?

. . . looks like a minister, I'm also looking well, do I look well?

At least we found the place, the traffic's awful in your neck of the woods, Konstant.

Oh, anywhere's fine, Dominee.

One would expect maximally developed social grace from you, Dominee. How uncomfortable you seem under that Norman Catherine painting of the screaming man. Yes, Dominee, not everyone hangs WH Coetzers on their walls to give a false sense of security in a city where lives are cheap and meat expensive. Pa really does look good, or maybe a little weary after the long journey? Did Pa come straight from where and whereto from here and why here?

I feel like a sheep. If only I were one, Pa would know me through and through: Come on now, old ram, open your mouth. Let's see: two . . . dammit, a six-tooth! Well, you don't have long to go: off to the abattoir with you.

Dominee, do little lambs also go to heaven?

Yes, my child, it's called Lambsend.

Right from the start, Pa's uncomfortable; he spills on one of the blue chairs. He's not himself.

Don't worry. No, Pa, it doesn't matter, just a few drops, nothing to worry about. Really.

I fetch a dishcloth. Pa's still not satisfied, and I return to the kitchen for a dry one. Afterwards the chair is cleaner than ever before. And that cat did get in. It rubs its cheeks against the Dominee's shoes. He's got a nice beer belly, this Dominee Pietie.

Out, dammit! And to think, Pa, it's a stray cat, and – 'strue's Bob – when I went to the kitchen, it had jumped on the stove and was licking the fat.

Licked the fat? What a strange way of putting it. Actually, no, we won't stay for lunch. A glass of water will do for me. You know what it's like when you're on the road. Your eyes are red, my son. Is there a problem?

It's the smog; Pa knows what it's like.

No. How would I know? The air is clean where I come from.

Was Pa always as reserved this? I don't remember him like this, strange how easily you forget your own father.

Strange how strange you've become here in the city, my son.

What on earth does Pa mean by strange how strange?

No, the heat is unbearable, too few trees and too many people.

Let me open the window. The traffic makes such a noise: we won't be able to hear one another. Wait, I'll close it again. That's better.

A lot is said about bugger all and something about everything.

It's a good recipe this, isn't it, Dominee? Works every time. Let me get more ice from the freezer. Maybe we should keep the cat after all. They say pets are therapeutic, even the goldfish on the secretary's desk helps with depression.

Three glasses of water for the three of us, with or without lemon? No: too much effort! Lemon wedges won't break your back, Konstant. Here I come.

On my way to the sitting room I hear my father say something to Dominee Pietie: Don't bother, Dominee. He's beyond redemption – always was.

Don't be surprised by my red eyes, Pa, just my daytime fix. If it weren't for mother's little helper, the tears would be streaming. From the day I left the farm, I've been deeply aware that Pa finds me strange.

And the hair, then, Konstant?

No, this is the way we make our stew here, Pa, lamb stew, I tried to make it just like Ma.

Fat?

Ja-nee, fat sheep, even here in the city.

And the hair, then, Konstant?

I don't care that they don't want to eat. My delicious stew will, thank the Lord, not be served. The heat has ruined everyone's appetite. I'll give some to our charwoman, for her children and her grandchildren. Christmas in the middle of the year, hooray!

Regards from your Ma, regards from Albert, lots of regards actually, from Hester, Mirjampie, Tilla, regards from me.

And old Boelie, old Bakkies, old Kaptein, old Wagter, old Ore – old Zimba, is he still alive?

Of course, Konstant, are you crazy, I mean stupid? You haven't been gone from us *that* long.

Yes, Pa, 'strue Pa, that's the stoody blew, Pa.

Have you heard about Van der Merwe and Van der Merwe and Van der Merwe? It's clean, don't worry.

Aai, this Dominee Pietie is a real card, geniality personified. How does Dominee remember all the jokes?

How's the farming going, Pa?

Going?

Jude arrives. Between twelve and a quarter past. In his monk's habit.

Jude, Pa, Dominee Pietie, Kitty the Cat, you know anything about this cat, Jude?

Dominee Pietie is *just* on the verge of experiencing a touch of joy at the sight of a fellow worker in the ministry. But those jewels, and those lips!

The pope also wears the family jewels, not so? Sorry, Dominee Pietie, we did everything in our power. Sadly, the stew just won't do. Nor will Jude. He's only popped in for a quick glass of water. Hell. And Pa didn't even smile during the introductions. Not that one always has to, but still.

Jude drinks the glass of water politely, though he remains aloof.

How refreshing it is for the thirsty Jude. There's nothing quite like a glass of cold water.

Then he excuses himself and the three of us are on our own again. I've never been so relieved to be rid of Jude.

The traffic is getting heavy again. We must get a move on. So who in fact *is* this Jude?

Ja well, true, the stew's ready, it can't wait, it can wait. Bye, Dominee Pietie, thank you very much. Bye, Pa, my hand is cold, sopping wet. Oh, I know, ja, that's the way it is. Once the traffic gets heavy one can't hang around for the sake of a stew. Won't let that stand between us, never has, never will. It's only a stew, really, long live goodwill.

As we part I notice the pocket Bible in Dominee Pietie's hand, with its well-kept nails. A man who takes good care of himself. Back in the flat I see an envelope cunningly placed on his chair.

Fuck off, cat! I yell.

In perfect longhand is written: Konstant Wasserman. The script you'd expect from a minister.

I'm afraid to open it. What's the worst it can be? On the white sheet of paper with Dominee Pietie's letterhead, a single question from the Heidelberg Catechism:

Q: What dost thou believe concerning the Holy, Universal, Christian Church?

A: That from the whole human race, from the beginning to the end of the world, the Son of God, by his Spirit and the Word gathers, defends and preserves for himself unto everlasting life, a chosen communion in the unity of the true faith; and that I am, and forever shall remain, a member of the same.

The last line underlined in red. Who is the *I*?

Were you here on a mission to the prisoner in the city of gold, Dominee Pietie?

As long as there's life, brother, there's a chance of salvation.

But Dominee Pietie, Dominee was full of jokes from start to finish.

Oh, we've got a completely new approach these days, brother prisoner, "al die veld is vrolik."

Not Pa. There was a sadness about his eyes, or was it crow's feet? A tear – or did I just imagine what I longed to see?

Jude returns and takes me out to a restaurant. Under whirling fans we pick at delicate quails. Jude insists on champagne to gladden my spirit. I talk about Dominee Pietie's letter, now put away in a drawer.

What arrogance. If I were you, I'd throw it away immediately, Jude responds heatedly.

For the duration of the meal I'm able to forget about everything.

A while after the visit, post arrives from the farm. Can't wait to sit down and open it. My stomach isn't too good these days: I'm drinking sour milk. The letters from home are all in one envelope, like warm eggs in a nest. A child's drawing slips onto the floor.

My mother writes about the plague of green grasshoppers chewing up her cannas so terribly, and Albert who's smoking so recklessly: that's just looking for trouble. And then there's Tannie Breggie: do you remember her? Gertjie Pienaar's mother, wasn't he at school with you? Apparently got a terrible pain in the stomach one day, poor thing, Oom Gert had to rush her to the doctor. They prayed their faith wouldn't fail them. Still, they feared the worst. We're all human, aren't we? It turned out to be stomach cancer. Oh, I'm so sorry for the poor people, life's like that, here today gone tomorrow, like grass in the fields.

And at the end of the letter, there's a reference to Jude, not by name, only by the use of *him* and *he*. An afterbirth, something te be discarded: And by the way, what does *he* do for a living?

In Mirjampie's drawing there's a man in an aeroplane: There goes Konstant. And Tilla sent a green and red creature with wings and nothing more. Albert writes: We don't talk about you much, we haven't forgotten you, life goes on, you know.

No, I don't, fuck you, Albert.

He adds: Pa said almost nothing about the visit to Johannesburg.

Why would he, Albert, you bloody idiot. Everything's sealed in cake tins and goes mouldy at home, haven't you noticed?

And: Ma misses you terribly – she doesn't dwell on it, though. Once she spoke about your leaving and Pa said if you didn't get rid of that person, you wouldn't have a snowball's chance in hell, and we could just as well write you off. It was the only time Pa mentioned Jude. What's so bad about Jude? I'm still trying to drag it out of Ma. Pa also said we'd never recognise you any more. What's up, Konstant? Or are they talking a lot of rubbish? Have you changed? Please send a photo. Tannie Trynie at the Red Store still goes on about your rudeness. One day I couldn't stand her any longer so I blurted out a Christian is supposed to forgive everything. Since then she's shut up. PS. I understand Pa better now.

You're also written off now, Albert. Trust you understand that too. This is, hopefully, the last letter from them before I depart: sincere regards, my son, from all of us here, everything of the very best and blessings from your father. May we never forget you. I enclose a cheque for you, fat one, isn't it? Hope you fly to hell.

Shortly before my departure I phone Deloris to arrange a farewell dinner. Jude has carefully proposed that Deloris comes to the apartment for an aperitif, and that she and I then go out to eat alone. Deloris can't hide her excitement over the telephone, also to see the apartment she's heard so much about. At the last minute Jude receives a call. Because the phone is in the hallway for the sake of privacy, I can't follow the conversation. Not that I make a habit of eavesdropping on Jude, but I have placed a high premium on Deloris's visit and am afraid something might go wrong. You can't help being human.

Jude announces that something's cropped up, and this and that, unfortunately I can't and all that shit.

You know how I feel about Deloris's visit, Jude. I want the two of you to reconcile before we leave.

I'm sorry about this sudden change of plan, that's just the way it is.

Jude grooms himself in front of the mirror for the unfortunate event, still talking away at me. His turned back makes me almost desperate. I shudder.

Don't construct all sorts of scenarios, Konstant. Especially when it involves joining together two completely different individuals. Don't allow your expectations to mislead you.

Expectations my arse.

I immediately regret my words. For one last time I try to persuade Jude to stay.

I've lost my appetite for meeting Deloris.

It's the last opportunity for us to enjoy something together like decent people. I wasn't thinking of any kind of joining together at all.

You're not being entirely honest with yourself, Jude slips a last earring into his left ear. Then leaves and closes the door softly behind him.

I run down the passage, shout he's a bastard who's unable to express any emotions, feel proud of my outburst, and slam the door so hard it comes off its hinges.

SAA GEMSBOK, KING OF the antelope – just my luck the plane is named that. We're flying over Zimbabwe, Malawi. Hard to believe there're still people who talk about kaffir lands. Oom Niklaas does. Pa always wanted to buy his farm. Glad he didn't: how could you ever be happy on a farm called Ontevrede?

The thing is, *I'm* the one remembering that phrase. I should leave Oom Niklaas in peace.

Will I ever see any of them again? Perhaps when Pa turns seventy or something. Prodigals usually return then for the fatted calf. Listen to me, I sound like a heartless bastard. Get rid of him, he's worthless! The irony is that I don't really know whether I'm pleased to be getting away at last. I thought it would be different.

Ma cried so bitterly over the phone: Love you very, very much. Always remember that. Wind out of my sails. Even Pa was so . . . how can I put it?

Though I *am* glad that Jude and I made peace before my departure. On my initiative. He's flying out in a few weeks' time, so I'm on my own.

I asked for an aisle seat. I can stretch my legs out as far as I want, and the black widow next to me is so shrivelled up I've got a whole lot of leg room to the right as well.

Her body trembles in anticipation of talking to me, but her English is weak. Finally she gets out that she flies back and forth between Germiston and Sydney to visit her two daughters. She's eager to chatter away. I'm too overwhelmed by the finality of my departure, and lose concentration. The widow mutters on a little, then seems quite content to fiddle with the rosary beads around her neck.

I'll be polite to her. She's a dear thing. A calcium-deficient bird. I'll even explain the menu to her.

The menu makes the meal sound much better than it will be. Look at that flab on the flight attendant's waist. Real spare tyre there. Something Ma dreads more than the plague. Thought cabin stewards are supposed to look smart and trim. Which is totally impossible with the Swiss roll he's got. Ought to stop this: I'm being too critical of my fatherland. It's best that I'm pushing off, there's no place for hensoppers here. I simply can't help picking this sort of thing up, it's as if my ears have been tuned in to it all: at the airport one of the black workers called a flight attendant *baas*. Don't think he helped the idiot right. Anyway, if he had, the worker might have felt awkward, it's the form of address his people have used for generations, part of their staple diet: poor bastard.

Yes, please.

Definitely, old Spareboy. Wine for the whine. I'll have three of those little bottles to soothe my spirit.

Red, please.

The widow's black eyes peer blankly into her lace mantilla when the steward asks for her order.

Come along, I encourage her, have one, signora, you'll enjoy it. She laughs toothlessly. Can't her children afford new teeth for their mother?

She's adamant: only communion wine will ever stain her lips. Once the trolley is down the aisle, and I've closed my eyes and swallowed my wine, her bony elbow digs my side. I'm startled.

Sambuca, she commands. I can't help laughing, and call the waiter. Sambuca exceeds their limited drinks list. He suggests a Scotch, at which she sinks back into her seat and waves him away. The skin on her hand looks like parchment.

I'm sorry for her. Sambuca is delicious. Had it for the first time with Jude. Two coffee beans floating on top. It would have warmed her tummy nicely. Poor dear, tiny old face like a saucer of intestines – not my way of putting it, but Ma's tennis friend's.

I wish Deloris could have come. What about my BMW? she shrieked. The last time together was really great. She promised to visit, though: I don't know, it's too far, too expensive. All I have is a B.A. and with affirmative action and all that stuff it's not easy for whites to get work and earn well.

Really deceptive term that – they're doing exactly what the previous government did. At least they're trying this time. Except old Winnie. A real anarchist. Like a bad child, always doing the wrong thing perfectly. Not surprising the Old Man couldn't handle her. Then again, he's too serious. Jude believes he's the only politician after Mahatma worth respecting. Though he was a dried out old stick in *Gandhi*. Passive resistance won't ever work in South Africa, there are simply too many guns around.

As far as I'm concerned they could serve wine and nothing else. I'm not hungry. Must say: Jude cooks very well. He's so talented. Pity the thing between him and Deloris never came right. Deloris was actually relieved the last night when she saw Jude had gone off. In the restaurant her tears dripped onto her kingklip. She looked so sad. She maintained that my voice and gait had changed. But we've seen too little of one another recently for her to say a thing like that. Maybe she was in love with me? No, she'd have admitted it.

Across the aisle there's a family of four. The father in shorts and sandals is closest, then the boy, blond curls like his mother, and a delicate mousy face. He's busy colouring in. Then the sister, cruelly endowed with the father's thickset eyebrows. Dark little lines on her young arms already show the promise of luxuriant growth. Finally the mother in a pink track suit paging through a woman's magazine. Mastag, Bokkie, the father says whenever his son shows him a finished picture.

Why are the stewards so scarce? Suppose they're afraid the passengers won't stop begging for more drink. Ticket is bloody expensive. We deserve all the drink we can get. By the time all the films are over and they switch off the lights, I want to be well and truly gone. There's one showing his bum.

So this is it, finished and done. Deserting my motherland in a blaze of madness. Damn, forgot to shake the dust from my feet.

Thank you.

Fleur du Cap. Why not more Roodeberg? The Roodeberg bottle is prettier. I ought to be grateful. To your good health, Konstant, old horse. Saddle-horse? Rather: all saddled up. Looking forward to tasting Australian wine. Jude says it's excellent, though it takes a while to get used to. At first it tastes like tree roots.

That story of Jude's . . . almost too much to tell. And a burden to carry alone. It very nearly left Jude so vulnerable he couldn't maintain his reputation of doing-everything-with-good-taste. I still see little Judy standing on the banks of the Berg River, tiny feet in the brown water. The baby tortoises in the sand. Buried under coals to be roasted alive. The other children thought it was funny, or were hardly aware of what was happening. What do children care about things like that? Splashing about in the water, all of them. Only Judy crying his little heart out. Don't! Please don't do it. Jude had never told anyone that story. My ears were the lucky ones.

Little Judy's daddy was braaiing baby tortoises at a picnic spot in Bainskloof. They must have been delicious and tender, just like sheep offal. Far off from everyone, the child stood all alone. Little sourpuss. Where was the mother? Couldn't she have comforted her child? Well, the fact is: the mother never went on picnics because she was afraid the father would get drunk. It was inevitable: picnics in Bainskloof meant drink. She refused to go anywhere near the place. And you can't blame her; apparently he beat her black and blue.

I could tell it was very difficult for Jude to talk about it. I wonder what the father thought of Jude: Man, a real spectacle, if you ask me. I'd give anything to hear his opinion.

It's okay, this Fleur du Cap. I've been drinking already, maybe my taste buds are deadened.

What I don't get is why the mother allowed little Judy and her other children to go if she knew her husband would get drunk. Or did he force them to go? I must remember to ask Jude. No: rather not mention it again. It only makes him bitter.

Maybe little Judy's mom sent the children along so the father could fuck them around instead of her. By the time he got home he was out like a light and all she had to do was to bath the children and chase them to bed.

And why the father dug a tortoise from the sand and took a pot shot at little Judy is beyond me. What a waste of a delicacy, especially if you're poor.

Was Jude exaggerating a bit? That's not his style. I've yet to hear Jude tell a lie – or laugh. No, I have heard him laugh. Are his periodic bouts of melancholy due to that flying tortoise? The father must have aimed well. And there it was: children and grown-ups clutching their bellies as they laughed at the poor child. It stained Jude's memory. He's been branded for life.

Mastag, Bokkie, I hear from across the aisle again. Bokkie's father bends down all the way to his poor mite. A child isn't really human, just a bloody mite covered in skin, property of his father: make him, feed him, clothe him – then break him! What more could any child possibly want? It's got nothing to do with me.

Fish for me, thanks. And another bottle of wine, please.

The widow points at my choice, and a tray lands on the fold-up table that I had helped her to open. Across the way children's fingers peel cellophane. The little girl with the downy moustache discovers a cherry in her fruit salad. But Mirnatjie, the mother whines, won't you first eat your chicken for Mommy? I avert my eyes and peel the foil from my supper.

The flying tortoise branded little Judy right behind his ear. That's why Jude still wears long hair. He made me finger the mark for myself in case I thought he was exaggerating. At first little Judy's whole face was scarred on one side. He says his mother rubbed ointment on it and it faded away miraculously. Only traces have remained behind the ear.

Apparently those wild throwing bouts only happened when the father was seriously pissed. And that last fatal time he aimed at his little Judy. He just couldn't stand the child bawling away all by itself down at the water. Little Judy did more than cry: he became totally hysterical. That night, tortoise feet squirmed everywhere, in the child's bed, in the room, in the cupboard.

Luckily it was only this once that the father couldn't stand it any more. Maybe he thought his buddies were laughing at *him,* though they were really laughing at his child who couldn't stop snivelling. So he dug the scalding thing from the coals and aimed it straight at the dark figure on the edge of where the children were playing.

One thing about Jude: you never see him wallowing in self-pity. Where does Jude's anxiety lie? Does anxiety lie anywhere? Mine certainly does. As soon as I lie down. It won't happen tonight. Besides, in an aeroplane you have no idea when it's night. Next thing you know, the sun is rising. All this wine will help. Jude denies his own angst, refuses to let it out. But I will.

I re-cover the empty punnet with the foil. Haven't touched the dessert or the pale salad. I check on the widow's meal. She's scratched around in everything without finishing a thing.

It's uncomfortably hot in this plane, even when you turn the fan onto your face. Have to aim the widow's one on me too. How hot would Pa be in this plane? He always gets so claustrophobic.

The toilet's cleanliness is impressive. I grimace at myself in the mirror, and without turning away unbutton my fly.

A handful of loose skin. Must be the heat. Cold sea water makes everything shrivel away. Women are luckier – nothing hangs out. Though Deloris has that train story of hers: when the woman opposite in the compartment changed, some sort of clitty thingy popped out, a fleshy red pencil, clearly visible from where Deloris lay, hand under her head. She can talk a load of shit. Wonder what she's up to tonight.

Damn. I steady myself against the wall as the aeroplane lurches, and can't help laughing at the crooked pee. I button up, tear some paper from the slot and clean my mess. I stare at the blue rinsing water for a long time, wash my hands with the white soap, and discover a fine hair on my left nostril. The aeroplane shudders so much that my thumb and middle finger – well-practised tweezers – are ineffectual.

Checking my nose and ears for whiskers all the time is obsessive. What will I do about fecund hair when I'm old and can't check myself? I'll have to forget this one; the plane is bouncing around too much. My beard is showing. It will get even worse before Sydney. I must look decent when I get there. Jude thinks I always look good: breeding shows, man, even when you've been boozing all night. Ought to drink less in Sydney. Perhaps I can shave in Perth. No, that's ridiculous. People know you look washed-out when you get off an aeroplane.

Hard beard. What makes a real man? Strong bum? Desmond Morris in that TV programme: the one characteristic all ethnic groups find attractive is prominent buttocks. Always been the case, right down the centuries. It indicates the potential for thrusting power. So why do whites joke about blacks' bums? Jealousy. Then again, *they* joke about our flat arses. And how does Wassermann qualify? Hard beard, hard body, look of steel: that's a man passing there! Like hell!

I take off my white cotton shirt, Jude's last gift, and check my stomach in profile. Must start sit-ups again. How many on the farm? 65? Then old Boelie would lick my face. Thanks, Boelie, you saved me from over-exertion. A person is essentially a kind of sloth . . . was unbelievably erotic, the sex scene with Emmanuelle and her lover in the aeroplane toilet. Don't know how the hell they managed it.

Before I let myself out I check again to make sure if there's any toothpaste available. I try one last time to pluck the whisker with my nail-tweezers.

Yes, it's available, I say to a greybeard in the passage when I come out. He can't open the folding door.

Wait, I'll help you, I turn around and open it for the old bungler. Not a look nor a word of thanks.

Rude. No wonder he's so grey about the gills. It's the colour of his flying phobia.

I must see that film again, just for that one scene. They must have filmed it in a normal toilet – an aeroplane's is just too small. Apparently there are lots of sex shops in Australia. That will be a stimulant after all the years of fathers Verwoerd and Vorster and boss Botha: O beloved nation, you may absolutely not delight yourselves in naked breasts, bums or balls. Well, if they're black we don't mind quite so much, ha, ha, ha.

The Immorality Act bred a lot of lust. That's why Oom Alewyn's Hardus knocked up that girl on his farm. Everyone in our part of the world knows the story: when the police came up the road in their van, Tannie Bets said to her son, whom she loved more than his sins: Run as fast as you can, Hardus. And, believe it or not, Hardus didn't think twice. He beat it all the way to the strooise and hid under his girlfriend's bed – so he could get a last chance to fondle her breasts. Ah! Old Hardus! I'll take you to see "Emmanuelle".

Are they looking at me? No. If I were on an alien carrier, El Al for example – oh, no, hell, they're too much of a target – I wouldn't give a damn. Here I'm surrounded by my own people, staring at me as if they know me, can see what I am and what I'm not . . . You can't fool a boer: the police dug old Hardus out from under that bedstead. The shame for old Oom Alewyn and Tannie Bets! She didn't set foot in the dorp for months. Poor Hardus was exiled from hearth and pussy to a banana farm near Hluhluwe where nobody knew him. Hendrik Frensch Verwoerd, if only you knew how your children have suffered. And the black girl? Her people were evicted from the farm. Or rather, that's what everyone hoped would happen. Don't you believe it: *that* would be the day, Tannie Bets said. When baby Hardy made his first sound she'd just cro-cheted the last stitch of his lily-white shawl. Dominee came to talk – to no avail. Tannie Bets never set foot in church again. Your own people keep account of your sins. Always watching to see if you fit in, aren't they, Tannie Bets?

This is the last time for me, they'll never see me, ever again.

I'm bored by the American film they're showing, take my earphones off, change my mind, put them on again. The widow has disap-peared under her aeroplane blanket. I can hardly resist poking the little body for a sign of life.

A bird, poor thing. Always wandering from place to place. Wouldn't she be better off under a plane tree with a bowl of raisins on her lap? Is this what she wants, flying around, or is she – do you become – too weak to make your own choices? Blessed are the poor of choice.

I remove the earphones again, scratch in one ear then the other, look to see if anything is on my nail, check whether anyone has no-ticed what I secretly did, then store it in the net at my knees.

What's Jude up to now? Bet he's already got someone to help him fold away, flatten down, pack up. Konstant's gone. Was a little short where it counts, that one! The whole apartment belongs to me again.

And tell me, where exactly you do it, my Jude?

Man . . . mornings in the shower, afternoons in the sitting room, evenings wherever we want. If only he would relax, this Konstant of mine, he's imprisoned by his own mind.

Wait and see, Jude, in my new country I'll turn over a new leaf. I can just imagine how dissolute you'll be there. You know, Jude, I sometimes wish I could dump you . . . Please, sir, don't take me for a cuckold. I tried to follow my head, you know, but my heart speaks the language of love. I'm inextricably bound to someone unbridled.

I undo my laces, push my shoes under my seat, and take the free slippers and blanket out of their bags. First I turn to my left side. My view is compromised by the proximity of old "Mastag, Bokkie". To my right side. Then decide that my original sitting position was the most comfortable. I pull the blanket up to my chin and snuggle the baby cushion under my head.

It's actually very good to fly. What's her name again?

I'm forced to forego my careful seating arrangement to fish in the overhead locker. The picture of Jude's friend who will be collecting me at the airport is in my passport. I sit on my blanket, scratch my nose and look at the picture.

On the back of the photo, in Jude's writing: Shane Jackman. The cursive, medium-sized letters slope backwards. A neat attempt, surprisingly uneven. Why do his letters go hands-up like that? They're the written proof of a repressed memory. When I lose concentration, mine sometimes lean backwards. The minute I dare look the other way something rotten slips out. That's the whole truth.

Shane Jackman. Strong name: don't rub me up the wrong way. The eyes are those of a gentle gazelle. Or am I reading something into it? She'll wear a red scarf. I know I'll recognise her easily. I'm good with faces. All those people in our town: Tannie Trynie, uncle Dirk Thingy, the whole lot. I remember them all, even if they think otherwise. What release to get away from there. "Ver oor die Diep Blou See". Pa always played that song so well. But as time went by he stopped playing the piano altogether.

Shane Jackman's got good lips. Jewish blood, maybe? Doesn't matter. Jackmanowski. Changed during or after the war. Poor souls. They'll be hunted like animals until they find their rest in the collective Jewish heaven. They're the salt of the earth, like the black people on the farm.

Farewell to all those tasty legs of lamb. My taste buds remember you. I could hardly get up from the table after those meals. If the black people don't hate us they're not, in fact, worth their salt. Perhaps they're happy after all – like Ma says. She ought to know: she's got a hotline to their happiness meters. Who are we to say, to decide for them whether they're happy or not? Look how they beat their drums on Saturday nights. And on Sunday mornings they're up at the crack of dawn to put the porridge on the stove. To fatten our bums up a bit. And let me tell you: that porridge has to be perfect, otherwise the baas goes berserk.

No thanks, I don't want anything more to do with it . . . here, Pindile, Pokasi, Samuel, here's a pasella for you. There were so many muggies the last night on the farm, in my mouth, everywhere. I nearly ruined myself financially trying salve my conscience and emigrate. The catch is: you can't buy a good conscience. We're all in it together. Will the Australians give me hell because of my white skin?

I could never miss Shane Jackman. Those dark brown eyes, looks like someone with guts. Hope she's got a job for me in her vegetarian restaurant. Jude *did* talk to her over the phone. Just keep on believing in old Albert's silver spoon. Farewell, brother, tuck into those legs of lamb to your heart's content.

Vegetarian restaurant. Sounds boring. Jude tried so hard to convince me that their food is delicious. Must keep my mouth shut, that's the most important thing to remember. I believe it's more than lettuce and carrots, much more sophisticated. Kind old thing, Jude.

You'll always look out for me. As long as you don't start throwing those prejudices of yours around, Konstant. Things are different across there. You'll have to work your butt off, and there're no black people to wipe it for you afterwards. Stay calm, do your best and don't stand around as if you've got nothing to say.

Jeez, Jude, you're going on like my father!

And laugh that lovely laugh of yours, Konstant, with those perfect teeth: do that and you'll easily soften hearts, bodies, everything, whatever you want. You're a bloody handsome guy so why not sell your pretty little face?

Oh, I'm not in the least bit scared. In fact, I'm looking forward to this more than anything ever before, far away from everything.

Yes, old Konstant Washedupman, you've licked arse and now it'll be piss-easy to shoot your mouth off about those of us who're staying behind.

What do I care? Bugger all! I'll work hard. That's what matters.

The cabin lights are dimmed, the last blind is pulled down, and everyone has curled up like a pupa.

I wake stiffly to a dream and heartburn. I've slept deeply for a long time. Not surprising after all the wine. Must get up. My one foot has gone to sleep.

I try shifting most of my weight onto the full-blooded foot, but still curl up from pleasure and pain as I heave myself up to go to the toilet.

It's free. Everyone's pissed already. How old my sleep-dead face looks in this light. The plane is all asleep now. Human bodies wherever you look. Sister Sleep awaits Brother Death. The Roman Catholics make much more of death during this life than we do. They're no dozers.

So vulnerable, lifeless puppies, all of them. It must be terrible to be attacked in your sleep. Like that farmer near us. They say it was one of his own workers who did it. He must have been so shit-scared himself, slinking into that most private of all places – his baas's bedroom. Wonder what went through his mind as he did it? I couldn't do something like that, not over my dead body. What if I had to? Never, not a knife into someone's heart. Shooting is better: at least you can do it from a distance. Strange the smell of the intruder's anxious sweat didn't wake the farmer. What can you – the victim – do in situations like that: so utterly alone with only your dreams?

I knew there'd be at least one old soul still sitting up. What's he reading? Stephen King? Story about an assassin on an aeroplane, has he done something like that yet? He's got the formula to write about anything.

Toy aeroplane, ours, nothing more. On its way somewhere or other, God could prick it and phewt everything's over before you can say lamb chop. I'd rather die on the ground. In the end it makes no difference. I snuggle down again, paralysed by exhaustion. I wish sleep would take me away.

I wake beforehand. This happens so often I simply *have* to take note. It's like a dog that starts barking just before an earthquake. On the farm the floor creaked every night. Just before the swelling or shrinking plank could sound out into the silent house, I'd wake up, time and time again.

So when the fasten-your-seat-belts sign goes on I'm already awake and nauseous. Through the small portholes the sky is pitch black. I nudge the widow, and with a sigh and a dribbly mouth she frees herself from her blanket. I point to the warning lights. The fear on her sleep-bedraggled face is so familiar to me. An old person's smell, naphthalene and sour milk, rises from the folds of her black dress. I lean over to help with her seatbelt. The plane jerks so badly that I struggle to slip the lock. She buries herself in her seat, closes her eyes, clutches her wooden cross and pleads for mercy.

Pray for me too, I whisper, pointing to my heart. She nods and shuts her eyes tightly again.

From Perth SAA Gemsbok flies east, and when darkness falls again the horizon swarms with fireflies: Sydney's bright lights. The widow encourages me to lean over to get a better view. Her tiny hands already folded over her handbag. Then she taps my shoulder for me to sit back. She's forgotten something. From her bag a wooden statue of St Theresa of Rome appears. She props it up and pushes its wooden nose against the window so that St Theresa can also enjoy the view. The world below only looks different to Johannesburg when the golden bow of Sydney's harbour bridge comes into sight.

That must be her, there's the red scarf. Has to be Shane Jackman, the olive skin, the nose? People here look the same as home. Hardly any black faces.

I walk towards her, try to peel my Afrikaans accent off my English, and introduce myself. Shane asks about the flight, warns me about Sydney's humidity, makes a remark about Jude, something about an "assumption", presents it as a joke then laughs before she completes her sentence.

As she arranges my case in the boot I quickly smell my armpits. Not too pungent, but certainly not fresh anymore.

Shane's got good wide hips. Her armpits show unshaven tufts as she slams the boot shut. The short green-bean green dress is cut away at the arms and gathered around the waist with a thin brown belt. Wide, flat silver earrings dangle from her slender earlobes. Her nails are short and rather neglected and she smells of something earthy, like sweet-potato syrup.

She lives on the North Coast across the bridge. It's the most elegant bridge in the world. The radio is tuned into a station called 3JJJ, and the Opera House is a fluorescent shell. A thousand times more impressive than I'd expected.

Oh, I love the bridge, she says. We can walk across it one of these days. It's a great feeling, fantastic views.

I've come to the right place, Albert, if you ever see this city, you'll get goose bumps, like me now. Can anyone really get so turned on by driving over a bridge, three tripple jay jay jay!

Shane tells that the domes of the opera house are covered with tiny white tiles and apparently, after all these years, only one has ever come loose, then laughs as I somersault about in my seat trying to take everything in all at once. At the end of the bridge there's an illuminated merry-go-round, and behind us the city of glass and light.

I simply must register my experience at the ministry of divine delights. Deloris, your eyes will pop out of their sockets. I can't believe I'm here to do my thing. What the hell *will* I do?

I look at Shane laughing, shiny eyes and teeth.

Is this is how all Afrikaans-speaking South Africans speak English?

We're a strange species, that's for sure, Shane. And we've had our day. We belong in a museum now. I wonder where Verwoerd's statue will go when it's taken down. It's been toyi-toyied to pieces. The statue had a pot belly.

White cotton shirt, grey flannel trousers, brown belt, shiny shoes. Well, as shiny as they possibly could be. Is this how she sees me? Us? Oh, hell, I'd better not always dress like this. Though most of my clothes look like this. They got me past customs easily enough. Clean and squeakily stupid.

Shane shows me my room. I can't identify the smells: blend of guava, pollen and something mouldy? I'll be lost for words in this city. There's an arrangement of agapanthus in the sitting room where Shane opens two wooden frames to bring the light of the harbour bridge a little closer. Across the road is a park of dark trees. I stop gaping at everything, and at her suggestion I take a shower.

I suppose I can use some of her shampoo. Everything is so natural here. Oh, yes, Jude did say the vegetarian restaurant uses mostly organic vegetables. Lots of the stuff on the farm was left unsprayed, wasn't it? So why do they think they're so special? In any case, what did I ever care about the vegetable garden? I'll probably never see boerewors again in my whole life. Why am I thinking about that now?

Have I become too cynical? Not *too*: just enough to have kept me in good health. Maybe I'll need a smaller dose here. Should I ask Shane if she's got a job for me? No; it's too soon. Be patient, man. How old is Shane? Mellow voice, very calm, could it be all those vegetables? The time Daniel and his pals ate only vegetables their hair became shinier than anyone else's and the flames couldn't get to them. It's the lamb fat that makes you roast so easily. Wonder if we'll be staying in tonight? My armpits need another wash. This soap smells like nothing. Sometimes it's just impossible to get rid of your smell. I know my own smell. And Jude's: burnt olive oil. Pa's also, old earth-Adam, he's probably forgotten all about me by now.

And, Konstant, Shane says when she bumps into me in the passage with only a towel around my body, this is your home now, so don't worry about a thing.

I'm, I'm not, I can look after myself very well.

Why should she say a thing like that to me? Trying extra hard to make me feel at home. Sweet of her. Like the way she just starts with "and Konstant" as if there's a conversation between the two of us that's simply being continued.

Not even a bit worried? She remains standing up in front of me.

Well, if you've got a job for me, I'll be less . . . I'm not really anxious about anything, quite the opposite. At the moment I'm just, what's the word?

Acclimatising.

As I talk, the end of the towel, tucked in tightly, starts to slip. My nails are scrubbed clean after the flight. I tighten the towel and fold the end back in. During the quick action I nail her eyes with mine. But she still looks down, first a little, then all the way: a few light, long hairs stray on the circles of my nipples and from my bellybutton a footpath runs downwards under the towel.

I'm glad to be here, Shane, I say, far away from everything – far away from what? – and thanks for collecting me at the airport, I add halfway into my room.

She reminds me that I've thanked her already – in such a way that it doesn't sound like a reproach.

She still hasn't answered me about my request for work. Was it because I only had a towel . . . No, Miesies, I just took a quick jump into that lovely hose of Miesies, now I wonder if Miesies got the job for me, Miesies.

I let the towel drop, hang it over the back of a blondwood chair with chrome legs, and stretch out naked on the bedcover. I take one of my cigarettes, lick the filter, put it between my lips. Am I allowed to smoke in this house?

What ti . . . where's my watch. Must have fallen asleep. Shouldn't have. Did. The body has its own demands. What's Shane doing? We were still going to eat, go out.

The entrance to her room is diagonally opposite mine. A wedge of light from my lamp forms a yellow triangle on the wooden floor of the darkened passage. Shane's bedroom door isn't closed yet. I peep out. The shadow of my head and torso breaks the light in the passage.

The rest of the home is in darkness. Why hasn't she closed her door? I'll close mine. On the farm no one ever closed their doors. Quite touching, come to think of it: everyone passing breath on to everyone else at night, all connected to one another in the dark house.

I'd rather keep my door shut. It's private. Who knows how and where your hand might wander, like on the plane when everyone was asleep and I was far away on Jannie Joubert's game farm one weekend in the Eastern Transvaal. My hand wandering under the plane blanket – the widow had no idea. Me and Jude in one of Jannie's huts, thatchy smell. The memory of a smell never dies. Jeez, we were too hot for the rondawel that night, as if it wasn't sweaty enough outside. Jude clung onto the table with both hands, arse up. And the mosquitoes!

I turn around and gently close the door.

HIJIKI.

Come again?

Hi-ji-ki or Hi-zi-ki.

Black seaweed curls, dried, bottled and stored with other things in jars on a wall rack. Cockroaches scuttle around behind them. If you simmer hijiki with fresh ginger, the black curls swell into fat worms. It tastes like nothing I've ever eaten, yet smells like something I know, like the roots of a tree; no, more like roots from the sea, like evaporated fish offal.

I've never come across a restaurant like Shane's before. It's a sliver of a space, almost like a wide corridor that's been turned into a kitchen with a counter. The customers are served steaming bowls of food straight off the stove onto the yarrawood counter.

Yarra? I ask, like bluegum?

No, yarra.

Djarra, hi-ji-ki, I say. The whole café reeks of it. Wait till they smell sheep's offal.

I'm washing dishes: huge stainless steel saucepans, oven pots, iron pans, wooden bowls, cake rings and chopsticks.

Liz Bird, one of the kitchen hands, is fishing for a garlic press in the murky dishwater. Her fingers curl around a blade. Blood mingles with water. A shriek, a shout. Everyone drops their work: carrots, lettuce leaves, roasted nuts, stirring ladles in the simmering soup. Everything comes to a standstill. Pandemonium.

Elastoplast! someone shouts. Blood squirts.

Mind the food! The steaming brown rice! The cake mix! The gaping casserole. There's a plague in the city, and who knows what's in Liz's blood? Who did it? Who dumped the knife in the washing-up sink?

It lurked in the soapy water like a shark, waiting for an unsuspecting kitchen hand. A golden rule has been disregarded, and who's going to pay for it? It's steaming in here. Is the window open? Open. Are the doors open? Wide open. Sydney's muggy air drips through the kitchen. Steam rises from the deep washing basins, steam from the soup pot, sweat on my forehead, drip-drip. How and whom am I going to pay for the slashed finger? The kitchen hand will be out of action for two, three days, and who will replace her?

Where're the plasters?

Grab some Miso.

Miso?

Brown paste from a wooden barrel to smear onto the finger. An old Japanese remedy.

Shane's efficient hand applies the thick miso paste. The blood from Liz's finger oozes through the layer of miso, drips onto the terracotta floor. There are no more plasters in the kitchen.

Someone run to the chemist, she orders. Quickly. Buy a roll of bandage as well. You go, Joseph. Never mind your apron; your legs are good enough; take a $10 note from the till.

Shane, it was me, I'm sorry.

I feel my face going red. No: it isn't shame. It's the heat in here. My neck is this red anyway, it's only extra blood welling up.

Liz Bird, forgive me, can I suck your thumb?

Don't be crazy.

My mum always sucked our fingers when we were small.

Times have changed: you're not at home now. Where do you come from?

Liz, hold your finger over this cloth and nowhere else. Shane takes control. Let it drip only onto here. Konstant, put the lid on the rice pot. Take the cake mix to the cellar. Move the broccoli crate out of the way. Wipe up every last drop of blood. I assume you know how to use a bucket and mop? Yes? No? Joseph, show Konstant. Add a few drops of eucalyptus oil to the water.

Shane, I'm sorry. Liz, I'm very sorry.

No worries.

Remember the golden rule.

I remember, I remember.

Liz pulls one of the high bar stools closer and sits down. Shane pours her some bancha tea.

Bancha?

Have you finished the washing up? Where's that knife?

Here it is. A Japanese vegetable knife with a rectangular blade and a beautiful wooden handle, perfectly balanced.

Take a look, Shane explains. If you hold it in your hand like this, you'll feel it has an energy of its own. Move your wrist up and down, slightly. The Japanese made it, chopping-knife experts. I'll show you how to cut a carrot?

No, that I *do* know. It's the easiest thing in the world! Shut up, Konstant, you know nothing.

First, place your cutting board on a damp cloth so that it can't slip while you're at it. If it slips, your fingers are done for. Place the carrot carefully in the middle, and hold it with your left hand, firm but not tense. Now curl your left-hand fingers around the carrot like a hedgehog, so that the flat part of the blade presses against the knuckles. Never work unevenly. Never get nervous . . .

You can't expect me to be dead calm already; surely that only comes with time?

. . . that way you avoid accidents, it's only when your fingers peep out that they get into trouble. You lead the knife with your left hand knuckles. Experts say that you cut with your left hand, not your right. See what I mean? Ah, it's not sharp enough. Wait; let's show you how to whet it. Where's the stone? Here, in its place. Second golden rule: everything in the kitchen has its own place.

A grey limestone.

Sprinkle water on it, place the blade at an angle to the stone and move lightly up and down. Then the other side.

I remember old Samuel when we were slaughtering buck.

No time for mulling over memories now. Is the washing-up done? Joseph, your rice-ball mixture needs a pinch of salt. What's the oven temperature? Have the roasted walnuts been added to the cake mix?

At some stage Joseph says to me: you ought to eat less meat and more vegetables, it keeps you mellow like soaked rice with the kernel of common sense intact.

Thanks, Jesuit Joseph. He's an outback oaf from Kalgoorlie

with a priest complex. Where's that? Somewhere in the sand dunes of Western Australia. Excuse me, Joseph, little shit: this isn't your shop, you know. Who do you think you are?

Freckle-faced Liz will lose up to three days' work.

It doesn't matter about the accident, Liz tells me when she notices that Shane has gone out to the storeroom. It gives me a few days off. I'll go horse riding under the Morton Bay figs in Centennial Park. Don't tell Shane.

A taste of kitchen politics.

Who'll stand in for you, Liz?

You, I guess.

Was it all a cunning plan hatched by my subconscious? Survival of the fittest? The dishwater mixed with the cooked hijiki smells like cantaloupe peels smothered in meaty gravy . . . won't touch those little black snakes.

I keep my eyes peeled. Got eyes at the back of my head. And listen attentively: maybe I'll pick up something useful. Shane moves into position behind her chopping board. She's wearing a neat dark-blue apron, shoulders squared, chin slightly down. She chops three medium-sized brown onions into paper-thin slices, and moves to the stove where one of the six gas rings is free. She takes a stainless steel frying pan down from a meat hook, and drizzles six drops of hazelnut-brown sesame oil into it, then lightly sautés the onions, stirring them with a bamboo spatula.

She asks me to drain the water off the hijiki and to set it aside.

Already thrown away. I blush.

Joseph's eyes turn to me. Arrogant Jesuit. I thought they were supposed to be compassionate.

I'm really sorry, Shane.

No worries, mate.

Yes, but I do worry.

She mixes the hijiki into the light-brown onions, and adds some golden sweetcorn.

Corncobs, keep or throw away?

Won't throw anything else away. You see, I'm smart: a quick learner. I *do* come from somewhere. I chuck the cobs together, with the celery leaves and broccoli stalks, into the bouillon bucket for the base of tomorrow's soup. My first workday ends.

Never in all my life have I been as tired as this. I can hardly lift my arms to wash my hair in the shower. The worker deserves his rest. Rip first worked himself into a frazzle and then dozed off for an eternity. Wish I could sleep forever. Shane has made my bed up with fresh sheets: white, starched linen – no, cotton. Must get myself a mosquito net like hers. Maybe just crawl into bed with her one night. Can't even . . . poor me, look how kaput! $100 for a cotton net. Will have to wait till I get my first pay. Mosquitoes will just have to suck blood till then. They're bigger here, their gaffs sharper. The hijiki didn't taste too bad in the end, with the fried onion and sweetcorn. Must get the recipe. Joseph surprised me during lunchhour when he came to sit next to me and gave me a sympathetic hug. Despite my sweaty shirt. We all smelled like food, like hijiki extract.

My first day and I've already bared my fangs: shark in the dishwater, a trap for Liz's hand – all so that she can spend tomorrow with that big bum of hers straddling a horse. Then the hijiki stock down the drain. Who'd have thought grey water could be of any use? They humble me, these kitchen colleagues of mine. They're like tenderly blanched cauliflower: we don't allow mistakes to alienate us from one another – we're all human. The Jesuit lost himself in his lunch-hour homily. I'd finished by the time he began to slurp his tepid soup.

Who'll stand in for Liz Bird today? I ask Shane at the breakfast table the next morning.

Jamal, the temporary cook. He's from Indonesia. Smooth brown skin. Does he speak English? A strange bird call comes from the Moreton Bay fig trees outside Shane's flat.

Just enough to know what he wants. That's a currawong you're hearing there.

Come again?

Cur-ra-wong. I stand in front of the open window.

Looks like a crow to me. Crow's arse, man. Hear how coolly it coo-kirr-i-aauw's so early in the morning.

Jamal arrives at the restaurant for his cooking shift with a cloth bag of candlenuts.

How much do I owe you for the nuts, Jamal? Shane speaks into his ears, brown like halved peach pips.

Nothing, no one owes me anything, the transaction was done and sealed yesterday, today is today, he answers.

Just listen to that currawong shouting at us kitchen hands. I look through the window at the plump bird on the ridge of the roof opposite.

No currawong that, it's a magpie.

But they're birds of a feather.

Look carefully. Everything's different here.

Shane, what where today, how long and until when?

Set your own pace, Konstant.

Whoever starts the day by asking questions even before the dishwashing water foams is no self-starter. My washing-up is soon done. Joseph raises his morning-weary eyes, full of wonder: this broom sweeps cleaner on its second day. No white man, no white person, no one at all is cut out for this kind of work, ha! Now it's the vegetables for the salad.

Here's the board, here's a place to stand. Where's your apron? Got going without one! Use Liz Bird's knife, she won't be the wiser, put it back in its cloth sheath this afternoon, un-nicked. Good. Chop the heads and tails off a bowl of washed carrots. Then cut them into equal diagonal wedges. Diagonally – that way you capture the yin and yang in a single wedge.

Gin and jan?

No answer. Never mind. Work hard, learn fast. An able hand becomes its own master. I feel invigorated: my body sank into the mattress last night. Such bliss. And carrots are easier cut with a sharp knife. Chop-chop, not much chit-chat, survive with senses out on stalks. Watch the other kitchen hands carefully. Between chopping the onions and apples, it's my task to wash their cutting boards with boiling water and rough sea salt.

See Jamal. Never tired, not a single drop of sweat. But the women – their armpit hairs drip like stalactites onto the side panels of their skimpy summer dresses, onto the green nori leaves in which they roll rice and daikon pickles.

Jamal always finishes first, his voice calm, his eyes a prayer, his hands like leaves. He's as tender as a halaal lamb. Every two hours he eats a red chilli. Chillies bring on perspiration and that's how he stays cool.

How long have you been on this continent?

Six years, alone by myself, without family; my family are my friends.

Jamal, do you know "baie" for a lot?

Yes I know "baie".

Do you know "bobotie".

That one I don't know.

Do you know "papaya" for pawpaw?

Flesh as sweet as a kiss, I know "papaya," yes.

Jamal, do you like "piesangs" for bananas?

The shorter the tastier, the longer the sweeter. I know "pie-sangs".

Do you know "tjalie" for shawl?

I don't know "tjalie".

Do you sleep on a "katel" for a bedstead?

I do everything on my "katel".

Do you know "tjap" for stamp?

"Tjap-tjap," yes, stamp-stamp.

Jamal, do you know "atjar" for pickles?

I make my own green mango "atjar," only tastier.

Do you know "verlang" for longing?

Longing I know well, early in the morning I long for my mother busy roasting fresh vegetables. I long for the smell of sweet potato, tomato, ginger, lime leaves. Scents that cut my morning prayers short.

My carrots are chopped. Where's the white porcelain bowl for my salad?

Wait, mate, Joseph cautions yet again. First steam your carrots in this Chinese bamboo basket, then rinse them in cold water until they're cool right through to their carrot hearts – and you'll see just how carrots shine. Now cut broccoli florettes and steam them lightly. Be careful not to over-steam – grey vegetables are anathema here. After that, start on the corn.

Mealies I know, don't try telling me a thing about green mealies.

Cut them into neat wheels. Steam, and mix everything together, carefully: we treat vegetables with love here.

He can't say a thing without sermonising.

Robert, the Dutchman, walks in, here to help with the dish-washing.

Wakame, he greets.

Come again?

Wa-ka-me. Robert, rolled ciggy behind the ear, believes that's how the Japanese greet one another: knees on the ground, palms facing the guest: wa ka me.

Spurred on by his lightheartedness, I shamelessly tell my kitchen colleagues about old Anna on our farm. How she spent her days sitting submissively on the ground under a tree, washing our sheets, shirts, underwear. When I've finished I feel I've put my foot in it.

For this, they laugh at me: it's not our business to box your ears. You didn't expect *that* from us? Washermanmate. Kalgoorlie, Karoo, Calabria, Canton – it's combination soup here: eat and enjoy lest we remember, if you haven't realised yet . . .

I swear I'll never spill the beans about my past again. That I swear. I loosen my apron.

That night the heat keeps me awake. I get up, bare-arsed, for a glass of chilled water.

Shane is at her kitchen table. In the glow of a lamp she uses chopsticks to pick miniscule stones from a pile of dry beans. She looks up. I halt in the shadow of the doorframe and cover myself.

Don't! Stay as you are, she pleads, her voice tender.

What's she looking at? Warts picked up from playing with frogs? She's pretty under the light. Why hasn't she gone to sleep yet? How silent the night is: my breath, that's all. How long will I allow her to gaze at me – a minute, minutes? I may be her employee, but that doesn't mean she can feel me up. How gentle her orders sound in the café. She never barks. Need trousers, things are hotting up.

I swing around, still covered, and in my room flatten myself into my jeans.

Bare-chested? Rather not. I'll take my ointment with me.

Shane pours us a tot.

The drink tastes sweet. Cockroach tentacles peep from under the bowl of papinos and jackfruit. I smell the frangipani through the open window and the essential oil on Shane's olive skin. Moist eyes bear witness to late nights. She talks about a new recipe, sago and citron, about her competitive sister who wants to have a baby before she does, about this city. It turns its inhabitants into somnambulists.

Shane, could you please rub some ointment into the spots on my back? I take my shirt off.

She sniffs the pale pink rose ointment then rubs it slowly into the fungous spots on my back. She doesn't miss any. I know how many there are, buggers.

Shane is thorough, in her café, too: don't cut too close to the cob or you'll get bits in the salad.

She finishes and closes the tin. I'm about to turn around when she takes hold of my shoulder and massages my neck, my shoulder blades and upper arms with her firm fingers.

I can smell her. Her unshaven armpits, her tepid breath, the bottle of sour dough fermenting on the table, the moist subtropical night. How constrained old Lady Macquarie's bosom and pelvis must have felt in her double corset when she arrived at this wild land with the First Fleet.

In two days' time Jude arrives. I'll move from Shane's flat to his house.

Shane, where is Jude's house?

Next to the railway line.

Far from the harbour, the bow of the bridge, are there currawongs?

There are Kooris.

Are they dangerous?

They're Kooris.

Are they ugly, do they look like the oldest people on earth, like pre-humans, do they look human at all?

Can tell where he's from.

Must watch my words. What would I look like after 40 000 years of dreaming – Oblomov was tatty enough from just one year's sleep.

Before going back to bed, I take a walk in the shadowy park outside the flat. The night smells of harbour water and damp moss. Like a true man of the wilds, I piss on the luxurious air-roots of a wild fig tree. And bump into the creatures I'd seen on my very first night in Sydney: brown-eyes scrambling up and down for something to nibble, rampant possum tails that whisk off into the shiny crown of leaves as soon as anything approaches.

The dark figure of a man walks up to me. I'm not afraid like in the past. Under the strip of streetlight, he briefly shows his face, offers a cigarette, gestures towards the deep shadows, and says something that his broad indigenous accent obscures. Later, between my cool sheets, I reconsider his words, deliciously salacious in hindsight.

Can't be, surely. Anything can. What would Jude think, knowing that so much has happened to me in such a short time? This really is a land of new opportunities. Can hardly remember when last I wanted a skyf. Bancha tea is a Japanese stick-like tea that lulls you to sleep, tempeh is a fermented soybean cake, wakame is green dried seaweed, agar-agar is a plant-like gelatine straight from the sea, kudzu – chalky crystals from the root of a legume. Shane says it grows on the coldest mountain slopes of Japan and is used as a thickener or a lozenge. Miso is the shinbone of meat-free soup; hatcho miso natto miso genmai miso mugi miso Shane says mugi muggins morrow morning early call curwong.

Jude returns, completely overwhelmed to see me. And as for me! Our reconnection lasts as long as a cup of bancha tea, then he's off to the street-level gym on Crown Street, going on about the damage the fleshpots of the fatherland have caused body and soul.

This time he's soon back, freshly sauna-ed and rosy-cheeked.

Come, Konstant; let me show you our place.

Jude comes to fetch me, an arm around my hips, the old honey-voiced heart-melter. What will Jude make of me, of us, what will I make of myself in this new city?

We stop for cloudy beer in brown, long-necked bottles. The city pulsates, waits for no one, everyone's doing their own thing.

Jude's place is down a narrow street. It's musty from being closed up. He opens windows and shutters, fingers a swelling where the wall has become damp, lights candles and incense on saucers in the middle of every room. I must sprinkle salt along the skirting. There are five dead cockroaches in the kitchen and three are swimming in the toilet. We wander into the walled courtyard. Jude kneels beside a blackboy. He examines the plant's sharp-edged leaves, smells the soil, tests for mildew, looks up at the darkening horizon. We drink the brown beer, elbows in the air. The evening is alien and pleasant, I tell Jude. He's pleased: this city *is* a strange animal, and you have to ride it bareback. We go out to buy Thai fishcakes in coconut milk with hot chillies, fresh ginger slices and fresh coriander.

Where do the Kooris live?

Opposite us. Come, I'll show you. Jude hangs a silver football-whistle on a thong around his neck.

Just in case, he says.

City sounds creep right up to Jude's front door: a dog hit by a car, a train departing from the station alongside the fence: "all stations to Penrith"; a seagull scooping crumbs from the platform. A billboard announces that defective condoms are a thing of the past. The beer has fuzzed my head.

There they live!

In the street with the bare lightbulb, the dishevelled mongrel, the tricycle that should have been taken inside, the wrinkled woman searching for her front door, the greengrocer on the corner without display shelves and no windows?

Jude suggests we take a train to a downtown bar.

On the way I complain that the floor is littered with leftover food. Jude realises that I'd rather be home. We get off, return, and spend the entire night in one another's arms without sleeping a wink till daybreak.

I return home in the evening to find Jude glistening with sweat. He's been painting all day. The passage, sitting room, and kitchen are done. All white. Jude smells of paint on sweaty skin.

Now?

Or later, or always, I'm as fit as a fiddle and ready to go.

The floorboards are cool under my back; the paint smells like jam, the candles have been dripping since last night. Jude and I soak the floor: this city sweats deliciously. The paint remains open while we busy ourselves, until a film forms on it. Outside, from far: "All stations to Penrith." The city goes about its business; we carry on with our own thing. And so this house becomes my home too. We don't wash, and paint on. Now and then we interrupt the late afternoon and night with oranges or beer and even some mind-numbing pot.

The house turns into a new pin and I can breathe freely at last. The painting was good. Long after midnight in the courtyard, I watch stars flicker far above the city lights. There's a cricket near my foot. When I move, he chokes on his chirrup.

Before Jude's furniture arrives by boat, we delight in a double bed, one table and two chairs. The floor gleams, the walls shine, and the neighbour walks in. She's Greek, dressed in black, and whispers unintelligible monosyllables. She points a surprised finger at our sparse furnishings, disappears, then returns with a plate of spinakopita, and an armchair which she drags in behind her.

The first train wakes me on my day off. I'm never tired, and never wake up tired. I lie in bed watching Jude in the mirror: hair up or hair down, something on the eyelashes, a little too dark – or is it too light? The four-point star made of Mexican silver or the beetle-yellow mass of beads around the neck? What do you think? Brown or black or brick-red for nails and toenails? The earbuds, the eyebrow tweezers. Perfume from the green vial or balsam from the black amphora? Phlegm in the washbasin. Hem too long, what do you think? The silver or the gold? Look at these arms, losing their firmness already. Squeeze this blackhead on my back. How do I look? Come, let's get some fish.

Jude and I battle through the traffic to the fishmarket.

Will there be snoek, mackerel, yellowtail, steenbras?

Stop making comparisons between South Africa and your new country, man, Jude admonishes me.

The market indeed carries fruit of a new ocean: oily butterfish, marrow-soft sea trout, muddy-pink yabbies, New Zealand green mussels, craggy crabs, tiny blue crabs with impish eyestalks, mauve pipis to be cooked with fresh bay leaves. Jude is confident among the stalls.

Am I imagining it, or is the fisherman looking askance at Jude in his unconventional Saturday morning get-up?

Jude chooses the stall served by a young boy in white Wellingtons. A curlyhead with a snubby nose. He lets Jude choose his own smoked eel. Then rolls the snake up quick as lightning. From his slimy hands it slips into a plastic bag. His eyes, currants, are already checking out the note in Jude's palm, aware of the next customer. He sorts the change in seconds, checks whether we check if it's correct, and if his second client is still interested, folds our package in butcher's paper, catches Jude's eye on him for a moment, then hands it over as something passes between them, too quickly for me to pick up. The change is right: One eel thanks mate yessir can I help you, sir?

Back home, Jude cuts the eel into wedges and makes a pumpkin pie that comes out of the oven with a golden yellow crust. Hunter Valley wine completes the meal. He's also baked bread using Shane's yeast, and the whole house smells of freshly-risen dough.

A dog pisses against the front door: the house becomes part of his territory. In the back garden I lure a magpie closer with grains of rice.

And Jude goes to the Crown Street gym every day.

I lie on the clean floor in an empty room. Waken to someone who says my name, to an ant, to a strip of sunlight on my hand. I carry a pillow into another empty room to read my book. Run my hands lightly along the passage wall, mop the kitchen floor with a bucket of warm water and a drop of eucalyptus oil. Do sit-ups in the empty cavity of the sitting room. All the ceilings look the same, white, until I discover a crack in the one in our room and a bit of fly-puke on the one in the kitchen - and I find a name carved into the wooden door of the spare room, at the bottom left hand corner, sandpapered to become illegible. There are 35, 70 and 35 lead panes in the sitting room windows. And rising damp on the wall to the left of the front door. I rest in the sitting room under the ceiling rose with seven knurls in its outside circumference. If I put my ear against the right-hand wall in the passage, the station sounds closest. In our room the air filtered in through the two shutters is the freshest. I curse the impending arrival of Jude's load of furniture.

Jude returns on time every time with a spotlessly steamed skin. And tries on new jewellery in front of the mirror.

I walk through the empty rooms, rub along the walls, and lay my ear against the shiny sanded floors. Jude will return by sunset. It's raining and warm outside. Here you can stay outside without getting gooseflesh. The walls, rooms, ceilings betray nothing of my suspicious mind. I fail in my attempt to maintain integrity, and can't resist the temptation to compile an inventory: one expedition to a bar – cancelled for my sake; one delicious eel and pumpkin pie, thick butter and Tasmanian goat's milk cheese on a slice of sourdough bread in bed – just for me; all the rooms white, the floors shiny; re-turn-times strictly adhered to – for my sake; my morning desire and evening lust are stilled in the echoing house – and even the station master shuts up then. What will Jude demand in return?

Jude's Koori friends don't have mangy dogs or snotty-nosed children sniffling along behind them. One of them, Cherril, invites us to an all-night party with the Aboriginal and Islander Dance Company on a pleasure boat in the harbour basin.

We depart merrily from quay seven. Men with curly black chest hair wave glasses of beer at the skyscrapers as they disappear, all cocooned in fog. Shane Jackman and Liz Bird are also on board. The boat passes under the bridge, past Glebe, Balmain, Goat Island, Birchgrove. Between Woolwich and Greenwich, dancing starts in the cabin. Trudie Aspeling sings to a band. Trudie's from Cape Town.

Hey, Truri, sing Walsin' Matilla for us, someone shouts.

I meet Doreen, Sylvia, Alec, Shorty, Leyland and their grey-frizzy-haired granny on a chair, Colleen Japaldjarri. While talking to her, Liz Bird sneaks up from behind and whispers in my ear for a dance. I promise, but later, after talking to granny Japaldjarri.

Dark waters churn by, a sausage slips from the food-laden table. Granny points out the twins she raised in the city: Doreen and Sylvia. They're exquisite, with their rich black hair. Granny's hair is terribly frizzy.

From eating pumpkin? I dare ask like an idiot.

She cracks up: yes, from eating Queensland Blues. For the rest she babbles on, so very convivially.

Has Granny tasted those Japanese ones, all the way from Hokkaido? I ask. I've checked the map myself, let me tell you, I'm not talking nonsense here – making her laugh again – it's the big, northern island, and it grows the sweetest pumpkins in the world. We should be really grateful. Hope Liz Bird isn't resenting me not taking up her invitation yet. She should understand.

Granny and I carry on chattering away about growing old. She's aged like ripe grass, gracefully. Jude joins us, not that I mind, but Granny and I *were* getting along pretty well.

Where does she come from? Jude chips in. Her people come from the Warlpiri region. And Jude adds something, something about the Chilla water hole and this and that. Granny Japaldjarri is surprised this whitefella knows about it at all and I almost congratulate Jude, but what the heck.

Instead, I watch Jude: the way he stands, his legs apart when the boat rolls, how he recovers perfectly every time; the way he sits, legs aesthetically crossed; the glass, the cigarette held so artfully – I have nothing more to offer here, and get up. Let Jude and Granny go it alone.

And their conversation continues:

I think white women are obsessed with the virility of black men, as long as they are not Aboriginal, Jude natters on.

As a last attempt, I ask what Granny's name means. She laughs at my question. Did she understand me? Am I really too gauche to mix with these people? Honestly, I never saw Granny as desert exotica that's blown in to the city. We talked so nicely about pumpkins, didn't we? And I still wanted to tell about my ma's pumpkin fritters with cinnamon. It's Jude who has burdened Granny with his personal fantasies – not me. Don't know how he gets away with it. And why did Granny laugh at me?

Time to get outside. It will be fresher on deck.

Granny asks Jude something. Her drink has slid along the shelf behind her.

Whe's yer friend goin', wha's this ferry doin', whe're my drink goin'?

I climb down to the toilets right below. The toilet hole is a circle of harbour water. The first Wasserman to piss in Sydney harbour: I've arrived!

Back at the bow with another beer I listen to three men singing to a guitar:

Will you marry me on a Friday night
don't forget to keep your promise
or else I'll cry my eyes out.

I climb to the top deck. The fog is so moist that drops of water condense on my skin. Someone's approaching. It's Liz Bird. We lean over the railings, about a foot away from one another. Muffled sounds rise from the water. Below, the dancers stomp, the band doef-doefs. Liz points out beacons: Balls Head, the tower block at Milson's Point, Shane's flat somewhere behind the park with the Mortan Bay figs. She tells of her first visit to Luna Park. Liz is soft in the mist.

At work she often makes time to explain things to me: Japanese noodles are shocked three times in cold water after they've reached boiling point; a sheaf of lemon grass is cut into fine rings – like this. She reminds me of a mushy pear with freckles. Fills her jeans and her white shirt, a man's shirt - could almost be my clothes. No rings, bracelets, earrings, nose-rings. Not even a watch. Only a delicate ring on her pinkie. Something a boyfriend fished from his trouser pocket on the playground during break and stuck on his flame's finger. Looks like she grew up on a farm, a sisterly type. Nice round breasts, firm bottom from all that horse riding. Bet the divide where the cheeks part is clearly visible in her jodhpurs. Sand-blonde hair tied back in a ponytail, the ears girlish, small.

Liz fondles my hand on the railing, and tells me a story:

Her brother was fifteen, she was only eight, blood of the same blood, when he began committing shame with her – lots of stories like this in the tabloids of my new homeland – and when she realised what was going on she put a stop to the thing with his thing.

But Liz, why are you telling me such intimate things?

Oh, Konstant, your face, your eyes are so winsome against the red and yellow lights of Luna Park. I'd hoped you'd want to hold me tight, against you, against my childhood misery.

She's still sensitive about the ring, given to her by none other than her brother at the time. And last Christmas when he noticed it at the family table, after all these years, he teased: My ring, isn't it? She blushed.

Why don't you get rid of it? Come, let's do it right now, tonight, throw it away, let the shame sink into the sea, now's a good opportunity.

See, the merry-go-round's going by, Konstant, she responds.

And there it is again: that peculiar image of Jude. When did I first see it? Just as Liz joined me: Jude below with Granny, I can scarcely make him out. He's become a mere outline, a line-figure in a colouring-in book waiting for a child's hand and a crayon.

I hug Liz Bird, our skin damp against one another. Shall we dance? As we go down, she frees herself and descends a level further to the toilet below. So Shane and I dance – wildman, wildwoman – until the boat rocks beneath us: Forget me not on a Friday night!

When I put the brakes on, Shane grabs any willing partner and dances on madly. Loose hips you've got there, Trudie of the Cape. Crazy reels. Everyone dances till the sweat simmers, they down beer till it overflows, japaldjarrijapaljapaldjarri.

The expedition to the Kuringai-Chase Park happens on a Sunday. Sandwiches are prepared with a long face. Jude's furniture should have been here by now, and he'd rather have stayed to unpack the familiar possessions, to fill up and arrange the empty white house.

Sydney glitters like gold, everyone's driving over the vibrating harbour bridge. Sunglasses, booming radios, children and bull-terriers, noses all smeared pink, guys with golf clubs and girls with flaxen hair like sea sand, surfboards under their arms. Robert, Liz, Shane, Jude and I head towards Palm Beach – a hand-picked spot under the bluest sky on earth.

A ferry takes us across Pittwater to Mackerel where a cluster of houses are set back away under bluegums on a shimmering fringe of sand. We leave our basket and precious chilled wine in the shade of a coral tree in the care of fellow bathers. Their satisfied bellies and lazy gaze assure us that our food is safe. Shane leads the way on a winding path past weatherboard houses to the top of a stony hill.

Robert is first to see the kookaburra whose witch-like mimicry we all hear. He's off before I can see him. The path leads us deeper into the reserve, further away from people and fresh water.

The air is laden with the fragrance of herbs, bluegum resin and hot sunlight. I follow on Shane's heels, Liz on mine, all of us along a path bordered by straggly banksias. I look back. Jude and Robert have fallen far behind. Far.

They'll catch up, Shane assures us.

The day goes on. We stop for a drink. Three rosellas trace a red and green rainbow above us, invisible birds cavort in the bush below. Out of breath, we reach our destination: a huge stone mound engraved with Aboriginal reliefs. Dolphins jumping over the moon, giant men with uplifted arms, echidnae. How old would the fingers be that engraved these rocks? Those mischievous dolphins – where's Jude? I'm doomed. I just can't rest in the moment.

We squat under shade bush until the birds are used to us. At last the bushes crackle. It sounds like hooves crunching branches.

I'm relieved to see them. Always happy to have Jude back with me again. What kept you so long? – any normal person would want to ask. Fact is: it's Jude I'm dealing with here. He's out of breath And neither he nor Robert – tough guys – say a word to me. It's not worth the effort, is it?

Jude's face is flushed, how often haven't I caressed it myself, like moss on a stone. Don't you look at me, Liz, you with your eternally available breasts, my hands don't fit them. And you, Robert – you look like the boy who pulled his tired finger out of the dyke.

Shane chortles to herself: Looks like the two of you had a bit of off-road fun.

I spend the rest of the day in Shane's vicinity, and the next day too, when, to Jude's great joy, the furniture arrives.

Won't be able to help, Jude.

I honestly don't feel like moving the stuff around to suit your taste, phone your mate, Mr Tough Guy – let him slug around and set things up for you. Ask his opinion: does it look better like *this* or like *that*, the picture up above, or upside down, which cloth fits best here, and how, and what, and where the dining room table's mat's

113

arse. Before I leave to have my crew-cut, Jude makes me sit on the single bed the dungareed guys have just carried into the spare room from the pantechnicon: Now we can each have our own room.

I've got nothing to say, I say.

Well, think about it, he waves me off.

I choose a barber downtown near Centrepoint. I'm not cut out for this expedition: my mind's wandering, like someone delirious with shingles.

From a glass of grey milk the barber lifts a pair of scissors and a comb. The cracks in the chair's vinyl, a pile of the latest *People* magazines for waiting clients, the baby cactus in the display window all suggest years of professionalism. Which makes it all the more difficult:

Sorry, Omie, jeez, you've really shaved badly, look here above my left ear, there's a barren patch. For sure my hair grows there.

Look carefully, mate, and you'll see that it's okay.

These people are so skilful the way they colour *mate* with such friendliness that you are almost overwhelmed – only to be hit by its sneering undertone later. They practised it to perfection, all those months on the ships getting here.

Look, I know I've got, I mean I know I've had hair on that patch. I'm really unhappy about it.

Did I really *have* to go and trip over my words there? It gives the old pockface a gap, and these boys are good at taking gaps. He defends himself vigorously: been practising the barber's art for years now, why would he go and mess it up . . . And by the way, where do I come from? Eighteen dollars, please.

You must be joking.

Meekly I count out the fives, take three dollars, and leave without another word.

Bloody cheek to ask where I come from – where the hell does he think his scum comes from? Stole a chicken in England, thrown on a boat, ate every rat in sight, and the moment they arrive here they suddenly play king and shove Aboriginals off cliffs at gunpoint. Where the hell do I come from, can you believe it!

Before I'm due to get off at Redfern, I glaze over, staring at a chocolate wrapper stuck between the train seats: You remember? I do! Konnie and little Allie and Hestertjie playing bazaar-bazaar on the front stoep on the farm, baking mud cakes in polish tins. And who put a snake in *my* mud cake?

I get off here. How strange the station looks this afternoon, have they re-painted it? There's been work going on here. From here the line runs west to where the sun sets. Never been further than Redfern yet . . . Suppose two dollars will buy her some bread. She sits in the same place every day, wonder whether she recognises me yet? Actually, she should call passers-by by name. Would make everyone happier and give her more coins in the hat. Definitely not every day, but today she caught me out. Poor thing, thought Aboriginals cared for their elderly and orphans, why's she left here so bedraggled? Needs a little extra for a tot, of course. I don't really mind. Anyway, she seems in much better spirits than most of the spookfaces on the train.

When I get there, the house is perfect. Flowers scent almost every room, and only a few boxes of the coffee-table books haven't been unpacked yet. A primitive vanity cupboard, a collector's item called bush furniture, graces the bathroom. Every corner, every cornice, picture frame and the kitchen; every pelmet, the toilet floor, every cupboard and all the bed linen: dusted down, mopped to a shine, disinfected, de-mothed and puffed up. Jude's not in.

By six in the evening he's still out. The pan waits, cold on the stove, the telephone has a plastic chill about it.

What should I do? Read EM Forster. The cave scene. The pages smell mothy, here it is:

"It was natural enough: she had always suffered from faintness, and the cave had become too full, because all the retinue followed them. Crammed with villagers and servants, the circular chamber began to smell. She lost Aziz in the dark, didn't know who touched her, couldn't breathe, and some vile naked thing struck her face and settled on her mouth like a pad. She tried to regain the entrance tunnel, but an influx of villagers swept her back. She hit her head. For an instant she went mad, hitting and gasping like a fanatic."

It disgusts me. What about a magazine? I still wanted to read that article by Rian Malan. Where's it? How many hours now? Maybe the blackboy needs water. Then I'll have to go outside. Can you . . . yes, I can hear the phone outside, in case Jude phones. Music, what? A skyf? No, that would be a mistake. Only intensifies the mood. I'll order a taxi. But what if Jude tries to phone while I'm . . . a cup of rooibos tea with soya milk – next best thing to mother's milk – hell, I must get away from here.

Jude stays out till six the next morning. Then he's back, in time for breakfast.

My feet are cold on the naked kitchen floor. Jude had better hurry in the bathroom, or I'll be late for work. A pot simmers on a low gas flame, smears on its lip. I lift the stainless steel lid: mealie-meal porridge.

Wouldn't have thought coarse mealie-meal was available here. All the porridge eaters from across the other side have created a big enough demand. There, Jude's done. Hate it when I have to shower and the bathroom is all steamed up.

I open the washing basket, grab a pile of Jude's smoky clothing from the previous night and sniff it.

Ugh, hell, do I really have to sink this low: I know where I came from, after all.

If you really *have* to know, Jude responds when I question him after my shower, as I'm pouring warm soya milk and honey over my breakfast porridge.

Of course I want to know, ignorance makes a fool of me. What's his name?

Mister J. Met at a club with a stage. Next thing, Mister J led me by the hand behind the curtain. All those years at a Catholic school had given him ample time to perfect his single greatest fantasy, and the moment had come for him to live it out. You must understand: while the prayer rites were being solemnly performed in front, the bit of stage behind the red velvet curtain became the locus for his erotic pleasure.

Locus of pleasure. You were at a club last night. There weren't any prayers.

How do you know? There's always a wisp of smoke rising somewhere.

Oh, Jude, there's nothing quite like mealie-meal porridge to stick in the gullet, so what did the Catholic schoolboy do with you, what did you get up to behind the curtain?

It's not necessary, or good – for your health – to know too much.

Jude circles the breakfast table and holds me from behind. He smells sweet after his bath, like an open jar of fig jam.

Knowledge drives me berserk. From the time I arrive home the next day, from four that afternoon until seven in the evening, Jude is away again. At the gym perhaps? I doubt it. Should I phone for peace of mind? Never! I'll never open washing-basket lids again. Jude's gym pants are lying on the bed, look, the black pair, folded neatly on the corner of the white bedspread. Suppose it's not a visit to the gym.

You don't need pants to visit a private Turkish bath, Konstant. How's your heart?

Where do you meet them all? And how? My heart beats feebly.

Why do you ask me that, my dearest desire? Don't you remember our very first night – weren't you the one who approached me? So you *do* know.

Whatever. What's his name?

His name has been engraved for his entire fleshly existence on his left arm in the shape of eagle wings – the most beautifully written name I've ever licked.

With your tongue?

How else would you lick a Maori skin, browned by the steam floating above our bath. And even darker under water.

Just like that, under water, or standing on the wet floor?

You don't need to know that. His bulging thighs, arms, chest filled the whole place.

Jude you're living my fantasies. You've also been careless: just now in the shower I noticed you'd forgotten your butt on the rim of our washbasin, probably while you were sitting. It's left a burn mark. Go look for yourself if you don't believe me, we'll never get rid of it. It's a blot on the ceramic.

And so, two days later we spend my free morning looking for ceramic bleach. Between twelve and six minutes past twelve, I wander about in aisle four of the hardware shop. Jude's off on his own tack, he's walking in another aisle, searching, on the lookout.

What aisle did it happen in, I ask Jude that evening at home.

Do you have to know that too?

I have to know everything.

But fantasies work best without knowing anything.

I prefer every detail to be spelled out. That way I can hold onto you when you're not with me.

You're losing your grip.

I've never had one on you. What was his name?

I don't know, hardware clients don't wear name tags, do they?

I thought he was one of the assistants.

Oh, he wanted to assist me.

So in what aisle did you find yourself?

Aisle six.

Two aisles away from the hammers?

No, at the screwdrivers – no, that's a lie – it was the hammers. He pulled the elastic of his trousers away and all I saw was tummy and a tool.

Weren't there any witnesses?

Not as far as I could see.

Konstant, you haven't washed this pot too well. Look here, there're lumps of sago stuck to the base. Is something . . .? Something is wrong, Shane concludes.

I know, Shane, pass it back here.

Sago clings like shit to a blanket. I tried scouring it off with this piece of steelwool so hard my skin flew off this knuckle, and this one here too.

You think it's Jude's absences that have caused these bags under my eyes? Just drop it. Not that I don't appreciate my job here, Shane, I simply don't feel like talking to you or anyone else, though I am trying. Promise. I lift my head from the washing basin. Something's floating on the dishwater, the chlorophyll residue of Liz's grated zucchini salad. I'd rather fixate on that than talk about myself.

I know, I know I'm slower than usual today. But check me tomorrow.

For the past two weeks now, we've had a problem waiting for

pots. You don't look too good to me, Konstant – something wrong? Let's talk about it, man. This afternoon?

This afternoon, no, totally out of the question. Must be home in time to wait for Jude, or the house will be empty if he arrives unexpectedly. I mean unexpectedly on time. Jude's always on time. And the paleness is just the new diet, you know, it takes time to get used to it. Those bean soups and blocks of tofu and the unpolished rice and plates of crunchy hard vegetables all burst out at the other end. What I need is a piece of fillet. By the way, I don't think much of Liz's salads: too much like chicken food. Remember her salads a few months back when she arranged the bowls so the clients thought they looked like tiny faces? Those were great salads, those. To tell the truth, Shane, and I think I can, Liz's work has deteriorated. She has no right to confront me about my work pace. Honestly, that woman's got a problem with me. I refuse to help her with her salads. I won't stand close to her again. She's got a hidden agenda with that freckled body of hers. Besides, my hands are trembling. Yes, Shane, that's the way it is – trembling hands can't throw salads together. Too risky. What if I cut my finger right off, worse than Liz's that first day? I know you don't pay for sick leave. No work, no pay. We all work bloody hard for you, Shane. You hear me? You realise that I'm so tired at night that I can't even sleep? Yes, Shane – can't even sleep. That's why my work's suffering. Or is it a matter of the new broom not sweeping clean any more? Must write to Pa that white brooms and black brooms sweep equally badly. It's a fact. Have to slog on, or who will keep our pot on the boil? Especially when there's no one at home. Do you know when last Jude and I slept together? Oh, I can't even remember anymore. It's not my fault! Jude cut me down to size, trained me up and found lots of pleasure in it all. Said so himself, I don't know how many times. No, the escapades have nothing to do with me. And I'll get over my grief about it, no matter how shaky my heart is, Shane. You know, don't you, all about that kind of heart, because yours is still in the right place, Shane. You're one of the old sort, as Ma would say. I almost get a fright when I think of my mother, you know, Shane. It's been so long since . . . And when last did my mother think of me? The thing about Jude, the thing is, well you know, Shane, it will be the death of me. Truly, the end of me. You've never told me about your people, Shane, though I feel as if we're part of the same brood. Why don't I spend more time with you? Have I told you yet, Shane, I'm amazed at the way you delegate. Always that delicate movement of your hands. Your touch gives soup its taste, and your thumb pad is like Fellini's grandmother's. You know the story, surely: what's the best salad dressing in the world? Grandma's. And why would that be, Federico? Because when Grandma sprinkles the salad dressing from the bottle, she covers its mouth with her thumb. Which means every drop of dressing is permeated with the taste of her thumb pad. Shane, I'd really like to teach you a song. It comes from the FAK.

It's the most moving song, Shane, about old Sarie Marais, she's so far from my heart, I hope to see her again. Bring me back to the old Transvaal, oh, God, Shane . . .

Shane leads me from the washing basin to the storeroom. We sit on old boxes.

Smells of mice here.

I know, Konstant, I know.

We must put out some bait.

If you want to.

I will, Shane, I will. Old Sarie Marais, Shane, old Sarie Fucking Marais doesn't want me any more.

It takes Jude from ten o'clock to half past eleven on Sunday morning to buy some fresh bread. I wait patiently, lost in our garden, which is calm and cool after last night's rain. We tend it with care, everything thrives, only the blackboy sulks without a single shoot.

Doesn't look as if it's dying, though, I remark when Jude stands next to me with a loaf in a paper bag. What kept you so long?

A detour through Centennial Park. It's so pretty there.

Why so many detours these days? What happened there?

Heavy load, I tell you, and all on the one side.

Why, was he that big?

He was still young.

Fifteen?

Sixteen, I'd guess.

Sixteen!

Okay, seventeen, then.

What's his name?

First Timer.

Where?

Up on the hill, at the bluegum copse. You know.

First timers don't cruise around there.

It was First Timer who wouldn't let me go; one, two, three times, he just couldn't get it down. Too excited. Comes from New Zealand. You know the place?

I know the place, but I've never gone in there. Trees are too straggly to hide goings-on like that.

Maybe you're too scared.

I'm scared of the plague that's around. Aren't you?

That's not true, Konstant, you also take detours.

The plague prowls around, you don't know where. Or whom with or when.

First Timer is okay. I've got it already is there more coffee?

Wait, I'll get the pot.

Can't be, it can't possibly be. Of course it can. It's the natural consequence . . .

I get up, walk from the garden through the sliding door to the stove. The espresso pot is still half full.

Please let me have heard right: Jude's sentence was ambivalent. I heard it wrong. Please.

Still sitting, Jude watches me return with the pot.

Haven't I told you already?

But Jude, that's just terrible, I put the coffee on the ground, squat, and my words are smothered in Jude's lap. It can't be, Jude, it's not possible, you can't have it, you haven't even got over the mark that the tortoise made.

I fall silent when I hear a thin, drawn-out sound coming from Jude. I've never heard him cry. So this is how he does it? A yowl from the depths, from the bones of someone called upon to cry out on behalf of all humanity, a sound that robs you of your senses. And then it's done.

Not that bad, Konstant. I've got eight, maybe ten, perhaps even fifteen, if I'm lucky. There're, yes, lift your head, there're people who are still alive after fifteen years. And as far as you're concerned, Konstant, I know by now how your head works: don't worry for a second. Everything is completely under control; you're as safe as a house.

. . . Of cards. Can't believe it, Jude. When were you diagnosed? Why am I only informed now? Hell, we live together, share the same bed, bath and bread. On the other hand, of course, you're away from home so often, there's never really any time to talk. Well, I'm going to shower. Shane's picking me up in a minute, we're going out. And don't tell me anything more about your expeditions. I don't want to hear *anything*, absolutely nothing, Jude.

That's an about-turn.

It's your weakness, Jude.

It's the engine that keeps me alive, "my affection hath an unknown bottom".

What's done is done. I must shower.

Konstant, don't leave it hanging in the air. There's so much I want to discuss with you, so much I've realised during this time with you, I really want to share it.

You may as well write it on that flat stomach of yours – you're always working on it anyway.

Have you ever wondered whether your wonderfully idiomatic way of talking, no matter how sharp it may be – and believe me, I can't begin to match you in it – keeps you a step away from yourself, a step away from reality? Konstant, don't go.

On the contrary. I'm kept a step away from your heart, Jude. All I feel is crust.

There you go again.

And your hand – all I remember is its stroke.

You're in no state to talk any more.

I am. Every day I talk to you endlessly. At night I wait for you without any rest. Although, my heart has become stronger since I've been eating only vegetables and grains. You've probably heard me already Jude, at night, when I lie awake with my heart next to your empty pillow waiting for the devil at the front door. Or maybe you've gone deaf on me. You've got your own rituals, Jude, and I'm just not part of them. But concerned about you: that I am – always.

You know, Konstant, Jude's voice follows me, I'm learning a lot from you.

That's news!

You could also learn a lot from me. You don't even know the designer of the chrome chair in Shane's guest room! And with that, he leaves.

Go skate on the ice, Jude. I don't give a sweet blue fuck who designed that bloody chair. The water is blissful. What would I do if I couldn't shower, especially after work? All those hundreds of rice balls leave a pong. Shane doesn't even know I've been giving Joseph a hand with the rice balls. Should I tell her? No, don't let my one hand know what the other is doing. And in any case, I've got more than enough to compensate for half-hearted work. I'm becoming a true blue. Must tell her about this new soap I've discovered. If there's any in stock I'll present her with one in a brown paper bag – it's called a *kardoes* where I come from, Shane. Won't bother shaving, tomorrow's another day off. I suspect Jude's the one who's become jittery this time. His grip on old Bignipples isn't as sure as it used to be. Well, I've got news for you, sweetie! Should I fuck up all your little bottles – your neat rows of containers and jars and other thingies – now or later? No space for my stuff here, is there?

I walk out, leave the extractor fan on, take one look at the bush furniture and sock it with my heel: a perfect ostrich kick. Bottles, jars, everything trashed, everything spilling out.

Fuck you, man, Jude. Fuck you.

TAKE ME AWAY, OLD head: it's no use fighting for sleep. When the front door opens, Jude has arrived. Only then. Off with this bedspread: it's a hot night. Could light the candle. I'll talk to Shane tomorrow, don't want to procrastinate any longer. At her place there are crickets at night. Here it's nothing but cars. And the first trains at daybreak, and the garbage trucks. Must be horrible getting up at four o'clock in the morning to hang from a dirt truck with sleep still crusting your eyes. The garbage men in East London never wore gloves. Christmas box, Baas; Christmas box, Mies. We were more generous than usual, holidays at the seaside, and could always find small change for them. With cupped hands they stood at the back door, wagging their tails, rotten from the pizza mould that burst from their bags as they heaved them onto the trucks. Here the lorry picks the whole drum up. What will I say to Shane? I want to resign? Sorry, Shane, can't wash dishes any more – domestic circumstances, you know.

Must get some sleep now, or I'll never be up in time tomorrow morning. Worst is when Jude doesn't return before I go to work. The bed, the room, the pillow, everything smells of him. I prefer getting all the details before I go off. What about my decision to let go? Let him be, Konstant. Hell, man, how much more crap can you handle? Could get my own flat, maybe share with Robert. Then we can compare notes about the two of them that day in the Kuringai-Chase. What did they get up to in the bush? No, rather let me have all the details, Jude. But why do I want to know everything? What's the point? At this rate I'll become senile before long. Night is the worst part of day: everything is bitter and black. What if I become infected? Jude wouldn't even know Jude knows Jude knows Jud

Must have fallen a . . . What's got hold of me? The bedspread . . . ah that's better. Legs together, hands crossed over my heart like a corpse. Won't have any problems laying me out in the right position. What will I do if I resign? Go back? Never! Rather die than return to that damned country. Would be self-betrayal. Now it's too hot. My heart, my whole body, too hot. Sheets off, this vest too. Pa, Ma, Albert, they'll all think even less of me if I go back – rather fight it out here. Fuck you, Judy, you too, Shane. You don't pay us enough, man, we work our arses off for you. Where're the matches, I may as well get up. My eyes are open. Wide awake. Water? Don't give a damn if you fire me, Shane, you pay us next to nothing anyway. Wouldn't have thought that of you, you're so thorough in everything. Joseph reckons it's because your father was a Jew.

Everyone's grumbling, Shane. Even doubt whether Jamal wants to become a permanent cook, and he's the last one to be greedy. Don't feel like going all the way to the fridge for wa . . . Oh, hell, Shane, I like you, man, but pay the price or face the shit, that's the law of the Transvaal.

How do you make a . . . If you hold your fingers like this next to the candle flame, you get an eagle. My finger-shadows all look like eagles. Pa could make bat-eared foxes, like the San. I *can* talk to Shane about these things, can't I? And her reply: Listen, mate, your work's not even up to scratch, and you're asking for more pay? Okay, let's make a deal. That's the way they do things here. Will, I really will ask for an increase on behalf of Liz and Robert and Joseph. Best would be to have a staff meeting. Though Joseph won't ever complain. Too pathetic. Couldn't be bothered. Robert, perhaps. Everyone's in awe of Shane. If only they could see her under that kitchen lamp, late at night, vulnerable as a moth. But why does she get sick so often? She's plagued by a bad conscience. No, these people don't operate like that. I've never heard Shane or anyone else apologise for anything. The thing is: this bunch didn't start off with open Bibles and churches. Jumped straight off the boats and got to work making and breaking right away. On the other hand, they're always at it, restoring, demolishing, building. Have never come across people who paint, repair, demolish, rebuild their homes so obsessively. It's an attempt to escape their convict image once and for all. But sorry about anything? Never! What's done is done: A complex set of ingredients determines every situation and every fault has to be related back to this situation. Yes, okay, Joseph, pain in the arse. Probably thinks I'm insane for apologising so endlessly about Liz's terrible cut that first day.

What's the time? The night never ends. I'll be exhausted tomorrow. Spent Wasserman will be a washout. Better keep my trap shut about the pay issue. Should I resign tomorrow or not? Where's my vest? My heart has cooled down. On thing is certain: if I carry on working in that shop I'll have to put old Freckleface in her place: Hey, Freckles, are you completely off your rocker? Everyone's laughing themselves silly at you, don't you see it, mate?

My eyes and my tiny heart are yours, darling Konnie, come rub me up. The coolroom is the best place, especially when I've got the hots for you. Right here, like this, yes! On top of the corn, sweet mate of mine, put your hand here, there and everywhere.

Not that I don't like you, Liz Bird, you've got the cutest little tits. It's just, well, since that night on the boat. Should never have let you grab my hand, who would ever have linked such an innocent gesture to such a mighty passion? You see, Liz, you created an expectation for yourself, and I wasn't even party to it. You assumed an intimacy between us, especially with that story about you and your brother, and everyone in the kitchen sees it, though not one of them will open their traps about it. Some days you're hardly able to get your salads out by twelve. You undress me, stark naked, with your eyes. And I'm not even that good naked, but how could you have imagined something like that? Sorry, Liz, I'm off the map, sweetie-pie. Tough titties – come to me and I'll teach you all about rejection. Bet you'll say I'm arrogant.

What's the time? Do I tell Shane tomorrow? Maybe I should get up, brew some coffee . . . Albert, I miss you, you bastard. You must visit, man, then you'll see how they make coffee here, espresso machines, everything.

I think you'll like Albert, Jude. Hell, man, that guy at the restaurant the other night, I could see he's still a mommy's boy, arse, eyes, still a baby. His eyes. Can't you see what's what, Jude? Doubt the boykie knows whether he's Arthur or Martha. Leave him alone, Jude, he's no match for you. You just couldn't keep your eyes off him, could you? What's in it for you? Strike me dead, I'll never understand you. Once you're obsessed with someone you lure him with all your magnets. You know what you've got, who can withstand you once you get going, Jude? You manipulate them all with your weakness. And your problem has become mine.

What? Five o'clock. It'll be daybreak soon. Maybe I should take something, could still get an hour's sleep in. An hour, Jude, an hour's grace. I will. Where are my pants? What's the good of sleeping naked if the bed's empty? No point. Can't help that I want you only for myself, that my love longs to sleep around with only you. Leave yourself just for me, Jude. I can't let go of you. Should I talk to Shane about it? Look here, Shane, this is how things are: Jude and I are separated. Bed and board. Though we do eat our porridge together, but it's the bum, oh! the bum, I mean the bed, Shane. Though I don't want to pollute you with my sordid tales. Still, I gather from Liz that you often have outbreaks of shingles on your head. Remind me to give you some of my Clocktower ointment. So I'm handing in my resignation, formally, here and now – and from this moment on I'll be biting my silver spoon again, look, it's got bite marks already. I'll hope for the best and keep believing: as long as I keep the faith. Jude, forgive me.

Where the? Better blow the candle out. Breeze could easily knock it over. Will quickly pick up Jude's bottles and pots, wipe them down, put them all back. Don't think he'll notice anything. I'll shoulder the blame for . . . my long night of waiting. Will just have to lie if too much of the perfume and stuff has run out. Thank the lord Jude isn't home yet. How could I have done it? Hope not too much has spilt. Will be okay, will . . . Day has dawned.

These are days of unbelievable progress, and I must give myself a slap on the back for the results of a diet that's become an integral part of my life. At home I'm certainly aware that the devil finds work for idle hands – but in front of the mirror I allow myself this: my shoulders are broader, my chest stronger, my bum as luscious as ever. And the other afternoon when I emerged from the waves at Nilson's Point, Shane flattered me: I looked good in my black Speedo.

It's mainly due to her and Jude's influence that I converted to a vegetarian diet a while ago. They rarely, if ever, eat meat. Sometimes I order a succulent shank at the Greek on Crown Street, and still licking my lips I pop my head into the kitchen to congratulate the chef. And gleefully leave the bare bones on my plate. What amazes me is my dark stool after these meaty delights. But I shouldn't exaggerate: it could also be from the many glasses of Western Australian red wine I down at these meals.

A surprise too the other day when Jude, back from the gym on Crown Street, joins Shane and me at the Greek for a wedge of baklava. There the three of us cackle away like galahs and experience a special camaraderie, especially when we talk about food and recipes. Demonstrative, Jude folds a pleasing hand around my leg.

What's up with him? Nothing, matey, this is vintage Jude. If you don't know it by now . . .

We repeat the union – so gemütlich, especially for me – at another restaurant. Besides that, the ever-prosperous Shane treats me to a variety of other establishments. Shane and Jude are quick to return their plates if they have the slightest problem with their meal. Both are connoisseurs. Shane does it with conviction and sends the chef constructive criticism via the waiter. Jude's refusals, on the other hand, seem fake. They can become so contrived that the whole evening is ruined for everyone.

But still, I take on something of their restaurant manners. I dine out alone one night at a window table in the Bayswater Brasserie to celebrate my mother's birthday – this after a relatively short but emotional call to the farm. And return my plate of food. It doesn't fit the colourful description on the menu at all. The waiter listens impatiently to my well-presented critique. For the rest of the evening I'm neglected and I leave no tip.

One evening Shane announces over plates of crisp chicken wings that she's appointing me manager for the short time she'll be in the outback. I'll also be doing the main dishes. I give her a delighted kiss then and there, across the table, and a sprig of fresh coriander from her plate sticks to my shirt.

Promotion for Konstant Wasserman. Dishwashing, salads – and now mains. No worries, mate. Bloody hell, I'm proud, man. Pa, Ma, do you hear me, I've hardly arrived here, and what do you know! Fact is, I wasn't stitched together carelessly: hold your knife in your palm like this – so that you can cut properly; brush your teeth every night – and do it properly, too; stand up when you greet someone – look him in the eye and give him a firm handshake, but don't squeeze his hand too hard, only louts do that; keep your shoulders back; doff your hat if you've got one; lift your willy and marbles, and wash all your tackle well. I've used everything Pa and Ma drilled into me to barter with over here where no one gives a damn about the white horse on Naval Hill. And so, in my own way I *have* honoured Raster and Mirjam Wasserman. May my days be long in this land.

And Ma often graces me with haunting visits, not so, Ma? How, I wonder, are you all doing? Must write again, but when I *do* get around to writing, it's always with a tight arse. I couldn't possibly tell you that I've given in to Jude's persistence and have made my own bed up in the spare room. And it's not too bad there, let me tell you, the late afternoon sun glows across the floor. And it's much better between the two of us, Pa and Ma; and, oh, the other night when we ate divine linguine pasta with a mussel and hot chilli sauce and got a bit tipsy like in the old days, I couldn't stop myself.

So I got up and sleep-walked down the passage. The house sang the route to me, so late at night. I'd never experienced our home as friendly as this before. And I knew that I was on the right road, the road of my heart. Although in truth I was reacting to the impulse of my hard-on.

My feet followed obediently until the corner of the double bed touched my shin, and there was Jude, fragrant between the sheets, and my back and butt ready to fit into his fold. Or his in mine. Afraid that there might be shank on my breath, I licked Jude's back to give my tongue a different taste. And prayed that the white muslin curtains would always billow in the window like this, that Jude's big toe-nail would always briefly touch the sole of my foot, that my thumb and index finger would always glide over Jude's eyebrows, that the sandalwood oil that burned earlier in the evening would always smell like this, that Jude's leg would always lie across my stomach, that the down in the keel of his back would always feel so soft, that Jude's auricle would always curve so pleasurably under my fingers, that my sex would always wait so warmly and patiently, that the bridge of Jude's nose would always sniffle like this against my neck, that the delicate scar above Jude's left ear would always float like a small island beneath my fingertips, that my nipples would always stand guard so smartly.

Can I expect all this from the shortest night of my life?

Early morning, and I splosh down half-awake streets in the shop's delivery van. A hunchback with a torn umbrella strides by: Hello, Kerneels, I greet him from the heated interior.

Two buck-arsed guys return from a round of dawn squash: Morning, Ratface, morning Biscuitbum, I say in my specially cheery way. Oupa Konstant always insisted on greeting pedestrians like that as he drove his black Mercedes out to the farm in the afternoons.

Morning, old Blackgall, I greet a scowling Aboriginal woman battling against the downpour.

People have a hard time here too. Surely I'm allowed to poke fun at them like oupa did? Roberts reckons I'm friendlier with our black clients. His arse! What would Oupa Konstant have said about my leaving? In his day people had more time for one other, less for idle chatter. I don't know any old people here; it's a shortcoming in my circle of friends.

At the shop I find the storeroom flooded. Luckily, the bags of rice haven't been damaged. On the dammed-up water, a drowned mouse and a zucchini stalk float.

Bad omen for my first day as manager? Not at all. Water is a blessing from God, the Setswana even call their money pula. If the floor were cleaner, the water wouldn't be so dirty. It's chilly: only the reject eggs are out on the streets this time of day. Shouldn't have called that woman old Blackgall.

While scooping out water with a bucket, I hear the front door open and close. I work fast, mop up all the water and don't think twice about flinging the rodent away by its tail.

Liz? G'day, Lovecheeks. Takes ages to get her raincoat off and her apron on. I know how soulless it can be to work for a boss on a nippy morning like this. Today I see my colleagues through the lenses of a benign slave driver. Oh, hell, she's probably in early for a bit of canoodling. Preposterous to be thinking about things like that now. You're crazy, Liz. Oh, it's Ava-Marie, the new kitchen hand.

G'day, Ava-Marie, can you believe this rain?

The new broom, she becomes more beautiful the longer you spend in her company. Unlike Robert, she deals with a pile of dirty dishes calmly and efficiently. She says she's a healer.

This kind of downpour is completely unknown to me. It can last as long as a week without a single break, and make you clammy down to the inner folds of your body.

There's Joseph with his untidy mess of rasta-locks. Always some or other inspirational meditation agenda with him. Hope he doesn't slack off while Shane's away for the next four days. Workers tend to behave like sheep.

The day goes well. Except that Robert disappears for his rollie every hour on the dot. I like him, even though he's jittery and a loudmouth. As long as he doesn't smoke in the storeroom. But that's exactly what he does: with the excuse that it's raining outside, he slouches seductively against the bags of rice and puffs away.

Must I close my eyes to it? After all, it's a gross transgression. My bet's on Shane: she'd never make a concession on this one. Nor will I: Robert will smoke where he should.

I was simply too vigilant for my own good that first day, and I arrive home still uptight and more tired than usual.

Stress gathers precisely *there* for me, in the buttocks. My stool won't come out like a perfect banana tonight. And that's got nothing to do with the move to the spare room.

I open the door to find Jude being swept along by jazz improvisations. I'd have liked to turn the thudding rhythms off, and have a quiet cup of tea to soothe my headache. With Jude, but made to my order: calm conversation like only he is capable of, and preferably not a word about food.

But sadly, my own long-suffering plan stops me from saying anything that might interrupt Jude's rite of unpacking, airing and repacking linen, cloths, towels and a host of similar items he's brought out of from the linen cupboard and arranged in heaps – each according to kind – all along the passage. From some of the piles Jude has taken sheets and pillowcases and hung them over the heater to get rid of dampness. With the result that the house has become far too hot. Jude is adorned with sweat beads, but he continues the process according to a pre-planned system without a trace of complaint.

He's even gone so far as to prepare supper for me. When I ask about the aroma floating from the oven, set at 250 degrees and adding to the heat, he informs me it's a delicious, grain-fed hen. The choice of poultry comes as a surprise. In this heat I can't be bothered to comment or compliment. I cat-foot over perfectly preserved Manchester en route to the bathroom where I strip and wash the day's labour away under lukewarm water.

At Jude's suggestion, I lie down on the white bedspread on the double bed in the slightly cooler atmosphere of his room. I remain uneasy.

Even so, any sort of rest will prepare me better for tomorrow's work.

I wake too soon – and with a throbbing cock. I strongly consider calling Jude over, even though the passageway sounds tell me the sorting is not yet finished. Yet the music has been switched off in deference to my weariness. I contemplate the wisdom of such an invitation for so long that the mere thought of it fires my passion. I utter a plea that must be familiar to Jude's practised ear, and completely forget that I'm supposed to have resigned myself to our abstinence.

When he enters the room I can tell from his neutral expression that I won't be getting any help this afternoon. What he then informs me regarding the absence of any sexual attraction to me, I'd rather not hear. Not now, not ever. Although I have to admit, I was the one to have provoked the declaration. I'm so upset at this confirmation of longstanding suspicions, that I half raise myself from the bed and ineptly seek his sympathy by lifting up my hands. As is to be expected, Jude, torn away from his sorting ritual, is in no state to respond appropriately to my demands.

Torrential rain rapidly cools the house. For the rest of the night I'm unable to shake off my melancholy.

Konstant, it's no good hiding it from you any longer, but K and I . . .

K? I interrupt Jude. That's my initial too, isn't it, is there a problem here, can I give myself the benefit of the doubt?

Can't do any justice to the chicken, despite the fact that my current, highly developed sense of taste assures me that it's more than delicious fare.

I ought to know from experience that Jude relishes the unexpected. Which is probably the reason he's unable to set up home with a single blessed fool.

So tell me again, who the hell is this K?

You ought to know, Jude, these days I've got to know many people through the café, and they . . .

I've wanted to tell you for quite a while now, Konstant, but there hasn't been an opportunity.

Does it surprise you, Jude? You're hardly ever home, no wonder you can't tell me anything.

If you want to sink to that level: you and Shane have been hanging out a lot recently.

Tell me what you have to. I'm not as vulnerable as I used to be. You haven't even said what you think of my hair like this.

I like it long, Konstant, it suits you very well. That's one of the things I wanted to tell you tonight. Hence the meal. Pity you haven't enjoyed it, but that's your choice. Let's see: I've known this guy, K, for quite a while now.

So how long have you been seeing him then?

I'm getting there. As I've said, the first time I saw K, I immediately felt attracted to him. I'd be stupid to deny it. Since then we've met a few times, and I'm sure this time it's different.

Have you slept together?

I knew you'd ask. No, Konstant, we haven't slept together yet, although I'd have liked to – very much – but K is very reserved. Our friendship is still developing. We're thinking of going to New Zealand, maybe . . .

So what does it all mean for me, or, rather: I know there's nothing in it for me, but how does it affect our relationship, our living together?

Have you noticed how you never talk about *our* house? But to answer your question: it changes nothing. If it were up to me, Konstant, I'd always want a relationship with you. And I'll always love you. Even if K and I sleep together, it would take nothing away between you and me. Anyway, as you know yourself, we haven't had sex for quite a while now.

Yes, okay, you don't need to spell it all out.

K is coming around later, and we'll probably go out together. You can meet him tonight.

I'll see how I feel.

Why are you so upset?

I'm not. I'm tired from the day's work. It's another story managing the café. Thanks for the dinner, Jude, but I've lost my appetite. I'm going to bed early. Please close the door quietly when you two go out.

I always try to do that. Konstant?

Must maintain today's clarity of spirit. I must remain standing.

Or lying down. Lying down is better for me. I can be alone in my room. All this because I relaxed on Jude's bed. Feeling the texture of the cover brought back so many memories. That's why it's actually no surprise, not so much the news about K – that's old news – but that Jude didn't nag on about my expectations and what they lead to and all that shit. Especially with me crying out like a stupid babe in arms on the double bed. What hurt me most is that Jude said he liked my long hair. The finality of it. Long hair emphasises the state of our current sexual alienation. It's ironic that it was my decision not to fall into Jude's lap with my crew-cut any more.

A tall man with a groomed goatee stops outside the café early the following morning. I watch him as I chop the cucumbers.

> Drop concentration:
> lose finger in the kitchen,
> spend life in grey gloom.

The man steps out of his Holden V8 into the rain, the rain flooding our storeroom. He marches in through our front door, clutching his briefcase.

It's probably asking too much to expect a knock. It *is* wet outside, so I won't hold that against him.

Is Shane Jackman here?

Can't even say please.

Liz and Ava-Marie look up in unison. Which confuses the man. And they won't look down again soon: such hunkiness, such height, and all of it so early in the morning on empty stomachs.

Shane's not here now, tut mir leid, bloody baboon – the ability of men to create a sombre atmosphere by their mere presence. Put your knife down, Konstant, you *do* want to act the manager, after all: Sir, may I be of assistance, sir, I'm sorry to say but Shane is away.

Can I help you, sir, please be seated at our lovely yarra counter. The man turns down my invitation.

Do I? Yes, I do indeed have to look up at him. He refuses to sit, to lower himself strategically before a migrant, instantly identifiable by the absence of: *mate*. Why did I refuse that user-friendly term in this situation?

Who's in charge here?

If I'm not missing the mark, mate, that would be me, not you, mate.

I'm the landlord. Your storeroom has flooded.

Our storeroom? But it's been sorted early this morning, why the song and dance, mate.

The masterful stroke of his single sentences, the piercing look, the advantage his height gives him, his undeniable good looks. I'm able to list all these characteristics during this, my year of maturity, and still be intimidated. It's unacceptable.

The storeroom must be dried immediately.

Then his wet briefcase is placed on the counter and a lawyer's letter in black print is produced. Without opening his chiselled hand, his finger – the nails flat and clean – slips along the legal-speak. Except for the finger that has come into action, the rest of his body remains planted in its place.

I look to the left and right, and behind me. Jamal, where is your support, where are your funny limericks, Robert, your redeeming mantras, O Jesuit? Stares are all I get. My colleagues are not unsympathetic, but somewhat amused, and left cold by the presence. The presence that excites the two women so much. I must take back my words – never look a gift horse in the mouth: it's none other than the newcomer, Ava-Marie, who speaks a healing word. Why don't you do it yourself, mate? You should be ashamed of carrying on like this, have you seen the rain outside?

All eyes swivel from Ava-Marie to mate.

I regain my equanimity.

Thank you, dearest Ava-Marie, offer him tea to wet his throat.

Two fingers rise and stroke the nostrils. He's merely responding to a complaint from the estate agent next door. There's rising damp because the storeroom hasn't been emptied. If we don't do something about it immediately, he'll be forced to use the key he now brings from his pocket for the purpose for which it is intended. With that he's done, and gives me a challenging look.

I explode. What about blocked gutters, blocked drains? Give me strength! If proper measures had been taken to deal with these endless cloudbursts you wouldn't be here bellowing at us. If there's to be talk of defects, it's without any doubt your Adam's apple, Mr Cocky, which is very obviously far too big. You've got a real crop there, you know. Besides: the owner of this shop is out of town, as I've already told you. If you speak to us more respectfully, if you simply want to talk about it, a compromise is possible. As matters stand right now, it's not humanly impossible to do anything. You realise we'll all get double pneumonia if we go along with your whims. And in any case, we're opening for business soon.

Like all primitives with emotionless facades, he answers calmly and rationally: The town council of Glebe has investigated my plumbing and drainage and found this building okay. What's more, I've received a certificate of commendation for my contribution to stormwater control, if you please.

With that, he places his manly hands flat on his legs, which he's kept planted wide apart ever since storming in, like men can do.

Please, please yourself, mate-sir.

I'm certainly not doing anything about it now. Hope I've made myself well and truly clear on that one. Liz's carrot, basil and tofu salad must get done. My lima bean, fennel and parsnip soup must be rounded off with miso, bloody fool, do you even know what miso is?

And so I go on: Spare me any of your type's affectations. You've put your body in a straightjacket, your movements are not your own, they've been sanctioned by generations of men before you. I feel sorry for your wife. Ten to one you need a dominatrix to get rid of your perverse impulses. Dominion and rule, gentlemen, your kind is so passé.

By this stage Robert must have noticed my features getting redder and have sensed a further rupture. He rushes to my assistance with the sangfroid of an ex-lowlander: Konstant, I think this mate here is talking about storeroom number two where we keep our tins of frying oil. We haven't opened it since the rain started. Can clear the water in there in no time, no worries.

Calm down, Konstant, Konnie can be calm if he must: it's storeroom number two, the one with our cooking oil, and we certainly don't want that locked up. How the hell will we deep-fry the rice balls? Shit, Robert, thanks for reminding me. It's full to the brim in there, and now the estate agent's soles upstairs are getting colder on a carpet getting damper.

We'll empty it out, I say, just cool it, mate.

Things immediately settle back to normal: taps are opened, lids lifted, semolina at the point of burning is stirred, and Mister Cocky - as his crop has emptied in the meanwhile - takes a steak sandwich from his briefcase.

Here's my chance to get even, once and for all: Excuse me, mate, but this is a 100% vegetarian-only environment. Please get out of my way, I mean my place, with that slab of flesh in your hand. As if I haven't been tortured my whole life long by your kind.

At which the man raises his perfect eyebrows in the direction of Liz, the person he's correctly identified as most sympathetic towards him, and proceeds to describe the ruler of the roost in words I correctly anticipated – hysterical and irrational – then he slowly gathers his things and leaves. Walking tall.

Good on yer mate, Ava-Marie says and places a cup of lukewarm bancha tea in my unsteady hand. Robert is amused.

Is that how it really happened? I ask myself afterwards, as my anger drags on at the thought of him versus all the friends I've made here over this counter. All those who recognise my good nature and are therefore more accepting of my non-Australian accent.

Even more than Robert or Joseph, I'm the one who makes time for the fragile ones who've reached the point of anaemia on a meat-free diet. And I'm the only one with a stash of plastic bags for customer Barbette who prefers every item packed just *so* – knowing very well that we don't tolerate plastic here. And despite my limited knowledge of this diet, I don't hold back in talking to hyper-allergic Melody, who has question after question about every single ingredient of every bowl of soup she empties here.

And what about Joseph who hides in the storeroom when some of our more finicky Jewish clients walk in? Isn't he supposed to be all charity? Also, I gather that clients King Rat and Servant Mouse, two grey computer geeks, want to whisk me away with their bags of shopping.

All this merely on the strength of my resolve to treat both man and mouse as human beings: constantly the same old washerman.

Shane can count herself lucky that she's got someone like me in her shop. And listen to my tattle-tales, now, Shane Jackman: it was Robert who was rude the other day to those two computer geeks. No need to report it to you behind his back, I've already told him off about it in the most tactful way possible. I couldn't stand seeing those two creatures so dopy behind the counter that they didn't even notice, sharp as only they can be, that the sauce of their tofu, kombu and chestnut-pumpkin casserole was drip-dripping out of its take-away container. Whether I spoke to Robert about his stupidity too soon – the two creatures still filing past the shop window, ears pricked – well, he'll have to decide about that himself.

Why exactly I carry the business so close to my heart, I don't know. Especially seeing it's so over-burdened already. Then there's the wanton Vivienne who arrives for her miso soup almost every day, greedy like a Viking, red tufts sprouting from each armpit. Vivienne invited me to one of her meat barbeques after our second meeting. And what about black-haired Doctor Paul who sneaked me his visiting card with this one sincere word: anytime. Not that I'll ever get sick enough for his services. There's also Deidre Rosenbaum who enters and leaves the cafe as if she's on stage. We've become so engrossed in conversation that once, in a moment of light-headedness, I dropped this bit of trivia: my great aunt Jannie van Staden was a personal friend of our country's Gerhard Beukes of "Let the candles burn" fame. Lastly, the unassuming David M who is very, very friendly towards me, despite his fame as an author.

If I'm so popular with all the people here, tell me Jude, please tell, why so shortsighted to choose K above me? And why has my distress been so lasting ever since you told me that K is the brightest and best on your ratings list?

God alone knows what I'm doing. It's late afternoon, and I'm wandering about downtown alone. Fumes from the David Jones perfume counters make me even more nauseous. I'm too tired to walk. You know, managing Shane's shop these last four days has really taken it out of me.

I see him approaching from far, but it's as if I don't recognise him at first. Then . . .

Robert!

He bundles me into a taxi and takes me to a pub on the edge of King's Cross. It has green walls and a eucalyptus hangs over its veranda, so that it's shady and cool outside. Inside it's as chilled as cold beer. A smoky twilight has the seductive smell of young people who spend their lives playing pool.

And don't assume they're aggro because they're wearing mostly black. Go up to that guy there, for example, the one with the heraldic unicorn on his delta muscle and ask for a light. He'll respond immediately, but without sucking up. Probably hardly look at you. By the way he cups his hand around the flame, he'll suggest a kind of mateship, and as you walk away he'll say something like: Pool table's been packed the whole arvo.

Or that one in the black tights. Here she comes across to bum some of Robert's rolling tobacco. Squatting at our table, she rolls herself a smoke and chats away: Don't you just hate Hunters & Collectors?

Olka bolka Roberty stolka. Man, it's a fucking surprise this. Fuck, man, didn't think you'd want to share a pint with me. You live here in the Cross, where they trade in flesh? You could too, quite easily. Let me say right from the fucking beginning: I like you more now than I did when Jude stalked you in the crackling bush in Kuringai-Chase. Clearly, I'm not through with that yet, or I wouldn't have mentioned it. On the other hand: love makes you forgive so very easily. Tell me: was it nice? Did you salivate? I didn't think *you* were unfaithful after that little outing: I'm too familiar with Jude's virtues. And you seem quite the man, sitting opposite me, open white shirt, black Levi's and all. Believe you me, as far as I'm concerned, you paid your dues for your bush shenanigans that humid day when you defused the situation between me and Mister Cocky.

Then I say: I can hardly believe there was no hanky-panky at Kuringai-Chase.

We did nothing, cross my arse. I sussed your Jude out pretty quickly. I won't be pulled in. Jude's all yours. Your very own dark horse.

The beer goes to our heads. Must be the beer. Before it has its way with me, I say: Robert, let me tell you where I come from: I was made the slave of faith, righteousness, and complicity. And so of guilt, penitence, and the consequent absolution. And last but not least, I was taught to say thank you: thank you very much. Thanks be to thee. So I'm grabbing this opportunity to buy you as much beer as you want.

After that we drink pint after pint of refreshing Cooper's Beer. It's cloudy stuff, with a high alcohol content. And the young men stand three deep at the bar, not to mention the buzz around the pool table. Hardly any of the black-clad guys are without tattoos on the upper arm, thigh, bum, or somewhere else inside their shorts.

It's a while since I've been in a pub. Not that I've become a teetotaller. Shane and I, or Jude and Shane and I, drink mostly pretentious Vasse Felix. And only occasionally in pubs. But here I am, chaffing away merrily with an easy-arse. To tell the truth, I don't know when last I've felt such energy. Here the truth is washed down light-heartedly, and to prove it, off Robert goes for two more beers with heads. Why not get shot of noble intentions and grab some of his Drum rolling-tobacco? Life's laid-back in Aussie-land: sun ya balls and sip ya beer.

Hell, I really like this country, Robert. From that very first night Shane and I drove across the bridge.

How long have you? Been here?

A day, Robert: one day in the life of Konstant Wasserman. You know, it's hard to believe that you and Jude weren't up to mischief that time in Kuringai-Chase.

Tell me, Konstant, you with all your friends – you make friends so easily – I've noticed in the café how lots of people take to you: why don't you dump that Dark Man? He's not for you, mate.

That's a helluva confrontational question to be put by a stranger. Have to sit a while on that one, Robert. Why do you ask? What about you?

From half past five, thirsty workers pour in and the bar becomes even busier. It's relaxed and boisterous. All defences can be washed away. And so, in a free flight of camaraderie I give Robert a hug.

Then he says: I've got a bone to pick with you. The other day, Mister Cocky the landlord was bloody aggressive and somebody needed to put him in his place. You made out like Shane's place belonged to you, not so? Now to get back to our cocky landlord. At his first crow, you, Konstant, reacted as follows: you looked around helplessly, begging for help from any quarter; then you attacked ad hominem and remarked on his enlarged Adam's apple; and then – completely disempowered – you became enraged. Which the rest of us, of course, all enjoyed very much.

Carry on. My rhinoceros hide is skin deep, man. For the first time, subjectively I'll admit, I notice his top lip: one of those lips that never forgive the slightest misdemeanour. And his greasy thick hair, and the stubs he clutches between his fingertips and smokes down to his tobacco-stained thumb. He's got a nerve to analyse me and Mister Cocky.

Another beer?

Yeah, sure.

I see it differently now . . . New Zealand? Surely it wasn't New Zealand? Fuck Robert, I've just remembered something: Jude surely can't have meant *that* the other night. Was he about to say that they, he and K, were thinking of going to live in New Zealand, hey, Robert?

Another thing, Konstant, I didn't like the way you told me off the other day before those two computer geeks had left the shop properly. And I was really pissed off the way you told me not to smoke in the storeroom. I know my place.

You know, Robert, some nights I even leave my bedroom door open just in case Jude comes back. So that if he does, my door will be open. You see? Doesn't matter what time it is. Even so, last time we did it, I mean I could tell it was more like a transaction to Jude.

. . . a bit of a white nigger with attitude, Robert talks on, the way you just dismiss people like you did with Ava-Marie that morning after she hid the till drawer in the lukewarm oven overnight, and all the cash notes were burnt to cinders. How was she supposed to know? She's just a new girl. All because you felt she lacked common sense, you simply dismissed her.

Ag, now you're really talking crap, Robert. I've learnt not to write anyone off here, to judge no one in terms of their work. Even the guy who mops the floor of the public toilets in Hyde Park started chatting to me. Asked if I knew who Christo was. Ha! Apparently he helped him wrap the cliffs at Little Bay.

I went too far the day I asked you not to smoke in our - in the - storeroom. Sorry, I admit, it's the only way I know how to do it.

Actually, I'm from working-class stock, Robert suddenly says out of the blue.

That's a lie, surely, Robert, you're all . . . wait, I must choose my words carefully: Look, those hands of yours, pure marble.

Still, the moment he mentions working class, I notice those thin lips again, his smoking habits, the open white shirt with its stained collar.

I can't be like you, he continues drunkenly, come all the way from the white tribe of Africa, chutzpah your way into a job and convince the boss you can do the work better than anyone else. It's hard for me even to chat to clients without feeling insecure. But still, I like your passion and energy, he says reassuringly. And for sure, you have the potential to be a good manager.

Another beer, Robert?

The evening comes to an end when, with my last beer, I get a nauseous warning in my stomach. Robert, who's so endeared himself to me, sends me home by taxi. And all ends swell.

JUDE, MUST I TAKE this, here? Should I pack that? And what about those?

All non-perishables. We don't want to deprive ourselves of anything out there.

And the flies you keep talking about? Where will we store the food?

We've got a dark, cool spot, deep under an overhanging rock, works like the old farm coolers. A kind of cellar. All the perishables go there, though they'll still wilt because of the terrible heat at the Wollondilly. Usually the food is finished before anything goes off. Once a goanna got hold of our eggs. He gobbled half a dozen and tore the carton up. We can also buy a watermelon, or a cantaloupe. There's a sandy beach along the river where we bury them. You'll see how cool they keep.

Are goannas like our leguaans?

I don't know about leguaans.

When my mother was small a leguaan went for her with his tail. She smashed her air gun's butt on him, and Oupa Konstant fixed it with some copper wire. It's still on the farm.

I notice you've stopped talking about "our farm".

Are you glad? I hold up a bottle of Vegemite. Should I pack this?

Not for me. But if you want some, take it. Actually, we should leave everything that's not essential. Mustn't overload the jeep. It's very steep on the way there, Konstant. The most important things are your fly net and leggings.

Has Shane got leggings?

Well, she certainly has money enough for everything. Hey, Konstant, have you seen the blackboy? It's covered in new shoots.

New spikes.

Jude, my dearest dear, no term of endearment quite fits you . . . Just you and me and you and Shane off to the Wollondilly River. Veggies under the rocky overhang; watermelon in the sand. When the moon rises, we'll crawl into the tent and zip the flaps shut. Shane had better make sure she's got all her tent pegs. She'd better not come begging for a place between us for no good reason. It's years since we were alone together. Eastern Transvaal? Wonder if you and I . . . Hope springs eternal. Don't forget your leggings, remember your piece of gauze for self-preservation: you're pretty concerned about me. Is it just force of habit? Maybe your new attachment, K, is so reserved that for the first time you're not getting the head on a platter? So you're keeping a door open to Konstant in case things don't work out. Jude, my door is always open for private business. To ascribe such thoughts to you is nothing but scheming: I wasn't raised that way. No, you've always been concerned about my welfare: this morning at the sound of the first train, your lips came to awaken me.

Konnie, Allie, my darlings, time to wake up. Today's the day: we're off to the sea. Ma, how many Dinky Toys can I take? But why's Konnie allowed . . .? Come on, hurry up, you lot! Wonder who'll see the sea first this year? We jumped out of bed with that grown-up feeling, a little tired, not having slept as much as we were used to. It was still pitch dark. Ma and Pa had already been up packing for ages. Though it was summer, early mornings on the farm were always nippy. And we children all gooseflesh from excitement with only T-shirts on. Cold underfoot, the dew on the lawn: Stay, Kaptein, you won't be seeing us for two weeks, la-lala-la-la. Okay, there's a good boy. The two of us charged around the house to see what Pa was packing, because that was the surest sign that we were off to the sea, round the house we ran to the bare yard, full of thorns, and now scattered with cake tins, suitcases, golf clubs: Ag, no, Mirjam, do we really have to go through the same thing every year? All these tins will never fit in. I wish you'd come and pack yourself, just for once. Then you'd sing a different tune. Pa's tone of voice was icy that time of morning. Ma: But my dear man, you're the ones who want cookies when we're there, and when she realised it was no use: Leave the damn stuff then, Raster. Leave the tins you can't fit in. It was the thin tone of her voice that struck me. Pa, Ma, you could never have guessed how much your bickering hurt – worse than a beating. Or maybe you knew all too well: let the parents teach the children how to argue. I didn't let it bother me for long those early years, soon the car was Wassermanned to capacity. Wave to Pindile opening the gate, throw him two pink toffees; wave at Pokasi too, at Zandile, old Anna, old Samuel, Thoza-mile, Joycie, Thembeka, all green with envy: Kleinbaas Konnie is off to the great waters, bring us some of that amanzi in a bottle.

But my mind, innocent as a boy's forelock, soon forgot the farm workers' simple request for a bottle of sea water. Until, at the end of the holiday, Ma sent me down to the beach with a rinsed-out whiskey bottle to get some of the purgative for Anna and the rest. Where on earth have you all landed up? Sometimes I imagine I see you, courtesy of the Australian Broadcasting Corporation, squatting somewhere in Gauteng or on the Cape Flats. We've died to one another. It's better this way. All the very best to you, Pindile, old Anna, Samuel. Take care, all of you.

Jude? Jude is packing the jeep. The sun's up, already hot.

Packed up and inspanned. Saddlebag stuffed with biltong and rusks. The trekkers really did know what food travelled best. You know what, Jude? I don't let it bother me any more. If you want, you can take this K of yours and go and live in New Zealand. I'll miss you. I miss you as it is. I'm grown up now, adult enough at last to make or break on my own. You've raised me well. As you say, you have a unique talent: you're able to lead someone to water, and once they're there, they must drink for themselves, for better, or for worse.

Shane arrives with provisions for our long weekend in the wilderness.

Settle down, hold tight. Everyone ready? Let's go!

I sing for Shane and Jude: "Hoe ry die Boere sit-sit-so".

What's that mad Afrikaans idiom, the one about the granny, Shane asks.

"Ek sal jou slaan dat jou ouma jou vir 'n eendvoël aansien": I'll hit you so hard that your granny will mistake you for a duck.

The long journey makes us all fidgety; the cabin becomes stuffy with bodies, and the jeep is bumpy. We stock up on beer and fresh food at Mittagong, the last town before the wilderness.

As we leave Mittagong and turn off onto the Wombeyan Cave road, we're already downing a second beer. We bounce around and our moods lighten and change track as we rattle along. The potholed tarred road gives way to a wide dirt road with knotted eucalyptuses on either side. We reach a beacon: a soft hill on the left, crowned by a monumental ancestral eucalyptus, its massive arms drooping with banners of bark. Shane and Jude impress upon me that this tree is a reminder of the joy of all visits to the Wollondilly, past ones and those to come.

A splash of parrots rise and fall above the eucalyptus, rise then fall again. Beyond the hill, the grassland dips to a muddy billabong where cattle lick their shiny rumps.

Then we enter the bush, sparser and dryer on the hill crests, lush and rainforest-like in the gorges. Flowerless ericas and the humble flannel flower grow along the rough verges. We've reached the end of the plateau: here the road drops steeply, along a stony ravine feeding into the valley floor. I can hear from Jude's breathing that his black clothing has become unbearably hot.

Hold tight, kids, don't be scared, daddy's clever and daddy's strong. Push it into second, no, first: let the gears do the braking. Hell, look at those rocks, how they've tumbled down. The road's tricky here: if a single wheel lands in the ravine, we're done for.

Shane laughs; shards of macadamia nut between her teeth. Jude, all concentration, says nothing.

Don't fail, brakes! Have they been tested? You can never play too safe. Hope for the best, half of life is owed to grace alone, anyway.

Hooray, the road evens out, throws an s-bend, turns right, through Burnt Flat Creek, and then we follow the last stony slope down to the valley floor. A couple of rabbits take flight. These aliens, with no predators, have bred like rabbits do. Jude glides in under a ghost gum, switches the engine off, breathes in deeply, sighs.

Well done, Jude, Shane calls out.

See my legs shake from all that braking, he answers.

Right, down to the river. The three of us walk across a hillock overgrown with river grass. We'll be restored again in this wild world! Jude leads the way with a sturdy stick, stamp-stamping the earth to warn snakes of our approach. Uprooted trees, the snapped remains of branches, torn shreds, and splintered trunks have washed up against other trees. The smell of a carcass drifts from somewhere on the wind.

This piece of land has remained untouched by human hands. Even the flies are lonely, but now scouts spy us out, and send signals to their mates. By the time we take the animal track to the river they are already swarming around us. A zooming cacophony, they land in a frenzy on any bit of body moisture or orifice.

Jude says they vomit on your skin and whip it up with tears, sweat or spit. They suck up the cocktail, then land somewhere else and start all over again.

I really wish they'd deal with the farmer who lets his cattle graze here, he adds.

But even without a single cow, the fly, the blowfly and the common Australian horse fly would flourish here. Let's get used to them, in the same way we have to sidestep the snakes.

The river too is a swollen, brown snake of a thing. Mercifully, there's a narrow bank of river sand for us, where the cool breath of the river at least keeps the worst of the flies away.

I'm first to rip my clothes from my sweaty body and to leap in, shuddering from the shock of the ice-cold water on my skin. Shane follows, shrilling, and then Jude.

Can't help noticing the brown body emerging from the black clothes, the bulging appendage. Look, Shane, have you ever seen anything like it?

I dive down, deep, my eyes closed in case I see something I'd rather not. The water tastes of fresh soil washed down from far away.

Judie-e-e, Shane, I yell exuberantly, and jack-knife so that my bum disappears underwater last.

You're behaving like a pixie, Shane shrieks.

The river sweeps you away much faster than you might expect from the bank. When you pop up above the water you see blue and nothing else: not a single fly. And under the blue, casuarinas up and down the river, and the surrounding land dense with native bush.

When I pop up again, I look straight at Shane. Her feet have found the bottom, and she's standing so that the fast-flowing water covers her body from just below her nipples. She lifts her hand to wave, and I hope that the image stays with me forever: the dark, wet fringe, the eyes gentle, the mouth that says so much, the tiny hand in the air, the vulnerable olive breasts just above the dark stream.

Meanwhile, Jude is getting dressed, and his body, far away on the bank, appears abandoned.

Our two tents are pitched separately in nice spots, not too far and not too close to one another. Shane unpacks everything she has brought: miso of course, vacuum-packed velvet tofu, lentils and ginger root, freckled avocado pears, soya milk and muesli roasted with almonds, vanilla flavoured soya milk, unbleached iodine-free sea salt, sunscreen, organically farmed apples, and a sharpened knife; candles for a wind-free evening meal, matches, goat's milk cheese, sesame seeds, olive oil, sulphur-free dried peaches, bonito fish flakes, a bamboo ladle, three bottles of noble red, a torch to lighten a hole in the dark, a break from her shop.

The food is safely stored in the damp pantry under the rocky overhang right at our eating place: a hospitable, cleanly raked opening where the campfire has already been stacked and three tree stumps placed as seats.

We go to the river's edge to wait for dusk. Kikois are spread. If we're lucky we'll see the kangaroos tonight. My head rests on Jude's tummy with a gauze cover to keep away the odd fly that may have wandered down to the water. How blissful, this body breathing under my head. Shane has fallen asleep. She needs a lot of rest.

A murmuring, cool south-westerly swishes through the casuarinas. When Jude lights a cigarette, I go to gather more firewood.

Gathering wood here is no sooner said than done, except that a snake may be hiding in every tangled pile of driftwood from which you pull kindling. We're indoctrinated to associate snakes with evil: deceiver of women, aggressor – trample his head and crush his body.

Under Jude's wholesome influence I'll learn that each has its own place. A black one lives under that hardwood there, Pietsnot is his name: bother me and I'll bother you. A brown one lives left of the pile of wood, where the well-worn animal track leads down to the river. His name will be Old Brown Eye: me in my small corner.

Supper-time arrives when the flies have quietened down. Shane prepares a green lentil curry in a cast iron pot. It will be served with apple chutney, yoghurt and basmati rice. The bush forms a dark circle around us. We talk about this and that, mostly attune our ears to the sound of the silence and the strange un-African kwaak of the frogs. And notice a giant fruit bat against the rising moon.

As the bush quietens around us, we sense our own solitude. Staring into the fire as all living beings tend to do, we realise before full stomachs take their toll how reluctantly the city releases us, how readily we embrace everything it forces on us. I had been warned: you can easily do well in Sydney, easily become a sex addict, but also a sleepwalker, nightwatchman, hedonist, monk, epicure, anything you want.

Shane's curry tastes well-rounded. The night ripens like fruit. Crockery is stacked away from the fire circle to be washed in the river at first light. Shane is first to get sleepy; Jude and I talk on for a long time. Our conversation is gentle and joyful, and on our first night the rough edges between us are already smoothed down.

I look forward to every night, every day. It's blissful inside our tent with only the membrane of the canvas between the bush and us. We embrace, carry one another right through the night, but it goes no further, and I'm glad of it. Towards daybreak, the thump-thump of kangaroos and Jude's under-blanket fart awaken me.

The days become even more serene. Sometimes we slumber at the river's edge, and are woken by the slight pricks of casuarina needles floating down onto our faces. Sometimes I dare a siesta in the unbearable heat of the tent and wake heavy as a stone after vivid but turbulent dreams.

And Shane makes the most wonderful food: a tofu and cucumber salad with semi-sweet rice wine, and pumpkin and garlic grilled to perfection in sesame oil with brown rice and nutmeg.

We talk about the shy pair of black swans who eye us through the trees. They're monogamous for life, last year there were two cygnets. The grey-brown kangaroos appear to tumble forward when they take their dusk sips at the river. Look more closely, and you'll see they are perfectly balanced when they bend over to drink. And then there are the cicadas that attach themselves to the trees, waiting, after a season of hibernation, for that one perfect day, to burst out in shrieks of delight. Fluorescent green now, they leave behind their sculpted shells with holes where the eyes had once been, cylinders into which the legs had fitted, and hair-thin feelers.

We also talk about the repulsive mass of flies you have to shoo away with one hand as they go crazy with greed when they discover your toilet spot. Our business is done more and more efficiently, and we spend longer on the river's edge where the flies are most merciful.

The days dam up, one into the next: the snakes become more restful, and so do we.

One day I play a spoor-tracking game alone along the river. I form sticks into arrows that I place strategically on flat stones and against trees. At each arrow I mark exactly how many steps the tracker still has to go until he reaches the next arrow, all the way to the final destination where something's been hidden away. I hope Jude or Shane come across my arrows.

I sit on the last stone. It's dead quiet and dripping with heat. A few lone flies hover around me. I run my hand all the way down my leg, then look down and back to see where my hand has wandered. Something is protruding from my skin. And for the very first time I notice the blue spot at the back of my right leg, diagonally below my buttock. A big dark spot with delicate reddish speckles buried in the blue just under the skin.

Can't remember knocking myself, wait, don't panic, let's take another look. Fuck, there's more.

In the hollow of my knee I discover another one, not as big as the first, but an even deeper blue. So I fine-comb my right leg: the thigh; the upper leg with its matted hair from wearing long pants; the knee with its boyhood scars, and the calf, front and back. Nothing, not even on my shin.

Then the left leg: three small ones behind the calf, not as dark as the one behind, under my right buttock, but unmistakably there. Another one on my left thigh, this time closer to my genitals. And two pale-blue ones behind, on my left upper leg.

I hug myself, stare into the distance without focusing, suddenly alert when a rock lizard wakens, his upper body raised high as he trots all the way along the stony bed between the casuarinas.

Spots everywhere, ma's poor, poor boy, has he bumped himself? Against what? Where? Nature's wild out here, no doubt about that. Could have been that stump, the one that sticks out from the pile where I collected wood. Last night I did . . . or was it the night before? The days here all seem the same; maybe it happened when Jude and I were here yesterday. The one below my bottom could have been from a rock. Surely I'd have felt it? Maybe it was in the water. Or maybe a river eel's rubber nose gave me a slight electric shock. It's so bloody cold in that water that you go dead numb.

Now let's see, come and lie down here for me. Yes, get undressed. Everything?

Yes, everything, why are you so shy today, we're all men here. No, take everything off. Hang your clothes over that chair and lie down here so I can check you over carefully . . . Ah, here's a nice big one, right below the bottom.

Present, Sir, blue spot number one.

There's also a tiny one here.

Blue spot number two, Sir, standing to attention, Sir.

And these three?

Present, Sir, Sir, Sir, number three, number four, number five.

And this little fellow, I mean spot, right here in the tender flesh where the hair goes fuzzy, like a baboon's. Good heavens, you're lucky it's not higher up, otherwise your balls might have gone blue too.

Blue cock, Sir, present!

And here, let's see – yes, another pair.

Number seven and number eight, Sir, present, Sir.

Seems that's all, son. That's all, Konstant. Just a couple of bruises. By tomorrow morning when you crawl out of your tent they'll be better, I guarantee you. And by the day after tomorrow or thereabout, all you'll see are dull spots. Have you got any Deep Heat? Now, if you're really worried . . .

I'm not, I'm not. I know it's nothing to be . . . do we have Deep Heat? Shane or Jude, Jude will have some. He's got everything. I'll get up and ask. Maybe one of them will notice my arrows. Why the hell does the one below my bottom make such a big bump? It's very sore when I press it. Unbelievable that I'm only noticing it now.

You must have knocked yourself somewhere, Konstant, you've got a blue spot right here. Now I remember your words the first night in the tent, Jude. They weren't worth a farthing then: I wanted to focus exclusively on you, how could it have been otherwise? Alone, naked with you, at night, in the bush, in a tent in you. Strange how something said a day or two ago echoes back exactly: you must have knocked yourself somewhere, Konstant, you've got a blue spot here. It's nothing Konstant, absolutely nothing, not worth even a single hair on your head, no point giving it a second's thought. Tell me, since when does anyone get worried about a blue spot?

Since I . . . since Ju . . . it can't be. No, it hasn't got hold of me. Not with your silver spoon in my mouth, Albert. Not that easily. I'm too smart for it, my life here too successful. I'm too happy. Definitely not: where's my faith now? Must get a grip on myself, get my thoughts under control. They're running away with me. Listen. Listen to the wind, how it chases after the river, how it whips through the casuarinas' horsetails. Said it the first day here: you can hear the wind through the casuarinas during the day as well. And in the early evenings, as the sun is setting: a slight breeze skips across the waters. It's so peaceful in our tent at night, the wind through the casuarinas. Can't be anything. Someone's coming, is it Jude? Or Shane? Hope it's, it's Jude!

Three metres, Jude reads the direction to the next arrow.

Konstant! when he sees me on the rock, How did you remember this game? You've taken me back to my Standard One year. No, Two, it was Standard Two. Of course, I totally refused to join the Voortrekkers, but my mother insisted, so in the end I went. She wanted me out of the house, especially on Monday afternoons, when my father sometimes didn't go to work. He had to recover from the weekends, and Voortrekkers was on Mondays. And then our corporal – what did they call themselves – cornet, or whatever it was, marched us off to the Eerste River in the summer heat, can you believe it, and there we played your game on the riverbank. I don't know whether to laugh or cry.

Jude, come quickly, let me show you, lay your healing hand on me, come here.

Konstant?

Jude, look, here on my legs. What do you think it is? I'm scared, Jude, of what it could be. What do you think; it isn't, is it, Jude?

I wouldn't get unnecessarily upset about it before getting a professional opinion. It's very easy to pick up a blue mark here without noticing.

We must get back, I want to cross the mountain, go back, I have to know.

Even if you get to a doctor today, you'll still have to wait at least a week; it takes at least a week to get the result these days. Konstant, don't get so worked up. You can't do anything about it, my dearest love.

My dearest love. Is that you speaking, Jude? Hold me tight, don't let me feel so sca . . .

Come now, Konstant, you're one of the strongest people I know, and the most handsome. Use your head.

Strong: I know I am. Luck lies just around the corner – it can't get hold of me, not as easily as this.

Do you know of anyone who's had blue spots and then . . . No? The fungal spots on my back? Who? That American guy? Why didn't you ever tell me?

I did, dear Konstant, and I even remember when. We were walking back along that pathway in Kuringai-Chase when I said: I suggest you get a diagnosis. I'm not altogether easy about those spots on your back. But you were so cross about Robert and me – I believe you heard, you just refused to listen to what I was saying.

Can't remember that at all. Can't even remember that we walked alone along that path. Where were the others? Blue spots – do you know of anyone?

Konstant, I think it's more important for you to calm down; it won't do you any good to worry about something that isn't even there. Come, let's go and make some tea. And there's still that watermelon to cut before it gets too ripe. Come.

You walk ahead, Jude.

With your sturdy stick. Me, carefully. I can't afford any more shoves or bumps. Will monitor the spots from now on. I'm strong: I'll get better. I've never managed anything without effort. Always take the narrow road, that's me. I'll take a nap in the tent this afternoon. Suddenly I'm very tired.

Jude turns around and stops in the dip near our eating-place. I'm forced to stop too. He lifts my fly net and kisses me long and hard until all my scary thoughts vanish, until I'm left with only the mossy smell of the driftwood around us. We let go of each other and walk the short distance to where Shane has already prepared something.

Quickly she lifts the cotton napkin for us to help ourselves before the flies descend. There is sliced papaya, its flesh a burnt orange, served with vanilla soya milk on three tin plates, and lukewarm rooibos tea with finely chopped fresh ginger.

The evening around the fire tastes of the dry and damp bluegum leaves Jude throws on the flames by the handful. Light flashes across his face, more resigned than ever before, and heavily made up: dark kohl lines around the eyelids, ox-blood rouge on the lips, the cheeks fragrant. Our Jude is deliberately more talkative than usual, to distract me from my own thoughts.

It's a pity, really, Jude thinks, that we don't eat meat. We could have made a trap for one of those rabbits and placed its entrails in a neat pile, down-wind from our eating-place, so there'd be fewer flies. That's how the Kooris did it. And still do: put the guts and of-fal of a kangaroo or any other wild animal out to lure anything that flies away from their food. Clever, isn't it? The tricky part is: whose hand will cut the rabbit's artery?

I will, I offer. Saw enough of it on the farm, though to tell the truth, never did it myself, but if I must, I'll do it, before you can say jack-knife.

And what about the dingo who's been lurking at the edge of the campsite the past two nights: sharp jackal-like face, pointy ears, yellow-red hair, his fur the colour of sand. We don't even have a lit-tle bone for him. Maybe we can put some bread out, a saucer with something.

Shane sits on the quilt spread with her back against a tree. I half lie on her lap, my eyes almost closed. I watch Jude push a stick into the fire until it turns into a red pinpoint that paints spirals on the night. A flame catches the silver of his earrings, the gold thread of his exotic dress. Then he puts the stick on the ground, gets up hum-ming, and fetches another log for the fire.

Now and then there's splashing from the river. It could be a kan-garoo. Shane says she heard a possum rooting outside her tent the night before. Other than that, she doesn't say much. She's already spoken to me about resignation and accepting what fate has de-creed. We stand by you, we are your family.

I won't let anyone fool me. What is my fate? If I knew, I might be able to prepare myself. Whatever the result turns out to be, I'll have only one opportunity to react to it. And the ones around the fire here will stand by me through thick and thin, even if I stumble. What am I going on about – how unbelievably easy it is to imagine the worst at night.

I do believe you, Shane and Jude, but how slight my knowledge of you really is. Shane hardly talks about her family, rarely about her mother, never about her father. Jude's the same. Who are you, Jude, you who have dragged me along with you? If only you were mine, then I wouldn't need to ask – but you are evasive, your true self hidden like the moon in purdah. Though I know the taste of your kiss, I have to entrust the rest to guesswork. If you stay with me, and it's like it is now, in the tent, here at the fire, I'll be the happiest man on earth. Then I'll embrace my fate, even if it's short-lived. Let's drink more wine, hum in my ear, my onnagata, and why not put a saucer of wine out for the dingo – one day his offspring will come sniffing at our long-faded footprints.

Black swans coupling:
a lifetime together and
still only each other

Shane, Jude, I'd like to say goodnight. Jude, take the bow on my behalf, I'm too tired to do it myself. It's been a long day and the wind has turned cold. I'm turning in now; it'll be cosy in our tent. My snores will seep through the tent canvas, the bush will listen. I'll close the flap, Jude, you know how it is. Feeling better now, thanks to the two of you. My own strength has deserted me; still, I believe in myself. The night is already too long for me: can't wait for to-morrow. Tomorrow we'll walk to that place you spoke about, Jude, where the rocks lie flat in the rapids, their backs white with guano, like prayers floating on water. I'll carry the watermelon on my left shoulder, and if I tire you can help. Can you cross the river with a watermelon? What about the bushpig hunter on the opposite bank, the one who aimed just as you took me in your mouth? Don't care if he saw us. He's after wild pigs, no other reason for him to be here.

Unlike us – swimming and lying about. There were two shots, no, three, I can vouch for it: I felt each one ricochet through my body.

Am I imagining it, or is it colder tonight? Probably because I've moved away from the fire. Don't need the torch, your eyes soon adapt to the gloom, what's more, it's never pitch dark here.

Stay a while longer, Konstant, you don't have to go to bed so soon, Shane says. She rises and squeezes my hand as I linger at the fire, ready to go to our tent.

You should floss your teeth.

There's nothing I *should* do, Jude. Why's tonight different? Why should I do it specially tonight?

Oh, Konstant, I don't mean it like that at all, whispers Jude. We scarcely hear him. Come to me.

I circle the low fire to sit with him. The wine-drinking and being next to the fire have left a glow on Jude's face. He's hotter than usual, and his clothing and the essential oils on his skin give off a scent of burnt resin and olive oil.

Well, I think I'll go to bed after all.

You're asleep already.

I need to be alone in the tent for a while.

Well, on your way, then.

I won't let the night stalk me. I'll listen to the wind and the frogs. I'm glad we brought this blanket along. Is it the one Jude got in Lesotho that time? It's soft to the touch, special enough to wrap a rider on a pony in the snowy highlands. I'm cosy in here: won't bother about the candle, don't want to examine myself again today. Must still put my shoes out, the dew will make them damp, I don't want them in here either. They must go. Anyway, the sun will dry them out.

It was so tranquil around the fire tonight. Always over-indulge on Shane's food. The wine was good, enough for a touch of heartburn, the familiar sour kind. Too much drink nauseates me these days: my constitution has become more sensitive. I've so much more energy, it's unbelievable what damage meat and dairy products do to your body. Actually, it's totally believable: the evidence is all around us.

Should have come to lie down long ago. The two at the fire don't understand my need for sleep. Shane and Jude are so compassionate. Must remember to ask Jude if K . . . Hell, no, I won't, can't be bothered any more: Jude has only mentioned K once here, when the two of us went to collect wood together, I even remember the spot. K's on an exploratory trip to New Zealand. I had nothing to say to this bit of information. Nothing at all. That must have caught Jude off guard. Jude, do you miss K? Will still put that to him. And won't forget to add: it means nothing to me any more, Jude. That's the whole truth. Here at the river you're so . . . It's a long time since I last saw you so contented, so utterly at peace with yourself. In the city the hunting season is permanently open: always on the lookout for an intriguing face on the streets, a gorgeous body on the train. Is there someone to catch my eye? Is somebody eyeing me in the pub? Especially the pubs, bookshops too. And supermarkets and parks: always on the lookout. Ditto the swimming pool and the art museum, the hairdresser and even the queue at the post office. Or intermission before the main movie starts. On the lookout: always feverish. It never stops. What an unbearable burden: being on eternal high alert throughout your entire bodily existence, just on the off-chance that your obsessive search for love might be rewarded. And rewarded again. Nothing more than a never-ending samsara. It terrifies me. Maybe it's my vocation to bring you to penitence. If that's all I have to do before falling asleep, I too shall be content.

Today I shat out a whole kernel of badly chewed corn. Shane

says you must chew one mouthful a hundred times – quite something, that. I prefer a shady spot to do my business. Where do the other two squat: somewhere with fewer flies? They're everywhere. I hate their tiny pads on my bum. The little buggers want to get right in. You should actually go do it at night, but it's difficult to regulate yourself.

What's that? Something, my foot, lying outside? Has Jud . . . Have the flaps been closed? My foot is freezing, though it's not really cold outside. Feet cold, body boiling. Am I sick, am I? What weird . . . Jude's asleep already. Snoring. Can't bear it: boozed too much, stinks of cigarettes, yuck! Simply can't help yourself, can you? Must always over-fucking-do it, you obsessive weakling. I'll still lose it here. Something's touched my foot: crab. Do they come this far from the water? Impossible. Maybe at night, looking for food. What . . . fucking toenail, Jude's, needs cutting. Comes with this and that: floss your teeth. Screw you, man. Hot inside here, foot, Jude's fucking foot touched me, can't take it any more, tent is too small for both of us. Warned Jude, but he always knows better. The bastard. I told you this sleeping together would lead to shit, and it already has . . . Juuude! I'd already dealt with you - I'm not your cuckold any more. Now you've softened me towards you again, use your weakness . . . must get out of here: smells of bodies here. Why's my foot so cold, my body so hot? That's what I want to know. And have I got a fever? My forehead, wait, let's check it out with Jude's, don't want to . . . a thing like that . . . Jude's farted or something. What now, where's the candle . . . must get hold of it immediately, check my legs. Konnie, right now. Now, I tell you, come, on your bicycle, now! Bicycle? What bicycle, Pa, why am I suffo . . . Stuffy in here since Jude came to bed. Happens in a tent. But no, Jude, you always know what's best, as long as . . . Take Konstant into the bush, have your way with him, tent is the perfect place, warm his arse for him, tent is big enough. Duvet over my head, blanket has covered me, can't breathe, Ma, can't get any air, my Ma. Albert, tell Pa he has to stop the Opel. Can't stop now, Konnie: have to push on, perseverance triumphs. The road is flooded, we'll be there in a moment, Middelburg's around the corner, let's first get through here. If we stop now, we'll be swept away, Konnie, washed away, man. You don't really want us all to drown for your sake, do you now? It's suffocating in here, Pa, pull over. Why do Hester and them always sit in front, the rest of us dumped in the back like dogs? Tell them: it's too stuffy in here for me, there are too many blankets. The tent back here's too small for all of us: tell them, Albert. You hear? Stop it now, Konnie, man, stop it, shut your mouth or I'll smother you. We have to push through here. Once we get to Middelburg we'll buy fish and chips, remember that shop next to the park? Shut up, Konnie, or I'll put this blanket over you, since when do you mess around like this? I'm going to tell Pa, he'll give you a hiding. Going to tell Pa Jude tried to smother me. Something's burning here . . . smells . . . candle, Jude's fucked the candle over, everything in the tent. Knew from the start you'd take me for a ride, Jude. You too, Shane. If only you knew how I tried to reinvent you, have reinvented you. Re-in, reign, from the back of your shop on a throne, queen of dollars: For heaven's sake, my slaves. Come along all of you, my eunuchs, come. Collect your dollars, as much as you want. I'll fill your heart's content. I went to pray at church, prayed the skin off my knees for you, queen on a throne with a heart of dollars. Didn't work, Shane, you've cheated on us all. All of us, do you hear me! Couldn't reinvent yourself. All your self-realisation courses didn't help: cat may don a top hat and bow tie, when mouse saunters by he's still nothing but a cat. You exploited us, you bastard. All of us to the point of starvation, Raster Wassermann. Always wanted to tell you this: you fucking didn't give a goddamn fucking shit for me. As long as I was what I am, you simply would not accept me. You wanted to create me in your own image. That's why on that last day at the station: I hope you get over all your nonsense in Australia. That was the last time you tried to force your will on me. Well, I did try. I did. So help me God if I'm not telling the truth. I dropped everything for you, Jude, just for you. You led me to your lair and then throttled me. Too late now. The matches, must get, must get . . . from here . . . My blue spots, it's you, Jude, I feel it in my marrow. I know it. You can't beat me any more, I've been struck down to the ground. Satisfied now? I know I've got it, I felt it inside me tonight, gnawing at me like an animal. Wasn't at my feet, not at my feet, d'you hear, I'm not as stupid as that: I know my body. It was wriggling in my marrow. Did you hear me clearly, Judas? I'd hoped to stay free from it: believed I was the horse with the white blaze and the four white socks. I *am* the horse marked with the blaze. Will get special clearance at the tollgate like in the old days: You don't have to pay anything, my mate, not with that swanky horse of yours. I'd get through for free, I promised myself. Now my faith's thrown to the wind and I'll be tortured for nothing. What have I done to be punished like this? Thought I was invincible, Albert. How many times did you impress it on me? How could you possibly have predicted what would happen to me? The torch, here it is, here next to my leg, must take a look. There's no more turning back, never again, Jude, it's finished. What to tell Pa and Ma? How do you tell people like that you've got eight blue spots on your legs, and that's only the beginning . . .?

Our poor son: it's all gone sadly wrong, well, that's life.

Ag, what a pity, Mirjam, oh heavens, Raster, our hearts go out to you, man. Let us know if we can do anything.

You phone them, Jude, you'll have to tell them I've got blue spots. Tell them in your mellow tones to look out across their mealie lands for the blue fucking crane. Pa will understand. It's like bluetongue, Pa. You know what a sheep with bluetongue looks like. That's all it is, Pa.

Damn it; give him a dose of blue vitriol. Immediately! A good spoonfull, and tomorrow he'll be dead right again.

Worry as much as you like, Pa and Ma, that's right. Except this time there's nothing anyone can do about it. It's too late, do you understand?

You, Jude, make sure they all understand, clearly, okay? Yes, Albert must know, Hester must know, the two little ones. From now on, their big brother is known as old Bluebeard. Of course you know the story . . . I'll go mad in here . . . must get out.

Get up and strip! Off with the sheet, off with the blankets, unzip the flap. The night is lovely: cool dew on my face, under my bare feet. Stars no longer in their places, shot by. Bluegums stand out darkly against the sky, exactly where they were when I went to sleep. They've stood guard around the tent all night.

Jude! Shane! Can you hear me? Bluelegs is here, he's arrived. Get up, little brother, little sister. You brought me here, come see what's become of me, Jude!

Shane is first.

Issit you Shane?

At my side, carrying a blanket or something.

It's cold, it's my head, Shane, I've caught a fever, I'm not putting it on, I swear, Jude.

What's he saying, Jude?

Wrap that blanket, wrap me up, that's all you can do, nothing more. It's too late to try to patch things up, my sweethearts, altogether too late, forever. I'm here to help myself, I've done well in my new country, haven't I, Jude? I was made manager; I earned my keep – even more – not so, Jude. You never even bothered to say to me: Well done, matey. Shame on you. Leave me. Throw the blanket over me loosely, so I can cool down. Leave me, Jude, as I am, naked, don't touch me, Shane.

Shane covers me with her blanket, the two of them hold me tight.

Is it morning yet, Jude? Can you tell Shane what the Karoo is like as the sun rises, when the cows sing for me. Jude, sing for me, you've got such a lovely voice, Shane, you . . .

What's Konstant saying, what happened?

I don't know. Don't know. Get - we need another blanket. He's freezing, feel his hands, like ice.

I'm not. I'm boiling. If you don't believe me, Shane, give me your hand. Here, put it here on the warmest part of my body. Let's call a spade a spade: you always wanted to feel me up. From now on no one will twist the truth with me. Sing for me, Jude, sing: "Ver oor die Diep Blou See".

Sing a song for Bluebeard, you know the story, don't you, Shane? They teach you to help yourself on all those courses of yours, don't they, darling? And they all lived happily ever after, and that's how it's going to end. You've no idea what I'm talking about, do you? Ask Jude to explain. My wise Jude knows everything. He can point out many ways with the greatest of ease. That's your trade, as you yourself so rightly say. Not so, Jude? Dance with me here on the grass, beyond the ghost gums, da-dum-da-da-dum-da-dum-da-dum . . . Don't fuss about the blanket. It's so good, so wonderful, here at the Wollondilly. Pardon my waltz, I won't. Never take me back to that tent, never take me back into your life again. You understand me, Jude, as only you can.

I understand, Konstant, come here. Stabilise your breathing. You know how: breathe in deeply, breathe out slowly. Empty your lungs completely on the out-breath. Right, you're okay with me,

Konstant. With us. Shane, would you mind bringing another blanket so we can spread it out here under the tree. It's lovely here: let's all watch the sun rise. I'm holding you, okay, Konstant, I'm right next you. In deeply, out slowly, I'll never leave you, Konstant, you're here with me. Forever.

I don't want to go back to the tent, Jude.

It's fine, Konstant, you don't have to go in there again. Thanks, Shane, we can all sit down here until daybreak, we might hear the swans' song.

IT'S ALWAYS WORTHWHILE WATCHING Shane place the washed carrot in the middle of her cutting board and levering the knife up and down rhythmically. Her right hand holds the handle firmly, yet relaxed. It's a high-speed see-saw action that transforms the carrot into five equally thick wedges in seconds. Noiselessly she lays the knife aside, positions a stainless steel basin below the edge of the board, and with a single sweep wipes the carrot wedges into it. Without looking up, she picks a second carrot from the pyramid in front of her and repeats the action. This slightly longer carrot yields six triangular wedges, like the previous ones, all equally thick. Again the basin is drawn closer and the wedges are swept into it. A third and then a fourth carrot are disposed of just as rapidly. Never the slightest hint of rush. But her secret involves more. She's established that the carrots are sweet before starting to cut them. Their taste, their cut, and the way she arranges them on the bed of well-roasted onion rings, also tested, together make for more than the sum of the whole.

The telephone rings and Robert answers with a spritziness that could get me through the day. Without having to watch her carrot, Shane answers the question Robert relays to her with his hand over the receiver. The twelfth carrot falls apart into six pieces.

You've got carrots on the brain, Shane, you never allow your rhythm to be broken by thoughts about your mother who so upset you over the phone yesterday; or your boyfriend who is smart in the bed, but not in the head. Like a predator, you focus on the task at hand, never missing a beat over the quickly diminishing pile of carrots. You could galvanise me into similar action.

I lift my head, drop my chin slightly, and a heavenly feeling slips down my neck muscles. It's as if a warm-blooded mother's hand is massaging me with fragrant Vicks. In anticipation of tomorrow's diagnosis, my muscles had gone all stiff. Now I'm able to breathe again on this blue Monday.

I lay into my daikon. My left hand grabs its top, holds it upright on my cutting board, and by rotating it clockwise – with a downward movement of my knife – I produce two-inch shavings. Imagine sharpening a pencil with a pocket knife. That's how Shane taught me.

Daikon shavings perfect for the pickle we are serving as a side dish with the tempeh and leek casserole today. The marinade for the daikon pieces is an original creation of fresh orange juice, fresh ginger matchsticks, rice vinegar, shards of palm sugar, and a few pinches of salt. After it's been pressed for an hour under a heavy bottle in the coolroom, Shane tests it with her pinkie and congratulates me on its cool, piquant taste.

Has Shane read the riot act to Liz Bird? She's taken up a normal collegial attitude to me since early this morning. And right now I can't help noticing the boyish beauty of her abundance of freckles. By chance, we land up together in the coolroom, searching for our ingredients, body pressed to body in the cramped space, without the slightest hint of discomfort.

Liz, have you any idea where those, the stuff, can't think of its name right now, simply can't, it's for Jamal's laksa.

Liz stoops down to pull her box of corn out from behind a crate of apples. She recovers and frowns at me with that brown forehead of hers.

Celery?

No, not celery, the stuff that gives a lime, I mean lemon-like taste to soup, you know what I mean, it frustrates me.

She guesses, correctly, that I'm after lemon grass. I experience her empathy and I need it today more than ever before. Jamal gets exactly what he's asked for, washes and slices it into paper-thin coins for his laksa enriched with coconut milk.

The day drags on unbearably. In order to uphold the unwritten code that we may not schlep our dirty linen into the shop, I work fast, neatly and silently. But find it impossible to maintain Shane's level of concentration.

Kitchen partners Robert, Liz, Joseph, Ava-Marie and Jamal, I'd just like to admit to you candidly that I'm counting the hours until I have to entrust myself to the doctor's diagnosis at exactly ten o'clock tomorrow morning. In preparation for which I would like to inform you that I have returned unscathed from the wilderness. There I was threatened, amongst other things, by snakes; and I sang with a swan about you, my work brethren and sisters, amongst whom I feel so contained. Now, however, I do ask myself, I do, however, ask myself whether, no. I'll hold the question back for now, I'll wait a little longer.

I'm asked to thicken the casserole of the day. First, squeeze two lemons. To do that I need the lemon squeezer. I know my place and I find it without asking. Finding the sauce thickener becomes another story.

What's those white crystals called again, like the extract from hooves of beasts? Those chalky crystals?

Hooves of beasts, Konstant! You keep saying the funniest things, it makes the time fly by. Hooves of beasts, well, for a start, we don't use any animal products here, so hooves of beasts it can't be.

Wildebeest, Robert quips.

It drives me crazy when I can't find the word, I gnash my teeth.

I'm not putting this on, bloody hell, it's the stuff my mother uses to make jelly. I'm not that stupid, I know that's not the ingredient used here. What I mean is what I'm not saying. What is its surrogate, I mean what's the word for it? See, I can remember such highfalutin' terms like "surrogate", but when it comes to . . . tell me, do any of you true blues know what "siece of pausage" and "civer lake" mean? Can any of you tell me that? 'Course not. I can't even begin to explain to you that it's my father who throws such curvies when he talks about his piece of sausage and his liver cake.

Please, Shane, tell me, what is the word for the thickening agent you use in this shop?

The answer is kudzu, Konstant, she says clearly and distinctly, and with that says all that's needed.

Pre-Wollondilly, she'd have hauled me over the coals if I'd expressed myself in a woolly way, but now, from the goodness of her heart, she treats me differently. It makes me feel good and bad at the same time. Remember this, Shane, my appointment is not until tomorrow. Nothing is final yet, and the three spots behind my left shin are much lighter today. Besides no new ones have appeared, did you know that, Shane? From the moment I laid eyes on you, I was hoping to work with you. I'll still take the shop to great heights with you, you'll see. When I'm sick, will I be able to meet the demands of this shop?

Draw closer, my people, it's time for lunch and a few questions which you may spare me your answers to. As always, we've worked hard today. Jamal, sit next to me, you always smell so fragrantly of cloves and it's not only from smoking your kreteks, there's something else in the mix. I can't keep my nose away from it, I swear a blind person could smell you coming. Your laksa is exceptional: did you sprinkle fresh coriander on it at the end? I've got a lot to learn from you, though I know our clients well enough: the anaemics will pull their noses up at all the chillies in your dish-of-today. Don't believe I've got a question for you, don't think you'll ever reject me. Wasn't it you who said: Well, everybody fancies everybody else, when you heard about Liz's crush on me? Now you're tucking into your own laksa with an extra helping of chillies. Strange, always thought chillies made one's body restless, but no, your fingernails are your prayer beads, you count off while waiting, and so your equanimity is preserved. You may have to teach me the art.

Robert. Would you still ask me out for a beer if you knew that I was sick? And you, Joseph? You'll probably have to meditate on it first. Don't forget to put your arm around my shoulder when we sit down to eat – and remember, you must still teach me a meditation technique. For the first time today I've . . . You know, just to give myself time, you know what I mean, so that I can be my old self here with you lot, I, well this is how it is: without wanting to deny the blue spots, honestly, they are there, if you don't believe me, I myself can't really get it under my knee, as they say where I come from. You know: Jamal and I may know what "piering" and "sjambok" mean, yet you fairdinkums still read us exiles like braille. What I wanted to say, for the sake of remaining on my feet, today I have – and this is what I wanted to make known from the beginning – today I have put on a pair of long trousers to hide those spots. I'm cracking jokes about it, well, I don't want to sit around whinging. I can scarcely believe that you haven't noticed my spots yet, especially you, Liz Bird, you see through me very clearly. Or did you hold your tongues, as does not befit you? You know, the other day I realised something. You were hooked up together: tall blokes Joseph and Robert, the latter bare-armed and tattooed with a tiny lizard, Liz with freckles, Ava-Marie with your natural tan, all of you confidently walking up a one-way street, fearless in your Blundstone boots, all in a straight line, as if you were ready to take off in a race. Boisterously you chose to walk up the middle of the road, jabbering like your kookaburras. Refusing to slink along the pavements, you claimed the whole street for yourselves. And when a police van approached, you swerved just enough for it to squeeze past, so self-assertive in this land of yours that you radiated a sense of invincibility. Not one of you looked at the two cops. What bravura. This is how I've come to know you, and although your experience of the art of waiting is limited to the five or ten minutes you wait at the bus stop, I have nevertheless put my blind faith in your humanity, which has cradled me from my first day here. Now that we're all sitting cosily here with bowls and chopsticks on our laps, it's perhaps not the right time to tell you chompers that I love you. I'll tell you this much at least: I rely on the fact that one day I'll be able to rely on you.

And you, Liz, to continue our conversation, I'm convinced you desire me as your lover - which would serve no reconciliatory purpose - for I know you heard birdies whisper that I desire you. It's true, you heard right, how could anyone think differently? You'll condemn me to misery if you claim I'm being presumptuous. Though if you say you're not flirting with me I'll know you are fibbing. Now let me confess something I'm hardly able to say out loud: I spurned you after your incest story that night on the party boat. Remember, until recently, with the best of intentions, I mocked pedestrians just like my grandfather used to. But in the meantime I've thought it over: don't poke fun at your neighbour – everyone is worth his salt. You too, Liz, you with your perfect breasts. I nearly say it out loud: YOU TOO, LIZ. But that might seem flippant again. And now, on reflection, maybe you picked up that I thought less of you after the boat night, and so, like a dog that had been kicked, you made yourself vulnerable by seeking reconciliation. Maybe it's me who's been misreading you the whole time. I ought to admit at least this to you, Liz. But not now, not before tomorrow. Hope you forgive me, and not merely because I may need you in the future.

See you later, everyone.

Home. My work is done, tomorrow morning early my built-in alarm will wake as usual before my alarm clock rings. Yes, my body is in tune with its own tick. Don't ask about me tomorrow, colleagues. I must go to the doctor before coming to work. On a single day I forgot the names of two of our ingredients – nothing to worry about.

It's great to ride the bike, my legs pedal strongly, spots or not. Not so smoggy today . . . should have my bike serviced. Always grinning, that bloke at the cycle shop, but I wasn't born yesterday. He's got something up his sleeve – don't know what. My relationship with most men is dysfunctional: I don't believe it for a damn moment, even though Jude is convinced. Wonder what he's up to now? Must have a beer with Liz and talk things through. Such a good soul. I enjoyed today, despite everything. Everything? There's nothing to be afraid of. I need a good swim, it's great exerting yourself until your last thought has been sweated out, until you're too tired to think.

Our front door needs oil, it's peeling in the sun. Nothing lasts here. A letter from home. Notice it right away amongst all the window envelopes. How many years has Ma been using the same envelopes? Makes me nervous right away. I'll make tea, no, first read it: Dear Konstant . . .

. . . and dearest friends, it's a great privilege to be able to do the honours here this afternoon, in the first place on behalf of Jude who looks gorgeous to himself, and naturally on behalf of Konstant and all our honoured guests. The reason we are gathered together is that these two lovebirds would rather not be given in wedlock. But, dear friends, we won't let slip the opportunity for a joyous reception. In fact, I believe it is Konstant who yearns with all his heart to be accepted, if I may put it like that, ha ha ha! And now, at Konstant's request, I'd like to read from the letter he handed me a while ago – it's hefty, and I'd like to do justice to it. Now, as you were not to know, the letter is from Konstant's parents, Raster and Mirjam Wasserman who, sadly, refused to honour us with their presence this afternoon. Firstly, if I may differ from Konstant, if you'd permit, oh, could the children in the corner there . . . thank you very much. Now, in everyone's life there's been at least one letter that has lain in wait for its reader like a scorpion. Well now, if you lift the stone, it means you have already decided to brave old stingman, and what happens next depends on your own preparedness. I must spell it out here – and this is where I differ from Konstant, if he'll allow me – the letter from his parents is as innocuous as a hidden Easter egg. Like all letters from a farm it starts with the weather, and I can assure you, my friends: it's a fair-weather letter. Let me read you a piece: We sit on the stoep every night. The mosquitoes bite us black and blue. As you know, this is the best time on the farm, especially to think about you. It's then that we miss you more than usual, and are bitterly sorry that we can't be there today. It's out of the question at the moment, every damn mouth on this farm must be fed, and, oh, it's a terrible burden to bear.

Well now, my friends, I'll skip that bit, as the English say, as I don't want to sour Konstant's life on this glorious afternoon. He's got his own worries about what tomorrow may bring.

Friends, it's a great pleasure for me to get to the next piece, about the recent Lord's Supper celebrated there in Konstant's home dorp, if you'll bear with me for a moment. One, two, three, yes it looks like a total of four short Bible verses . . . Oops, there's another one tucked away here. We therefore have a grand total of five short Bible verses in this letter. Now, if like me, you grew up with Konstant, you'll know that he doesn't sit around the same fire as a Bible verse. At most, one could quote that well-known one about the wine, how does it go again? A glass of wine every night won't hurt anyone's stomach.

Thank you, thank you very much to our friends over there at table nine. As I said: Konstant and I grew up together, and I'd like to tell you this one quick story: We were two youngsters and he and I regularly visited one another on our parents' farms, and we liked nothing better than sitting behind the kraal wall baking balls, if I may be so bold as to put it like that, thank you, dear friends. Thank you, shall we then? Yes, here's a toast to that from the stunning Jude. Almost forgotten about him.

Well now, as I was about to tell: one afternoon we were sitting happily engaged behind the kraal wall when Konnie's Pa suddenly arrived down-wind and caught us in flagranto, and he – well, he's not slow to take any opportunity – he grabbed a piece of plastic pipe that happened to be lying there and gave my old friend such a sound walloping as I'd never seen before. Blood literally flowed. Konnie spilt not a single tear. Yes, dear friends, this is the point I'd like to make: Konstant swallowed his tears. And do you know what gave him his strength? His anger. Such a pure white rage, dear friends, I'd never seen anything like it before. Well now, by that time I had made tracks, as far away as possible from that crazy father of his who also wanted to get at me. I cleared out, and looking back I could still see my old friend's face upside down as he bent over. Wasn't a pretty sight. Which is why I won't dare reading any of the Bible verses.

The next thing, and we're nearing the end now, I know you're eager to get to the best part of the afternoon, let's see, yes, we must mention this here, and I feel it's most fitting, as Konstant does after all know Trynie of Oom Giep van Straat. And, well, it's written here: Tant Trynie is in hospital, very seriously ill with . . . we fear the worst and we're all praying for her, only a miracle can save her now.

A last quick note, my friends, you would have noticed that Konstant's mother does not use the word "cancer", and more than this I don't have to say. Before I end with the toasts, Jude asked me to apologise. He's unable to stay the whole time, as duty calls. With a certain K. Excuse me? Oh, yes, it's his birthday tonight, I understand from Jude, and if I may: if *we* may, what does that K actually stand for, Jude? What? No, friends, Jude flatly refuses, wait, here it is, he's going to say something after all. Friends, our lovely Jude thinks it's a load of crap to get so personal at receptions, those are his words. According to Jude, Konstant hasn't been doing the job satisfactorily for a while now. As he quite rightly puts it: We all know how sensitive Konstant is about it. Well then, before things get out of hand here, I'd like to conclude in a fitting way, with the last sentence of the letter: Regards to *him*. Excuse me, I just want confirmation from Konstant here. Yes, it's as I thought, the letter concludes with regards to *him*, that's Jude, of course.

At this point, Jude would like to excuse himself, please. Many thanks, friends, we'll drink a toast to Jude as he saunters out, could someone please start up, thank you very much.

Children by the dozen, children by the dozen . . .

Before I take my seat, I'd just like to remind you to tuck in to your hearts' content. I'm told there are still plates of these delectable dainties. A moment, friends, one moment, a quick request from Konstant: he specially asked the caterers for devils-on-horseback – or, rather, devil-on-horsebacks, ha ha ha – because he wanted to keep the food as traditional as possible. My friends, I thank you, and enjoy! Remember, time is running out.

I wake this morning, not unafraid, but unexpectedly sheltered by my sleeping body's own smell that lingers as I peel the sheet from myself. There are touches of pastel morning sun on my walls; the clink of a spoon on porcelain comes from the kitchen, and the departure and arrival of trains beyond our house is strangely reassuring. I had a good night's rest, and my blue spots are neither better nor worse.

Under the shower, first lukewarm then ice-cold, I rinse the haze from last night's dream until I'm able to recall it.

An arrival – mine – at dusk on our farm. It was that time of evening when the day's fierce heat had been tempered. Behind the hills the horizon had softened to a shy blue and pale yellow. That was also the time when the birds returned to the trees around the farmstead, the old cypresses, the lombardy poplars, the willow.

The dogs lay in front of the house, their jowls flat on the scrap of lawn specially planted for us as children. They too seemed to rest from all that had busied them during the day, and only became annoying when unusual sounds disturbed them and they charged around the house to bark into the darkening sky.

Fresh in my memory too: my parents on the stoep, the still evening enfolding them, each with a tot, whiskey, water and a block of ice. Besides taking a sip every now and then, and perhaps saying something as they do so, a gentle sigh or single sentence to draw attention to something out there, they sit in silence, waiting for the first sounds of my car at the gate.

Clearly, this was a return after a long absence. Both their faces were sad, and so both also appeared older than the last image I had kept in mind of them.

That's all. No distorted images, no confused messages. The sum of it all was farm life at the end of the day. It's the time when farm people allow themselves to sit quietly without any duties intruding; even unfinished tasks may then be left. No one feels the need to say anything. Even my aunt with verbal diarrhoea, my mother's youngest sister, sinks into silence at this last hour. I've only seen farm people, and mine in particular, experience this melancholic time in this way.

I have carried this mood from my dream and I remain silent over my porridge. And say nothing to Jude either. This time Jude misinterprets me. I'm not depressed, neither am I entirely without anxiety, simply ready to hear what I must today, and to accept it well.

Admittedly, doctors' hands are always immaculate, often translucent and pale as well. Don't they ever get to the beach? I'd have thought Dr Paul would. A shaft of sun through the window makes his hands even paler. Strange that he doesn't draw the curtains. How is he able to determine my colour, or that of his other patients, properly in this light?

The fact that I know him doesn't make me less uneasy. Everything off? You usually keep your underpants on. Since Jude and I have been together, my underpants have been whiter than ever before. It's sweet of him to have come and to be waiting outside, patiently.

I'm not shy of my legs, I mean calves, they're more muscular than Albert's. Could do some work on my upper legs, though; cycling might do the trick.

The way Paul inspects my legs bit by bit. Thorough bloke, this.

Slight frown. Doctors aren't supposed to give the game away so soon. Maybe he allows himself freedom of expression because he reckons we know one another. His expression doesn't generate any new suspicion – I've been on edge since the Wollondilly.

What do you suspect, Paul? Tell me, I've prepared myself.

It could be serious.

Doctors here don't mince their words. Jude assured me. What's more, you use your doctor's first name from the start, whether you know him or not.

I'd have wanted things different, to have a bit of a breather at least: Mister Wasserman, could you please come for a second consultation after a full week, you may arrange an appointment with my receptionist. I'd like to inform you then about the cause of the plethora of blue spots, although, sadly, I suspect the worst. In answer to your request, I will allow you a week's lease on your life. You owe me nothing, I owe you the truth, please convey my best wishes to your spouse. That's how the old school did it. Especially with cancer. Tight lips sealed in everything, like a blocked rectum. For the observant patient, that was the first sign. The second: his nearest and dearest who, after a private discussion with the physician, looks on with sad eyes. Poor, poor man, he's got it. *It*? Yes, it, the doctor's given him six months. Maybe not even as long as that, it's . . . it's? Yes, apparently it's quite advanced.

I'll get your blood sample tested right away. Do you have a history of STDs, Konstant?

Yes. No. Well . . .

I need a blanket to cover my heart, Paul. Your black hair makes your skin look even paler. It's cold here. I'd hoped, prayed so hard, but you can't move a mountain with prayer. I'm glad Jude's here.

Don't go home, Paul requests, have a cup of coffee round the corner.

Don't even dare go off too far, Konstant, in an hour and a half's time you must see me again, brace yourself for a knockback, mate. Sounds worse than I'd ever imagined. It's incomprehensible that I'm feeling as strong as a horse. Is this how it works? Does he strike down the healthy first? When God takes a walk to pick himself some flowers, he doesn't take the wilting ones, no, he picks the most beautiful first. Who said that? Ma? Can't untangle myself from the farm. What am I going to do for the eternity of an hour and a half? I'm glad Jude's come with me.

Does Paul also need to look down my throat? My heart, it's my heart he must listen to. Nothing wrong with my heart. I don't eat meat, don't smoke, and drink in moderation. What will I tell Pa and Ma? My throat's already constricting.

Piss too, he wants to check everything. Can't get a pee out here, must stand behind the screen. Doesn't even look at me. Nothing unusual for a physician; it's their job to listen to the pip-pip of pee in a pipette. This is no pipette, a pipette has openings at both ends. The wisdom of the pipette: open to all sides, what a blessing. Here it comes now: the yellow tears of Konstant Wasserman. Now what do you do if your piss is more than the test tube can hold? Probably put your pinchers to work. Like all shitpants I've got good pinchers. Here it is, Paul.

It's not over yet. Must lie down again, no; stay seated for two more blood samples. Yellow is okay, but if I see red, I become anxious. The time for euphemisms is over: it's not red, it's blood red. I'm not anxious, just totally freaked out. Is it routine to see patients in such a state, Paul? I'm scared, Paul, there's something very wrong with me: Paul, how much time do you give me?

Questions like that are part of an antiquated practice, according to Jude. As usual, he knows everything. Jude, my old favourite, what on earth would I do without you?

Well, I'm sad to say, you're on your way, Konstant. Don't make it even more difficult for me. You're such a strapper. Haven't I told you already, I give you one and one half hours.

I need coffee. Jude too. Back to the waiting room – fishbowl, light-blue walls, all to soothe the fearful – Jude immediately looks up from a "Vogue Entertaining" and embraces me with his eyes.

Maybe it's not a good idea to drink coffee at this stage?

Nonsense, a cup of espresso won't make any difference.

It's not going to make any difference any more, Jude could also have said.

I mustn't wriggle my legs under the table: it irritates Jude at the best of times. Today he doesn't mention it. That hurts. He's treating me with kid gloves.

I've been so calm the whole morning. There, my leg's at it again, I can't help myself. Will the people in the espresso bar notice my anxiety? Keep your poise: in any case, you're tucked away in long trousers.

Can't believe Jude is having so much white sugar. The lump of cheesecake he ordered will be loaded with sugar too. It's old Afrikaner eating habits showing through. Jude, shame on you, you're the one who warned me: sugar damages your immune system.

Jude, did you taste my adzuki bean mousse the other day? I used real vanilla beans for it.

Jude places a hand on my knee: I did, it was delicious. You make the most divine food these days, Konstant.

No one can ever tell me that Jude doesn't love me. The proof of our love lies in the fact that I don't find him inscrutable, as most other people do. Ha, my Jude, do you think you'll ever find anyone else who can cope with you as well as I do? You imagine yourself free of me, but it's become impossible for you too. Separate bedrooms were about as much as you could bear. If I do get sick, you'll suffer too. For that you seem to have prepared yourself already.

Jude, I must phone Shane right away. I can't work today.

I've already done it for you, Konstant. After he's ordered another espresso, he takes my hands again as they lie on either side of our empty glasses.

What did you tell Shane?

Just that I thought you'd gone through enough today, regardless of what the outcome of your test is. You need to relax the rest of the day. Shane agreed. It's so nice outside; I thought we could drive out to Palm Beach, if you feel like it.

Are my hands slightly colder than usual, or am I just imagining it, Jude?

It's a term I'd last heard a long time ago. Not since matric biology has it been necessary to remember about *blood platelets.*

Paul pulls up a chair and explains the results of the blood tests slowly and articulately like a television announcer. So that I'd have no doubt about the authoritativeness of the result.

Blood platelets are miniscule colourless bodies, present in their thousands in the blood of a healthy human body. They enable the blood to congeal after a wound. Blood platelets are manufactured in the bone marrow; the process is called haemopoesis. A certain set number of blood platelets should be present in a specific volume of blood.

By separating a sample of my blood under a microscope, it's been determined that my blood platelet count is lower than it should be. What's more, it is so low that it has become life threatening.

What is more, Paul, what is more. When next I lie down it will be on a hospital bed for a blood transfusion. And if my blood boils again, ever again, there'll be young blood platelets in the mix.

The logical cause of the blood platelet shortage is compromised haemopoeisis. As to the cause of *that*, Paul cannot and does not wish to speculate: hopefully, the analysis of further blood samples will throw some light on the matter. My current condition is not necessarily similar to that of a haemophiliac. The blood of a person with that condition has almost lost its congealing capacity altogether because of an absence of congealing factor VIII. The case in point may perhaps be explained by the simple absence of enough blood platelets. And it's impossible to stress too strongly that even the slightest wound can lead to a serious loss of blood.

What Paul has just conveyed to me I grasp so fully, and have processed to such an extent, that I'm able to distance myself from his malediction and my own awful condition, so that I become aware of his physical proximity to me. So that I must accept, and thus do accept, that he's made this disclosure with as much sympathy as is possible for a physician, without disempowering himself. Soon he'll be expecting his next patient - perhaps with equally serious symptoms and hopeful eyes.

I press his white physician's hand gratefully and tell about our holiday on the banks of the Wollondilly, and how my initial exuberance was overshadowed by the discovery of the blue spots. When he learns about the harshness of the terrain, the river with its drift stumps, the rocks in the rapids and the poisonous snakes, he's surprised that I didn't knock myself and bleed to death.

I leave his rooms, am bade farewell with a firm handshake. But my spirit is faltering, it's hospital time, remember.

In the hospital, Jude won't allow me to abandon myself to loneliness for a single moment.

Shock will set in later, when I'm truly alone. Real shock can lie dormant for years. Must ask Jude about it, right now I'm too tired.

My response to Paul's diagnosis was serene. Shock can also come too late.

So here I'm lying with the needle in my vein. They found a vein easily: my veins are still pulsating with blood. Can't understand that it had to happen to me. Poor bloody fool. And who was it, who was it?

Shane arrives within minutes. How did you manage it, sister? She shoves her nose, wet like a dog's, into my neck, hugs me for a long time. Sincerely. She's from Sydney, see.

With her I can . . . Can hardly, why does her snotty face suddenly make me cry. Her constitution is also fragile. Why cry now, why now?

From an inner pocket of Jude's black monk's habit, knitted from second-hand hemp, a pure white handkerchief appears. And his ringed hand doesn't pull back when I take the handkerchief, but rests on me warmly.

Do you still remember the Indonesian silk cloth, the silk handkerchief the silk ha the sil . . . I'm crying too much. Will . . . I will recover. I can be proud I've been compos mentis the whole day long. Will get my grip agai . . . Me, you too, hold me.

I feel better now, it's good to let everything flow out, I stutter. Jude, do you remember the silk handkerchief, that first night in Melville, I remember it like yest . . . I can't talk.

Cry-it cryitout, cryout, when I get sick, I've always wanted to. When I'm sick, like all babies, I want my mother. Will tell Shane later when we're alone. Jude can't stand my parents. Fancy pyjamas he's brought for me. Everything must be aesthetically pleasing. Save me from looking as if I've been dragged in from somewhere just because it's a hospital, not so, Jude?

Now I know why I've been so obsessed with the farm, with Ma, recently. First the uptight letter, then the dream. Images haunt me and give early warning: call mother Mirjam, you're going to want her badly soon.

When I was small, my legs ached at night. Don't know whether I eventually called out, must have, otherwise she wouldn't have woken, as I looked up, the torch's beam entered our room and my mother came to sit at my legs, but not before laying her hand on my forehead. Then the blanket was pulled back, to massage first the one leg, then the other. That's the way it's been as long as I can remember.

It's hard to teach yourself later in life not to call for your mother when you're sick. Like blood that must congeal once it's left the body. Sad when blood's forgotten how to clot.

Jude's request to spend the night with me in hospital is taken as routine and granted without objection. Even though I'm not hungry, I enjoy the conjee Shane brings later. Warm rice soup covered over in a cloth in a stainless steel billie with an airtight lid. Specially made for me at home, using only the best ingredients. I can imagine how she sought out one of her wooden spatulas and folded soft kombu clockwise into the rice porridge, folding-in-and-fold-old-fold and

Must have fallen asleep. It's a good thing after such a hellish day. Jude is fast asleep, exhausted by all the stress. Wish they'd switch the passage light off, probably need it in case someone rings the emergency bell. Someone *will* need medication during the night. I'm still lucky; I'll soon be up and about.

I've became so totally free here, like never before. So self-assured. No other country gives you as much space to be who you are. I could do anything here, achieve what I wanted. Even Jude's escapades couldn't get at me any more. Shoot me if I'm lying. I felt so good. Couldn't care less what anyone thought of me. Only this afternoon in that espresso bar: did they notice my anxiety? And how will people see me, and what will they think of me? Is it true that all the time with Jude I imagined myself invincible, so untouchable in my golden haze of happiness that I refused to confront the reality of his infectiousness?

Flew too high, the old people will say. Not without reason. I have migrated, succeeded in my work, and made myself loved. And it wasn't as if I was big-headed. I really tried to offer others something, even though the honesty of my opinions was sometimes hurtful. At least everyone knew exactly where they stood with me. I sang, don't know how often, for them all at work. Soon Shane will make me permanent, and no one will boo or baa about it. I'm going to negotiate higher wages for everyone. 'Strue. I can. My leap from meat culture to here has taken everyone by surprise. There's a new recipe with udon noodles, try it out myself first. Shaen w n't belie 't when she tastes it . . . What was in tahini arame can't believe I ate yesterday

I'm sleeping well here. I'll soon be better. Warm-blooded, I am, truly, guess who it comes from? Not true what Jude says about me. Okay, I admit: when I stand next to a man in a public urinal my piss won't come, don't know why. Was never aware of it until he started prodding: Why do you always take so long when you go to the toilet at a restaurant or the theatre? Jude traces my piss problem to a problematic father-son relationship. How does he manage to bring piss and pa together? Easy for him to analyse me. Trading in trash, that's his speciality. Maybe it lay in wait for me in a public toilet. I torture myself at night, there's something about lying awake that stokes my anxiety. It doesn't happen much these days. I must remain calm and cold-blooded, ha! May have to take a few days off until my condition stabilises. Don't want to lose working hours, I'm enjoying it there as never before. My last letter to Albert: my life's peaceful, not much to upset me. Alber th nothing come believe me if you won't come see me now believe me you will you're all we can't be afrai all be afrai wonder when will I home to my curtains dull nice material . . .

. . . dice rolled right for me: I'm the one to buy the meat tonight. Nothing at home: shows you how things fall apart without me. I kept everything going. Fridge bears witness that I'm missed. Just get it at the supermarket, doesn't matter, meat is meat. No need to always buy from so and so. I'm not going to pull the wool over Jude's eyes, he doesn't even have to know where it comes from. Must buy fruit to stew, guavas.

Konstant: Excuse me, sir, excuse . . . Why is no one listening to me?

Supermarket man: It's our new policy, sir. We're pushing meat sales. I've got rock-bottom prices on our spring lamb, sir.

Konstant: Thank you, I know my way around. I know my meat.

Supermarket man: Yes, I can tell. But don't you believe in the win-win principle: I can only be happy if my customers are happy?

Konstant: I'll do it myself because you guys are too slack.

Supermarket man: No worries. Before you go, first tell me if I'm wrong: you're a member of the superior white tribe, aren't you? Wait, I'll stick a meat badge on you.

Konstant: I want maple syrup, Camp, the little bottle. Sweets have to be very sweet, that's the only way I can keep my Jude home. Once there's a bowl of stewed guavas on the table he can't resist staying home, it's as simple as that. I'm too clever for Jude. Bloody hell, Liz, you got ants up your arse?

Liz: No, Konstant.

Konstant: Not here, Liz, can't you tell that this is far too public? It's not fair on me. Are you following me?

Liz: Don't deny me what's due to me, Konstant.

Konstant: Liz, you're only good for one thing outside the kitchen, sorry to tell you, but everybody else is too wimpish. Honestly, Liz, you've got nothing upstairs.

Liz: Won't matter if we do it here. Remember, Konstant, you're well and truly covered.

Konstant: I know, I know, I'm wearing my David Jones pyjamas. Tell me, Liz, since when have you been living nearby? Did you move specially to be closer to me? You're a true believer. Okay, Liz, I'll make a deal with you: our fridge is empty, so I need twenty dollars. Oh, there's that waiter, do you know him? When the sparrows come to roost in the evenings, people leave home to buy food, it's the law of the supermarket. It's the waiter from the Bayswater Brasserie, with his name on his shirt for all to see.

Konstant: Brad, I need twenty dollars, our fridge is empty. Come, I'll take you home for a cocktail to pay you back.

Brad, the waiter: Can't make head or tail. You're a hoon, you know, and I couldn't give a damn.

Konstant: I'm addressing my needs for the first time in my life. Please, I need twenty dollars. Well, don't be a tight-arse, you can be my guest for the night. Liz, tell him what I want.

Liz: You're only remembering your debt to Brad now that it suits you. You were the one who sent him back with your plate of food. You saw fit to return lovely mussel soup, the best in town. First you must grant me my request.

Konstant: Your breasts are full, total giveaway. You've slept with Brad, haven't you? That's why you're siding with him, what's more, you don't get our attitude towards restaurants. It was invented by Shane, practised by Jude, fucked up on me: no more sleeping around, it's far too risky, you'll burn your pudding.

Liz: Brad, gimme a hand with this man. Sometimes the only way to learn is the hard way. It'll be quick and swift. Once in the cool-room all will be over.

Brad, the waiter: You never understood me, Konstant. I always wanted to know you. That's why I followed you to the supermarket. You see, you never even bothered to look at me in the Brasserie. Too intent on making yourself feel secure. You were alone and a bit nervous and never realised that I could give you the comfort you longed for. You fixated on yourself. The only way you could prove yourself, you constipated idiot, was by pretending you know how a real mussel soup should taste.

Konstant: I was given a meat badge the moment I entered, it protects me.

Liz: You are beyond protection, only we can help you, Konstant.

Konstant: You thought I forgot the name for lemon grass the other day in the coolroom. I never did. I just pretended in order to cool it between you and me, Liz. This is your last chance to have yourself acknowledged.

Liz: You haven't got a say about yourself any more, Konstant.

Brad, the waiter: He has, don't intimidate him further, fatpuss. He's already invited me and I'm going to forget all, it's the easiest way out.

Liz: You haven't heard the latest, dickhead. Konstant, why don't you show us a leg?

Brad, the waiter: I don't care any more.

Konstant: Liz, all you'll ever know about me is what I tell you. Jude will be here soon, he'll never forsake me.

Brad, the waiter: Take my advice about that Jude of yours. Have I told you that I know Jude too? And there are others I know who know Jude, there are lots of them, the whole city is full of them.

Konstant: Whatever you have to say is of no consequence to me.

I don't care about you and your kind, Brad. Take this, Liz, you can have my meat badge. I'm sorry, I have to leave immediately. Have to get out of here.

Liz & Brad, the waiter: You can't escape, my mate, can't escape, never escape, never ever.

Konstant: I'll just take this cab here, it's a bakkie, Shane, you don't have to sit in front, then the driver can't molest you. We'll just stand in the back.

Shane: It's not allowed, it's forbidden to stand in the back of a bakkie here.

Konstant: If you have a gun with you and you're hunting, you can stand at the back. Please, sir, would you take us to Centennial Park, please? Shane, why don't you have your boots on? I'll have to piggy-back you. This will do, thank you, here at this stony hill, thanks.

Pindile: Kleinbaas Konnie he must wait, not shoot yet. I'll walk this way round the trees, I bring buck here where you lie, then I put my hand in the air, then you shoot.

Konstant: Hey, Pindile, don't come with "kleinbaas this, klein-baas that" here; here we use first names, even for the doctor. Pindile, you herd the buck past those bushes there, there are always people cruising around, Jude too. Take the buck to the east side where Shane and I will wait behind those rocks. Come, Shane, I'll piggy-back you. Hold the gun.

Shane: I'm fine; there aren't thorns here like in your part of the world.

Konstant: Shane, lie like this, flat on your tummy with your legs open in a V towards the back and at a slight angle. Like this. Wait, I'll slip in here next to you. It's easier for women, you don't have a knob in the crotch that bruises. We may as well rest the barrel on the rock. It's cheating, but I'm not such a great shot. Can you smell the gun oil? Nice, isn't it?

Shane: What kind of rifle is this, does it kick?

Konstant: It's a Vixen .222. If you press it hard against your shoulder, you'll be okay. Come, let's lie on the monument there in the meantime. You go first, be sure to make yourself comfortable first. Place the cross-hairs right on target. Try to get a clean shot, best is in the head, obviously; next best is in the neck, though you'll lose the neck meat. If you hit the leg, that's bad – then the best meat will be bloody. Breathe in just before you pull the trigger. Hey, Shane, I'm glad I can teach you something for a change.

Shane: My elbows are getting sore.

Konstant: Wait, I'll make you a cushion from a tuft of grass. See, they're already approaching? I can see their ears sticking out. There they are, beyond that row of wild figs. Liz should actually go with her horse around to the other side: she's faster than Pindile. What's she up to? Can tell she's a city chick. They'll be here right now, you'd better get ready.

Shane: I really don't know whether I can shoot an animal, it doesn't feel right.

Konstant: Shane, you must do it, otherwise everyone will think you're a sissy. Show them, man, show them you can do it. Men don't have the sole rights to shooting. Any bloody ape can do it, as long as you show him how. You know, Shane, no one ever really showed me how to handle the tractor on the farm. It was somehow assumed I'd know how, and when I didn't show enough interest, that also wasn't good enough. Right, there it comes now. That one in front, it's a young ram. Get him. Liz, just don't . . .

Shane: I'm shaking, I don't want to. I won't be forced into it, take your Vixen.

Konstant: Remember, when you shoot your first buck, you have to eat its liver raw. You're going to miss a great opportunity here. That's right, I'm ready for him. Easy if your rifle is rested. Come along, bokkie, just a little bit, so I can zap you nicely. You see, Shane, I had no choice: there was no choice on the farm. If I'd refused to go shooting, the men would have thought even less of me. There was so much pressure on me, you know, where have you ever heard of a fucking farm boy who's never shot a buck in his life, let alone one who refuses to go hunting? No ways, rubbish like that deserves to have his balls cut off.

Shane: Where was your mother at times like that? Thought you said she understood you; didn't she rush to your side?

Konstant: My mother achieved much in her own quiet strong way, but she swooned before my father's sceptre. What's more, she really wanted her son to shoot his first buck for the pot like all the other farm boys. Don't forget, she was a farmer's daughter too.

Shane: Be careful. Liz is coming fast from the right, can you see her through the telescope? She's running in between you and the buck, watch out!

Konstant: Yes, okay, Shane, don't shit your pants. I saw her long ago; do you think I don't know how to take precautions? What the hell is that woman up to now, is she off her head?

Liz, screaming from her horse: You can't escape, Konstant, never escape.

Jude, I call urgently, are you still here?

I sit up in my bed. A nurse has removed the drip. Only a plaster remains where the needle was. Jude is still here with me. Fast asleep, snoring a little.

Jude?

Should let him sleep on, snoring like a piggie. As far as I know, I'm the only bedmate to have witnessed his snoring. To think, Jude, I have personal rights to your snores. It's sweet, this is when you're at your most vulnerable. You breathe in far too greedily, look how your nostrils bulge. You may be a master at organising your socks and stuff in crisp clean nooks, but here in snoring land you've surrendered control. Here it's just snatch-and-grab. That's how I know you. Must take a photo sometime as proof, although that would make you into public property, whilst at the moment I'm the only one to know. You definitely wouldn't like it. Not refined enough for you. And far too revealing. I like it: even though you may use your boundless energy for life to my detriment, it's a take on you that only I possess. You ought to snore more, Jude.

I must get back to sleep. Paul said I need to get as much sleep as possible. I can do it, no worries. All that new blood has made me wide awake. Doused me with oxygen. Paul is a good doctor, only failed me once. Thought I wouldn't hear him: case in point.

I've been clinically reduced to a case, an anonymous drop of blood. Even the eye of the physician through the microscope has become redundant. Cell types in blood are determined electronically. There's not a person in sight who gives a blue fig that this blood belonged to Konstant Wasserman.

I didn't want to entertain even a vague hope that there might have been a mistake with the cell count. Didn't even have the courage to mention this to Paul. He is a good person. Shouldn't be too quick to pass judgement. As a physician he can't exhaust himself over every patient: case in point.

Wish I'd never heard it. Will keep an eye on him in the coming days, anyway: no one will treat me like I'm just a piece of thing. I remain in control, don't give a damn how sick I am, people will treat me with respect. If they don't know it already, they'll know it soon enough.

The first few days after the hospital pass quietly. It's time to clean the house. I can't take this thing lying down.

Jude and I are summonsed to Paul's surgery again. Calmly we listen to more blood-test results. Read out one by one. They don't hit me like a bomb. Paul demands an explanation from me: why didn't I get myself examined earlier? I shrug.

My T-cell count is average to poor. He recommends the maintenance drug azidothymydine. No need to worry about the blood platelets for the moment. At a later stage I might need another blood transfusion. I don't have haemophilia.

I love my blood too much for that, I remark.

I'd like to write a carefully considered letter home – it might be less of a shock than a telephone call. When can I start work again? Know only too well Shane depends on me, but she says nothing.

Meanwhile, she's found a house to rent in the Blue Mountains. A comfortable weatherboard house belonging to a friend who's overseas. Needn't worry about work at all, Shane assures me. She's good at keeping up a brave front, but all too soon shingles appear on her scalp, the most painful place to get them.

The house in Katoomba exudes a tranquil atmosphere. A large timber veranda that runs the whole width of the back keeps us outside. From there you look out onto bush that teems with birds. I spend a lot of time there.

If I were to fall, on the steps or while walking in the bush, I won't bleed dry. I prefer to say *dry*. Neither Shane nor Jude nor Paul would put it differently.

Must still tell Shane about my dream. The hunt will make her laugh. The single question Jude asked the other night – the way the question stood out at the dinner table still echoes: Have you asked yourself what's the real cause of your illness? That's all. No qualifications, which is unusual for Jude. He's out to test me.

Why did I get sick in the first place? Questions are unnecessary now. Reality demands that I rather look out for opportunistic illnesses. I have to be carried around like a brittle pastry on a tray.

Shane and Jude need to return to the city. Shane to see to work, and Jude to see to K. It affects me, but during my long nights all alone with my thoughts I keep fear at bay. For the first time I also try to meditate following Joseph's instructions in my own amateurish way. I get to know my neighbours. Jude leaves the car for me, though if needs be I'd rather take the train to the city – it's more convenient. I explore the shops in Katoomba and Leura, always in long trousers that are not conspicuous, I mean that keep my blue legs from being conspicuous. It's chilly high up in the mountains, and I stay out on the veranda too late. A cough soon develops. Mustn't worry about it, still, I wish that it would go away. I'm cautious, but not over-anxious. However, for the first time in my life I worry about the slightest ache or pain.

It's important to stay positive. That in itself boosts immunity. I floss my teeth religiously, and don't allow any shoes further than the front door, with or without dogshit on them. The only problem is a cat prowling about in the kitchen in the mornings. I've discovered that anyone with a compromised immune system should not keep any pets, especially cats. No idea where the bugger gets in.

I'm taking more care with my diet than ever before. No sugar or beer passes my lips. A lot of root vegetables like sweet potato, carrots, parsnips, braised onion, ginger root, and also well-cooked grains to make my body strong again. The cough refuses to go. At my request, Jude inspects the phlegm I cough up. Mention it to Paul, he suggests. One can't be too careful.

How do my colleagues explain my absence so soon after the Wollondilly? I ask Shane about it. She encourages me to give her the words to tell them.

The day after tomorrow I go to Paul for a blood test to determine whether my T-cell count has dropped. Hopefully they still deserve their sturdy name of helper cells.

The protein layer of the invader cell latches onto the helper cell, and instead of the helper doing his work and destroying the invader, the opposite happens. With this new vocabulary that has forced its way into my life, I unwillingly compose a letter home.

How am I to convey only the truth? My blood congeals at the thought of their reaction. Should mention it to Paul, it might put some colour in his cheeks.

My dear Pa and Ma, I'm sitting here on the back stoep of a wonderful old wooden house in the Blue Mountains, that's the mountains about a two-hour drive west of Sydney. I hope your ears are also tingling with the birds that make such a racket here, so that your hearts will be strong enough for the announcement that follows. I don't want to begin on the wrong foot but this is how the matter stands: my blood platelets have suddenly become so few I could bleed dry from the slightest knock. Nothing to worry about for the moment, I'm running like a 4x4 over mountains and dales, pumped up with blood. And that's basically how I feel. Some nights I'm unable to close an eye. I put it down to the extra oxygen in the extra blood. It all began with the blue spots on my legs, Ma, you must remember how my legs ached when I was small. Not that I want to link the sore legs to my sore heart, yes, it is very painful to tell Pa and Ma this. I was doing very well here, and I, without blowing my own trumpet, I was really, oh, I don't know, I, I . . . What's wrong with me . . . How is Tannie Trynie doing? I've got the same thing. Everyone is so good to me here. Shane brought me food in hospital, and all the nurses there are good. Even the old tannies who polish the floor, they don't manage English too well, don't know where they come from. Eastern Europe, perhaps. Such screwed-up little faces, worn by concern for their children. At first my doctor, a competent guy, thought it was haemophilia, and what could be worse than that? Then the blood tests indicated something worse, I mean different. Do Pa or Ma know whether there were any cases of haemophilia amongst our ancestors? No? That's what I also said to Paul. Pa and Ma must be strong now.

I've wondered, or rather, I sat here the other day and wondered how things were going on the farm. Oh yes, I did receive your last letter the other day, very distressing – it must be – for Pa and all of you, all the names being changed like that. All the names people give things, dams, airports, towns, illnesses. And before you know it, a new lot is in power with a new attitude. It's only a name, what really matters is the Samaritan-heartedness. Yes, I haven't forgotten a thing, even though you think I have. As I was saying, I was sitting quietly the other day wondering whether Albert, now look, I know there's a drought again. Oh, Pa, my heart goes out to you all, you hear? Just wondered, I really want to pluck up the courage to ask if Albert could come and visit, if there's maybe a bit of money lying around for his ticket. I know it's very expensive, and Pa never lets money lie around, which is a good habit I've forgotten here. No, this is a simple request. Nothing serious. Just thought if Albert were here now. I've developed a cough, nothing to speak of, really. Then I thought to myself that if Albert were here he could rub my chest just like Ma's hand used to. I'm homesick, although I won't admit to it now. Money is no problem this end: if Albert could only get here. It would do him good. Thought I'd mention it. Don't feel under any obligation. I'll be better soon, tomorrow, the day after tomorrow, I'll be back at work. Have I already mentioned that the doctor's fees, hospital, literally everything, is free? Have I told how good Shane, everyone is to me? Of course my mate here as well, but I don't want to go upsetting Pa and Ma with names. Give lots of greetings and a big fat kiss to Hester and Mirjampie and Tilla. They have probably stretched quite a lot by now. I suppose I wouldn't even recognise them if I passed them in the street. And for Pindile and that lot too. I don't mean a kiss. How's everyone doing? And please convey my sympathy to Tannie Trynie. P S: some people here speak of the plague, however that's not how it should be seen. It not a shame; it's an illness. Remember, cancer can also infect – though only succeeding generations. And who gives a damn? Oh yes, it's also terribly dry here, especially in the outback. Seems to me to be too backward for words there – they don't even feed the poor sheep. Shoot the innocent creatures just like that, too bloodthirsty for words.

My return to the city is taxing. During my absence Jude changed the interior completely. The one wall in the sitting room is now a gelato green. A broad obi, the brocade geisha girls wear around their waists, hangs below the ceiling. There are crocuses in my room, with a bright welcoming scent. Everything to delight me. But instead I'm afraid that at night I may bump into familiar objects placed in new positions.

When I return home after the umpteenth visit to Paul with the baggage of my latest diminutive T-cell count, the trains are noisier than ever before. I collapse into the sofa in the newly arranged sitting room. No loose trimmings in sight, no scarf or jersey on the back of a chair or left forgotten on the floor, no hastily folded "Sydney Morning Herald" to pick up. I find myself right in the heart of Jude's choice of green and purple and gold – colours repeated in the foliage and purple blooms of an arrangement of larkspurs – a calculated beauty underlined by the minimalist furniture. What enchanted me in the past makes me feel uneasy now.

After a bout of coughing, green phlegm squirms on the back of my hand. Can't possibly wipe it on the squarely puffed cushions.

Even alone in the house in the Blue Mountains I never experienced the kind of anxieties that assail me all the time here in the city, like the stretch of badly fitting Jockeys. When I rest my head, the loudspeaker at the station starts scolding. When my dark maroon silk gown reveals my legs, the blue spots – faded, thank heavens – clash with Jude's colour scheme. Even the kitchen smells of day-old ash and mould. Something unfamiliar has been prepared for me.

In obedience to Paul, I may not get upset, must not hear the trains, nor the screech of the gulls on the station platform, nor the Koori beggar at the station entrance. I must also disengage myself from the bass sounds pulsating from the V8s of rednecks, and the rowdy sounds of university girls passing by our house. Nothing may upset me any more.

I position myself on a double blanket in the middle of my bedroom, with the curtain half closed, the door locked. Meditating is no involuntary decision. In the absence of any other method, I use Joseph's.

Sit calmly, be silent, back straight, legs crossed, lotus position if possible – can't yet – eyes open a quarter, eyelashes like sunfilters: I may not alienate myself from the world, nor allow its mundanity to define me. Hands lightly on the knees, palms upwards, only the index finger and tip of the thumb touching lightly to keep in the flow of chi. Shoulders broad, so that the chest is free: now sit still, sit strongly, sit mightily like a mountain. Lower the chin. Invite two channels of pure white air into the nostrils and accompany them over the nose bridge, up behind the tear ducts and further upwards and let them follow the curves of the skull bone just below the skin of the scalp, from there down along the neck, still further on their separate journeys along both sides of the spine: down all the way – deep breaths – and allow the two channels to cross below at the tail bone, the left-hand one to the right side and the right-hand one to the left.

Now the channels of white air become ice-blue, ready to continue their different routes, this time upwards along both sides of the sternum. Breathe the blue air out fully, to the very last: don't force it, in case the face goes blue . . . Old curtains these, will get myself some thick ones, Jude can make them himself, he's clever. Nice thick ones to muffle the street noises. Look now! Attention wandered: the desire for curtains! Okay, thick curtain cloth, I do not banish you in any way, rather take a good look at you, fluttering and waving, banal in your mundaneness, material, dust. Goodbye, goodbye . . . now where was I?

Two channels of pure white air enter the nostrils and there they go again to where no plant no ground no water no animal no person no desire no anguish no joy no emptiness no fullness no beginning, if this bloody fly. Okay, fly legs tickling my nose. Not a hope in hell of concentrating like this at the Wollondilly, far too many wild things there – in the photo outside the tent Jude looks altogether as if he's pregnant. In fact, we all took another look at that picture. Did Shane also see it? Didn't want to say anything, Jude can be so touchy. It was a picture of complete union: perfect phallus-belly. Haven't posted my letter to Pa and Ma yet. Jude just thinks I have. Why so insistent about it? What's the hurry . . . where are my thoughts wandering?

Further and further away, must bring them home, stop them from straying along the mountain road. The fly legs, then the clouds of flies at Wollondilly, then the photograph of Jude: okay, how did I get from the photo to the letter? Whatever the case, I'll sidestep you all, all you old head fillers, I'll leave you all behind. Fly off to Wollondilly where Jude is waiting for you, with an open envelope to pop you all into. Goodbye, you lot, fly far, fly well.

Pure white air in and up along the two routes and then ice-blue air, deeply and fully . . . What was Rinpoche's wisdom? The moment between breathing in and breathing out is the most precious. That moment must be held without knowing that you are holding it. During that unattended moment your mind empties. Hold it, Konstant – okay, Joseph, what? The moment of wisdom is contained in the completely emptied mind. That's right: white air in and up along the two channels, do not deny a single thought, but observe each one that enters, and let it go again. Then breathe in fully. Blue air represents the rancid smell of the anxiety I have become so attached to, the dark colour of pain that clings to me, the grey suffering of the Koori woman at the entrance to the station, the inconsolable grief in my mother's eyes, the irrational fear of my blue spots; everything, yes, everything is drawn up into the immense blueness of the two channels, like from a well, up and out! Everything out. And gone. I remain sitting broadly, shoulders strong like the ridge of a mountain, and I free up the lungs, open the chest and let them out, let them fly high, freely, and hang quietly, calmly in one place and then sink and descend to the third eye just above the brow where the blade of grass wilts, the grain of sand blows away, history fades into nothing. Empty. Fill up with emptiness, breathe in – Roxanne. Do they really have to? Police wasn't that bad. Why do people have to play the thing so loud as they pass our stoep, why ghetto-blasters were ever invented . . . Breathe in. Go! The two white routes of pure white air, and bye, bye, Roxanne, all rolled up! I roll you in a packet of chewing gum and that's that! Spit Roxie out so that she knows what's what: cheers, Rox; and, and, virginal white air enters the wide-open doors again . . . How long have I been sitting here? Surely there's a reason I didn't bump myself at Wollondilly and bleed dry? If I'm supposed to die, it would have happened there. It's a sign. You are only sick because you want to be sick: it makes no sense. Re-focus on the centre point above the eyes: no days or birthdays, no sorrow; also no joy, no wealth, no desire for it. No grave. No milk? Jude can't, Jude is able . . . want to get up tomorrow so that I can start work earlier. Roast the tempeh beforehand, then set it aside. Garlic and ginger root in sesame oil, with a touch of lemon zest. Then a small teaspoon of garam masala and one block of solidified coconut milk . . . Wonder whether my blood will congeal if by accident I bump into something that's been moved, Jude ought to know better than to be moving things around now. I'm no longer perfect enough for Jude's interiors, too fallible, too f . . . Breathe in, breathe, don't grasp the air, avoid cramped-ness, never be greedy, rather breathe more air out, all the bad energy – hate that word. Joseph, everyone trades in it: energy this, energy that, energy my arse . . . Where had I got to? The Irish say: Your arse in parsley. Stop! Get rid of all ill-placed words, all false wit-nesses, all shoddy works of the head, all vendettas, all dirty wash-ing, all ills. What did Ava-Marie want to say to me, would really like to hear . . . My back is sore now. Once more, it's a grand effort – not so, Joseph? – pure white air in, ugh-ugh.

I place my hand on my chest to calm the cough, become breath-less for a moment, then overcome it after all. There's dust here. I must vacuum tomorrow when I get back from work. Whole house needs a good vacuum. One more time: nothing, no, there's a mountain . . .

I end my day early by sorting out my drawers. I was set a good example. I set my clothes out for my first day back at work, and on a sheet of paper write down the ingredients of the soup and cas-serole for tomorrow's menu. Even phone the shop to check if there are dried chestnuts in stock. Ava-Marie answers. She's glad I'm re-turning to the land of cooking and I'm glad she is glad. She insists that I see someone she swears by. For the sake of sound health.

It's good to be working again. My colleagues greet me enthusiastically, as do the magpies on the roof opposite. Everyone is so eager to break out and go their own way that I'm amazed the kitchen manages to contain its cooks within confines as fragile as an eggshell. Liz soon announces that she has to finish earlier to saddle up a new horse. Joseph's hands are seriously rolling rice balls, but his eyes are vacant, and he is only shocked into wakefulness when a chopping knife accidentally clatters onto the terracotta floor. Robert can't stop going on about his new series of photos.

I almost envy their longing to be elsewhere. I see now that it implies abundant well-being. As for myself: I could not wait to be here again.

Only Robert asks about my illness, and questions the partial truth of my explanation that it was a kind of blood problem, not quite the same as haemophilia. I get the impression he expects more than this from me.

I take my time with the tempeh and coconut casserole. The knife handle finds its place in my palm. My feet plant themselves squarely on the floor. The cheeks of my bum are relaxed. There is not a single reason why I shouldn't be here. Today, tomorrow, in a week's time if God wills, because I will it. So help me, my T-helper cells, be strong, be fruitful, multiply and fill my body.

The coconut I fold into my casserole adds a richness to it. I let it simmer away. Does it need a touch of sweetness? I ask Robert his opinion. Today I prefer his reptilian frenzy to Joseph's fossilised serenity or even Ava-Marie's Victorian seriousness.

You need extra sweetness, he says.

I test it again to reassure myself that I must follow Robert's and not my own judgement, then, on his recommendation I dissolve a few shavings of palm sugar into the sauce. Plump bubbles plop in slow motion between the brown tempeh pieces and emit a luxurious old-fashioned aroma.

As soon as we open the front door a wave of lunch customers rolls in. They effect hungry bellies. Those with faces greyed by office tedium seem the most credible. I always try to serve them first. The sudden pressure makes my colleagues forget their extra-mural activities. And that's the way it ought to be if we want to cheer up humanity. Various customers welcome me back when they taste the casserole, assure me they have missed my food. My actress friend, Deirdre Rosenbaum, comes inside and adds something lavish on cue.

Of all the people I know, Konstant, you are the clearest.

Clearing out, Deirdre? That's a joke. No, just joking while I still can. Please repeat what you said, even though I don't know exactly what you mean, it sounds good, a soothing lozenge.

Your eyes are always so clear, she attempts to explain, I'm convinced that your intentions are pure.

I laugh appreciatively.

If Deirdre only knew how much a successful casserole and an added compliment mean to me, especially today. I am indeed lucky.

There's something old-worldly about the compote of tongue-smacking eaters, pots blowing off aromatically and then being smothered with a lid, Sarah Vaughan turned softer then up again at the request of a soup-slurper, a Jewish auntie making sure she won't be neglected, and Liz at the till, shrieking as Robert nips her bum. I truly regret that I'll have to withdraw from the scene.

In the cramped space of the toilet – the light stays off – I cough my bowels out, anxious to be totally alone, when only a few minutes ago I was surrounded by a cordial crowd. In a corner where the wall joins the roof, a daddy-long-legs has made its nest.

I wipe my mouth, piss, and do up my pants. Notice one of Robert's cigarette butts on the floor. I'm a notch shorter on my belt now. Mustn't worry too much about it, that's not good either. It's been such a happy morning: I must make the best of each new day. Some people deteriorate rapidly.

Can't think that it's something serious, hey my daddies, a bit of phlegm this, nothing more. I won't harm you, okay. I'm the last one you need be afraid of. You're cute. Now listen, net all those bugs and gnaw the carapaces with salivating jaws. Gawkies! One would swear you were still adolescents.

Someone starts fiddling with a tin of tahini outside. It could only be Shane. She must have heard me coughing. As I leave the toilet, she looks at me questioningly and gives me a hug.

My T-cell count is becoming a bit of a thorny issue, Shane, I whisper in her ear, and loosen myself from her embrace to check whether I'm still needed behind the counter.

Everything is under control. Thingy – what's his name? – and Ava-Marie are skilled servers when they choose to be. I may as well saddle up and be off.

First the letter to my parents must be finished and posted. I can't put it off any longer; it'll be a shock to them. The request for Albert to visit is perhaps expressed too apologetically. Oh, hell, bugger it, I'm not changing it now, it must go as is. Who knows, it may help lessen the impact. Wish I didn't ever have to tell them. Dear Pa and Ma, why I have to protect you, I don't know, you yourselves affirm and believe that not a hair on your head will fall. Alas, I've waited too late, veiled myself in layers and layers of clothes for too long – the layered look, you know – and now I suddenly stand before you stark naked. Measure me: take a good look at me. Look a little like Pa's. I don't want to cover myself any longer. I can't even avoid the pain of this unexpected honesty that I always, cross-my-heart, wanted to spare you – it's staring me in the face. From now on deal with me as you wish, but for heaven's sake be merciful.

I'll cook something special for supper, fish for a change. Should I do as Ava-Marie suggests? She was so self-assured about her recommendation, so persuasive about the clairvoyance of her Gordana. Can someone who is serious about it really have a name like that? Like all true Calvinists, I'm born sceptical about such quackery. Never felt the need to look into my future. Facing each day demands enough courage as it is, why go and mess about with your future: no thanks.

However, Ava-Marie is not that easily put off: it's precisely the *past* that Gordana leads you to, and with absolute professionalism. It's like a rebirth, and you don't have to be afraid of anything, she knows when to stop, and that's important.

I don't have any need to awaken repressed memories – it will make me want to vomit. What have I repressed? Save me from pinning the blame on the hem of my mother's dress and father's trousers when my emotions run amok, that's the point I'm trying to make. Thank you, Ava-Marie, I'm putting the business card – purple, isn't it – in my wallet. You're my witness.

I lean my bike against the window of a fishmonger in our neighbourhood and check the display. Dead fish wherever you look, sunken marble eyeballs and slimy discharge around the scaly bodies. Shane has taught me that you don't touch fish like that.

I decide to cycle downtown to see what the luxury deli has in stock. I arrive utterly out of breath and have to rest on the entrance step, feel desperate, and reproach myself for peddling so far and so fast just to prove to myself that I could.

Later I feel strong enough to stand, wipe the discharge from my eyes and enter the deli through the faux marble portal. Behind the display cabinets, opulent with polished fruit and freshly imported products, meticulously trained assistants with white tops and black trousers are ready to serve.

I shudder when they touch vegetables or my hand with their see-through plastic gloves. If you approach food too clinically, you lose granny's thumb pad on the salad dressing bottle. Must write that up somewhere for the neurotics so they can use it as a mantra. Still, there's a vintage feel here of real espresso, mature brie and air-conditioned air. And sheep's milk cheese – rather expensive – makes it worth the effort. When last did we have any? It's reassuring to know that I don't have to deny myself anything. Since I've been preparing main dishes, my purse has been full. Gordana's card is in there too. Ava-Marie recommends that I attend more than one session if I find her pronouncements credible.

Arriving home, I find Shane and Jude at the kitchen table with crumbs of lemon cake on their lips. I sink down into a chair and belch out the remains of my afternoon like a garlic wind. Jude comes to massage my neck, playfully, but his sticky hands irritate me terribly. Instead of excitedly unpacking my shopping as I had planned to, of being happy about Shane's visit and grateful that I can be grey in the presence of these two without compromising them, gloom envelops me. I feel so derailed that I can't even tell them that I'm powerless to escape it. Even that would have put my inadeqaucy in perspective.

They sense my mood, and lose their earlier whimsy. I interpret their questioning looks as condescension. Shane senses this, looks down, and a hand, hesitant as a shy pet mouse, crawls across the table and rests lightly against mine.

I place such irrational demands on them. I can't reproach myself enough for doing this. Even getting up from the table is too much to ask. My fingertips feel a red glow on my face. I'm wasting blood over nothing.

I've lost every bit of control I had over my life, I scream, and rise so abruptly from the table that my knee knocks it and one of Jude's fine white cups shatters. I scream.

I'm powerless! Totally powerless! You have no fucking idea how it feels, you know nothing, I scream and cry all at once. I kick open the back door and run into the garden before coming to a dead stop. Will-less. Choking on my red-hot fury. I will never get my rage shouted out in this life, there's too much of it.

You know nothing, and you, Jude, I screech at the blackboy, now totally beside myself, *you*, *you*, but at least I don't say it.

Both Shane and Jude get up. They don't know what to do. Jude hovers, petrified, somewhere behind me.

You know me well enough, don't you, Jude, you know what I wanted to say, and you'd rather not hear it. And I, I don't want to turn into your worst nightmare, my Jude, I don't want to pay you back in kind.

I don't care, don't care about anything, I scream myself sense-less, Shane, Jude, I turn to them, it's irreversible: I am dying.

The word frightens me. I've never said it before. They've never heard it from me, maybe thought it, but waited for me to say it. It's better that it's out.

I'm better now. I'll be able to have some tea, forgive me, Jude.

It doesn't matter, Konstant, my dearest darling.

When last did he call me that? Must I drive myself to such extremes before he admits he loves me?

Thanks, Shane, just a small piece, thanks. First a glass of water, thank you both, thanks man, Shane.

Shane suggests I try alternative medicine; it might be the answer. It involves infusing pure oxygen through the total volume of blood in the body. They bleed you systematically, infuse oxygen through your blood, inject it back in. I could undergo daily treatment without even interrupting my work. The clinic is not too far from the shop. The process takes about a month, and it costs a fortune.

And the success rate, Shane, has anyone been healed yet? What about side effects? Have you ever heard of anyone dying of too much fresh blood?

She doesn't know, but would very much like to pay for it in full.

During the following peaceful weeks I stay at home at night and engross myself in familiar old cook books as well as my new ones. I first test the ingredients and then launch my new dishes at work. The result is that clients lick their plates, congratulate me, and smack their lips over surprising fusions. Shane reports a small but noticeable increase in her restaurant's turnover. I'm enjoying myself so much in the kitchen that I allow myself to be heard from again.

I'm having a run of luck here, and there's no place like home, isn't that so, Pa and Ma? And I add a few upbeat thoughts. I select a postcard with care: a kangaroo mother with joey in the pouch. In all probability a desperate attempt to lessen the shock of my previous letter. Not over my dead body will I say a word about the fact that I'm still deteriorating. This time I spell out the urgency for Albert to come over.

Jude is home virtually every night. K is overseas. It's all the same to me. Jude talks to me non-stop. I resent all he says, and remain silent. As more comes to light every night, as he pushes me further and further, I'm made to feel that I'm not in the driver's seat. In time I realise that I'll have to unload my rage somewhere. I'll never manage it on my own, and even less in the presence of Jude, who though possibly one of the objects of my rage, is not its source.

I uncover Deloris and Martie's addresses like long-lost recipes and write each a two-page letter on unbleached paper. After pondering for a long time, I decide to mention that I'm seriously sick, full of hope, well loved, and free as a bird, verily I say unto you.

Back at the shop amongst my colleagues, I discreetly put a lid on the cause of my indisposition. The old fear that I'll be rejected comes back to haunt me. I wear wider shirts and looser trousers to cover up ever-thinning limbs.

I cry bitterly one evening after my bath, not at my mirror image as such, but at my constantly wasting wrists. They're bone, after all, and bone is bone and it's a fact written in stone that bones don't thin, only in cases of osteoporosis, and I'm guaranteed against that by all my rabbit food: steamed bok-choy, choy san, cos leaf salad, sea vegetables. I really do look after myself.

I fine-comb my body every day for new lesions. I try to find my glands under my skin. If they still slip from my grip, I'm safe. It's always been a pleasure for me to take care of my hygiene, now it's an obsession.

With a touch of neurosis I squat with the soles of my shoes on the toilet seat. I refuse to stir with a teaspoon that has been lying around. Flies shit everywhere, and quickly too. Before you know it, you can be swamped by an opportunistic illness.

I look after myself as never before. I become demented the moment I see our old Greek neighbour's cat in our garden. I dart at the poor creature, manage a thwack with the broom and end up breathless in the kitchen, rubbing my contorted mouth. Then the dry sobs. The grime of futility settles over me: I must have seemed like a witch to the cat. To save his own life, he jumped the back wall to his Greek mama. I smelt my own blood, my life shortened once again. What's happening to me?

My reaction was again almost violent the other day when an insurance salesman wanted to enter the house with his shoes on. He nearly died of fright. Me too. It's a pointless waste of energy while work exhausts me enough as it is. Haven't weighed myself yet today.

Shane is working out a diet for me to match one provided by a naturopath. I'm developing a slight aversion towards such people.

The acupuncturist promised to cure me. I'd have liked to be able to look beyond his naivety, but I don't have enough faith to waste any on him.

There were times in the past when the vases stood empty in the sitting room. Now Jude doesn't skimp, they're always full of the most amazing flowers. And Shane is the bearer of good news: she never arrives without a surprise for me.

This time she reports that her friend is offering the weatherboard house in Katoomba again, and at a reasonable rental. Shane doesn't think she'll return soon – the friend thinks the sun shines out of all Europe's orifices.

After five visits to the ozone sangoma, as Jude christens him, there's a small increase in my T-helper cell count. Paul, paler than usual, as if he really does nothing besides inform patients about their steady decay, listens sceptically to my explanation of the treatment: it's a type of oxygen called O-three that is produced from molecular oxygen, released electrically to reactivate the blood, drop by drop. Almost like a tonic for your blood. I'm shocked that he could ask whether the apparatus is one hundred percent sterile. I hadn't expected his scepticism to go that far, especially as he could be viewed as an initiate – at least as far as alternative food goes.

After that, I don't consult Paul as often and I miss the calculated frankness that, strangely enough, is not practised by the ozone sangoma. I meditate, with reasonable success. I suspect I've developed my own meditation method by singing myself into a kind of trance. The sharpness, the here-and-now presence of pure meditation is of course lost this way, still, I enjoy my way so much that I allow myself to do it.

One morning I happen upon an erotic childhood experience that I want to live through so badly that I don't re-centre myself back in the meditational vacuum via Joseph's rigid technique. Later I ask his advice: What to do if, during your meditation, a thought enters that you absolutely want to remain with for a while?

Joseph, amused in a wizard-like way, says he's never heard of a meditator who is so inexperienced. He encourages me to keep following the principle of not blocking any incoming thoughts. Can't I give him an example of what it was? He asks. I hesitate; sharing this sort of intimate knowledge always brings me face to face with my old bottled-up self. I start saying something, am interrupted by a cough, and the cough refuses to dry up.

On a sunny bikers' afternoon I park in the vicinity of Gordana's shop. I balance on my bike. Passers-by with children and bags of oranges self-importantly take on the business of their lives. I don't want to reveal that I'm not afraid. One of Sydney's down-and-outs shuffles by, humming something operatic. It could be that moving Saint-Saëns aria. Must be the singer Shane is always telling me about. The one who searches out acoustic hollows in the city centre when others are sleeping, and then performs aria after aria. Here on the pavement it would be a privilege to listen to her when she really lets go. These days I go to bed so early that my chances of hearing her are minimal.

A crystal or two dangle in Gordana's window. I have nothing against them. But don't ask me to swear high or low by these glass baubles either. For the rest, the place seems respectable, painted white and light-blue. Must have been her special wisdom not to present herself in exotic colours to a bunch of Anglo-Saxons. Gordana. With a name like that you could cast spells. Well, it can't do me any harm dum dum dum . . .

. . . know about blackouts, don't panic. Don't. Suddenly pitch dark. It's so easy, things can change so quickly, they already have, often. Stand firm. It's a blackout, Konstant, nothing serious. How many blackouts have you had in your life? When you get up from a crouching position, wham! Fist right in your face. Passing over, this one. The sun is quite hot. Shouldn't go out without a hat. There it is, my bike's fallen. My hand must have shot out automatically to break the fall of my body. Survival instinct.

You 'right, mate?

Sight returns, light won't set so easily over me. Someone's stopped, stopped me. I haven't yet been outlawed to a marginal figure.

Yes, tannie, no tannie, just need a pick-me-up, nothing serious, don't worry. Tell me, do blackouts also frighten tannie like this?

Yes, I'm okay, thanks. I'm fine, had a blackout.

Had a biddovva fall there, mate, can be a bummer.

Oh, it's not a tannie, it's a sheila and her bikey, peacock feather patterns on the leather jacket, sexy bum bulging from torn jeans.

He helps me up by the arm, she picks up my bike and takes my other arm while steadying my bike until I'm able to take it from her.

Thanks, I appreciate . . . Thanks a lot, guys.

No worries, mate, look after yerself, see ya.

I'd better make a detour to Paul. What's the time now? Will start getting cooler soon. No, rather leave it: you don't want to be so puny that you run to the doctor for everything. Raised that way. Shall I make an appointment with Gordana now? Tomorrow, I'll ring tomorrow, it's less confrontational on the phone. I can always pull out then. Every day has its own cure, I have to be prepared these days, keep the candles burning.

My visit to Gordana is fixed for two days' time. In the meanwhile I keep busy: my knife sharp, my work exemplary, my words fewer. Every day is a day too soon. At the shop they notice that I'm quieter – they are missing my songs.

On a bench under a Mortan Bay fig, Jude, Shane and I enter into a kind of pact. We almost go so far as to cut our wrists and mix blood-brother blood. They *will* get me better, if it's the last thing they do.

We affirm the right to act according to our own knowledge, Jude swears.

The two are like watchmen on my walls. Who waits on them? That's what I want to know. So, together the triumvirate will heal me. Even if it costs me my life, I almost add, but bite my tongue, and rightly too, about the healing power of the cynical word. So much still to unlearn.

They are glad to hear that I've booked a session with Gordana. Jude has a report about a wonder drug made in China. Clubs and pubs are abuzz with it. He'll find out more about it.

I am punctual for my appointment with Gordana. And I've wiped away my prejudices like a clean slate. She can deal with me as she feels fit. Only the tremor of my heartbeat betrays me.

Gordana is friendly and invites me to the back of her shop where, predictably, it smells of chakra-unlocking oils. The walls have been left plain white, it almost looks like a clinic which, in the circumstances, I find reassuring. I am made to lie down on white and blue covers on a massage table.

The bedding shows no sign of human hair or skin. Ask me, I've developed an eye for this kind of thing. I would be embarrassed if someone were to see me through Gordana's Venetian blinds, embedded in a rebirthing experience. Who cares, here I am.

She makes me close my eyes and circles my body, placing crystals and other cosmic trinkets around me. A cold one is placed on my forehead and a last small stone lands on my solar plexus. Next I have to follow an extremely exhausting breathing technique and imagine myself encompassed by a golden haze. She performs all sorts of abracadabra movements over my body without touching it. Although my eyes remain shut, I register a slight breeze, see the shadow of her hands, and hear the tinkling of bracelets. I carry out additional softly spoken instructions. Breathe in fully, breathe out fully. It's very tiring. I keep going.

I arrive at a place with grass clumps and a peppercorn tree along-side a dry riverbed. A little girl sits against the tree, she has short black hair and red cheeks, and although I can't see her eyes, I know they are blue. They contrast with the starched white of her pina-fore. Next to her, there's a basket. Her hand rests on its handle. I can't tell what's in the basket, it doesn't seem important to me.

Is anyone else there? Gordana wants to know from me. Her voice forces me to continue.

I can't see anyone else, so I rest in the wild peppery shadow of the tree with the little girl. I'm not getting anywhere, the little girl means nothing to me. Until I see someone else ambling along. Over there. An old man in a going-to-town hat and a white shirt. I can tell from his high forehead and the straight line of his nose that he's a man with a sense of righteousness, sent to keep me on the right track. His decorum is awe-inspiring.

Ask him to take you down to the river and along the riverbed, Gordana says.

I hesitate.

Come on, Konstant, take yourself along, allow him to lead you. It's for your own good, Gordana encourages me. I ask the old man to take me with him. He agrees. I wish it was rather the little girl.

While I strain forwards, with my back facing the upper reaches of the river, he pulls me further upstream, faster and faster, so that I can't stop.

Mind the rocks, hell!

Backwards, back, can't stop. Convulsions through my solar plex-us, I collapse half-spastically, like a coir mattress, a tremor jerks my legs up, my chest jerks up.

You've got a blockage there, Konstant, Gordana says, nothing unusual, something like that, seems to be someone you need to meet, looks as if you don't want to.

Gordana suggests another route: Go back to the place with the grass clumps and the little girl under the tree, then look at yourself.

That I can do easily.

I rise up, high up, far above, it feels really good, the sky is so blue, the autumn sun gentle.

What do you see? she asks.

I see myself, far below, doing somersaults on the grass. It's really weird seeing myself like that. Sometimes I fall and stones hurt me. It's not sore. Nor does it matter. I'm wearing a blue sailor suit. I've got a tame rabbit, he's staying put, we're playing, but I'm careful so as not to hurt him by accident. It's pleasant, not too hot. The tree casts a deep shadow. I laugh all the time. My one shoe comes off, it's a bootie, my mother doesn't even tell me to put it back on.

Oh, is your mother there?

Yes. She's not watching me though, too busy with other things.

What's she doing?

She's busy with my father.

What are they doing?

I don't want to know, the old man is back, he's leading me away again. I don't want to go with him. I won't. I start crying and kick his leg, he won't let go of my hand. I look again, don't know how many times, my mother and father get busier and busier, smaller and smaller. Now I'm thirsty, can't come up, something is holding me. Something warm is moving upwards, inside me, my nostrils are half closed.

Gordana places the palm of her hand behind my head, raises me slightly and holds a glass of water to my mouth. I taste life in the water, I roll the wetness round in my mouth and empty the glass.

Bring me back; I want to finish, I say urgently.

There's an unbearable pain in my upper arms and shoulders, as if something is weighing me down. I realise that I have existed like this before, and that it can go on for ever, just like this, and the anxiety at the thought of continuing to exist like this forever is powerfully discomforting.

I have to get out of here, I say, I'm dying of claustrophobia; under no circumstances do I want to go with that man. I don't.

Can you go back to the little girl?

Leave it, let me go.

Gordana offers me another breathing technique. It's up to me whether I use it. I take it on. My breathing pattern changes, it becomes shallow, normal, and I open my eyes. As I come up, she offers a second glass of water.

I'd like you to go further backwards, up that river; I couldn't tell what was going on there.

Yes, I mumble, so pooped I can hardly stand.

Stamp your feet hard, up and down on the ground, like a Red Indian.

I stamp my feet. Gordana is still talking on, I don't even try to follow, couldn't care less, I just want to get out of there.

I think we should work on this once more, Konstant, there seems to be a lot you still need to face.

Yes, yes, and I walk ahead of her out of the shop. The afternoon smells pleasantly of exhaust fumes and bread. There must be a bakery nearby. It's a relief to be outside; even the sparrows in the acacias sound angelic. I unlock my bike, hop on and say goodbye to her abruptly.

Sorry mate, I don't know if I want to go to her again.

Gordana could tell I felt awful, still, she insisted that I go to that old man with the white shirt. A grumpy, overly-courteous old fuddy-duddy, I've seen through him. Why couldn't that little girl have led me? She's also a guide, who was she, in any case? Hestertjie?

Before turning left to our house, I look back, still riding, an unusually risky action for someone who's compromised like me. There's that Koori woman at the entrance to the station. It's as if she's keeping her eye on me, I owe her nothing.

Constipated days follow, when my body is forced into cramped spaces, then is unexpectedly driven out with the crack of a whip. Whether I sit or stand, I feel uncomfortable. I can't find an equilibrium. Something is lacking in my dishes, my soup smells cabbagey, the sauces of my casseroles are too thin or too thick, and when I have to serve upstart Robert during our lunch break, he makes a fuss before taking his bowl of soup. He tries my patience, and when I lose it, he mocks me for being arrogant. Just to trivialise the whole thing. And I have lost my appetite, that worries me more than anything else.

At night the faces from Gordana are not repeated. It was far too conscious an experience to be repeated in my dreams. I'm trying to put off what can't be delayed any longer. I'm destined to walk up the river with the old man in the white shirt. I phone her from the shop and make a second appointment. My sweat smells like Joseph's rice ball mixture.

I also have my last session of the ozone treatment. Paul draws a blood sample and I pray for an improvement.

Gordana waits at her door. What kind of person is she to make gains from the woes of others? Nevertheless.

She leads me to her massage table. This time I have to battle through the breathing technique before I reach the place. I don't see the little girl.

Is the old man there?

He is, he's beckoning me. He's already rock-steady a little way up the riverbed.

Go to him.

I don't want to.

Her hand flutters above my forehead.

I'm afraid I'll go spastic again. The riverbed is rough in places.

Go, I hear her, go to him.

Old man with the white shirt, here I come. Respectable old bugger, you can't teach me a thing. And remember, I can't afford to stumble.

If I'm able to walk here, then so can you, you're still young. There's someone waiting for you on the bank under that thorn tree.

It's only Jude. It's you, Jude, only you would brave nature in your wide Indonesian dress. I'm so glad to see you here. Only you, Jude, you of all people. I'd never have expected it.

Konstant, I'm here to escort you.

Jude, you're speaking the same language as the old man. And why are you so festively dressed in that bridal gown of yours? It's only for special occasions: look at you, all dolled up. Why do you look at me like that, Jude? I know you by now. You can't hide anything from me. Such a strange look you have. Almost as if you've come to celebrate our parting, why do I smell a rat? Talk me out of it, Jude. Don't let me believe it: only once your pixie has gone to la-la land will you be truly free, not so Jude? Is that why you're all dressed up? You and K together forever without care or complaint or Konstant in your lives: that's why you're dressed up, isn't it Jude? You hesitate to entertain yourself with such thoughts; you'd rather leave me to spell it out it for you.

Konstant, you're being silly, let's get to the point, honey, I have bound you to myself with ties that cannot be broken. This is how it works, or must I explain it all to you again: I gave you a present, man, a cell wrapped up in a fatty layer of protein. You were free to do with it what you wanted. As you know, you wanted it so badly that you tied it to your own T-cell. Do you understand now that I'm inseparable from you?

We must press on, young man, the old man's harsh voice eggs me on, you can't tarry here.

I want to stay here, old man, here with Jude.

Look here, young man, it fills me with distaste to say this, but you ought to realise by now that blood bonds have been forged between the two of you, nothing can separate you any more, what the devil more do you want?

Go, Konstant, go! What he says is true.

Jude, why don't you take me away from here? You've got a leasehold on all wisdom, we can easily get out.

Konstant, I am with you, always, know it once and for all. First you have to go, you must, Konstant, listen to me: you must.

This once and never again. Come, old man, not too fast, ho if I say ha.

Joker, you'll be making jokes right down to your last gasp.

And what's wrong with that? A joyful spirit is housed in a healthy body.

We'll have to see about that. There's someone, can you see him? He's waiting for you on a canvas chair.

It's my father! I recognise him from here. Wait, let me go to him myself. It looks as if he hasn't seen me yet. Let go now, old man, I don't need you, don't touch me any more. I'll go to him by myself, I'd like to greet him first.

Hello, Pa.

Dammit Konstant, what a fright you gave me. Welcome, man. Mastig, I'm glad to see you've made it, my son. We've been looking forward to your arrival very much, you know.

Yes, Pa, but let's not beat about the bush, lets call a spade a spade, I don't have much time left.

What are you talking about, my son? Where to now?

Back, Pa, come, let's walk a little further upstream.

Careful now, Konstant, this is a river without end.

That's not true, Pa. Come, Pa will see.

What do you see there, my son?

I see the two of us together, I see my chubby baby legs, does Pa recognise us?

It's a strange sight.

The two of us are in the dining room, me in my nappy, Ma is busy, I can't see her. Doesn't matter, I'm with Pa, aren't I, and it's very good that Pa has to look after me for a while. We walk round and round the table, just the two of us, and it's very good, I'm a little plover in Pa's arms, in the nest of Pa's arms nothing can get to me. Little dribbling mouth and pricked ears.

Pa's big boy, Pa's little man, Pa's bull. Look at him, whose little bull is this? Tell Pa, who does this little bull belong to?

Pa is very, very happy; Pa's joy is great.

You were my first-born. You came to be baptised in the name of my great grandfather.

Yes, but that's not the whole story, Pa. We must go further and have a look at what happened that Sunday at the hot springs, the day we had the picnic. Pa and Ma were braaiing and drinking beer with the other grown-ups under the bluegums. I come running sopping wet, and who picks me up? Don't have to think twice, Pa swoops me up and throws me high in the air:

Pa's little man.

I feel Pa's hand, rough from all the farm work, against my bottom where my bathing trunks pull up at the back.

I loved you very much, my son.

Yes, but that's not all, Pa, we must go further. I'd had enough of swimming pool water, but of Pa, as I got older and bigger, of Pa I never got enough. Pa keeps busy, never stops working, Pa slaves away for all of us. No more time for games, Pa put me down that day and never picked me up again. From then on there was only time for a stiff handshake.

Hell, Konstant, you're getting too serious now. I'll break my back for you.

Look how grey Pa's hand is turning, everything going grey, we're becoming loyal citizens of the state. I obey everything, and obediently I'll nurture my branch of our family tree. Then I grew away, Pa. The day came when I couldn't look Pa in the eyes, right until today, never in the eyes again.

You've lost so much weight, my son. No more than a reed. Aren't they feeding you where you come from?

Pa, the time for this drivel is over: I want to know why the day came when I wasn't good enough any more. Why did you abandon me when I started taking myself in hand, when you noticed that I dreamed of going the other way, from that day on . . .

Look here, Konstant, you're completely rubbing me up the wrong way. Understand me very well: I did my best for you. Remember, we were very, poor and look where we've got to now. You got everything your heart desired. I bought you nice warm slippers.

Slippers! I could keep warm without them. Instead, I became colder, more distant; words escaped me when I was alone in your presence. What has become of Pa? That's what I'd like to know.

Damn it all, Konstant, you know I've always loved you.

You felt I didn't do well enough at school. Oh, I knew it from a word here, a sentence there. Ma let it drop on the odd occasion. The one time I was awarded a trophy, you and Ma disappeared.

After school, my hair was too long and my trouser legs too narrow. When you got to see me in Johannesburg my hair was too short and my attitude too precocious. I used up your money at university only to dump my degree in the water and drift further away with my friends, beyond redemption, as they always were to you. No, wait, give me a chance, let me finish, this time I'm the one doing the talking, this time you'll see your child and you'll hear him. Aren't you the one who believes that you talk it out with your neighbour before you bring your evening sacrifice? Do you still remember Deloris? She also wasn't good enough, despite the fact that she came from a respected family. No, in her case her bum was too big. I don't even want to talk about Jude. He's scum, in your eyes. I must mention one other incident, the wounds are raw, still fresh. Pa, you remember how you beat me when Albert went and ratted about some small change that I didn't fully return? I wasn't angry with him; he's not the one who betrayed me. He was too scared of your commandments, which made him tremble. He couldn't do otherwise: he had to spill the beans. And me? I bought a handful of toffees with the money. And then the day I went out to shoot my own buck for the pot, as to be expected, I didn't get any recognition for it. All that I've achieved in this short space of time, all on my own – hell, I've become head chef in a respectable place and earn a tidy sum of money – but never, not once was there a single word of encouragement. And now, I'm too thin again.

You've got us onto the wrong track, Konstant. I can see it now. You want to drag us into perdition. Your mother and I have seen it coming for a long time – but to have to go hobbling through the driftwood now . . .

Wrong track and Ma's whatever. Yes, my tongue has become harsh. The branch of the family tree breaks off with me. Nonetheless, I don't believe I owe anyone a single cent, nothing, except that

I want to put my fist right in your face. Ha, do you see me? Do you recognise yourself in me? Do you know where my rage comes from? My rage is like that of Raster Wasserman. I've already asked myself whether an emotion like that, a disposition, can be passed on in the genes from father to son. If not, I don't know where I get it. It's an awful fire, a propelling wave of flame. I've seen it with you already, man, how first your forehead, then your ears begin to glow, how your beard stubble stands upright, like prickly pear thorns, how your hands and fingers swell up. Do you have any idea how terrified your whole family was of you when you got like that? Your jaws locked, your breath came out in gasps, you couldn't speak any more – all you could do was to stutter. Do you know how I and Albert, Hester, Mirjampie, Ma, all off us backed off, away, out, then? Did you never see it, Pa, were you that blind?

No man, you've gone mad down under. You're taking things too far, I see that only too clearly now.

That's it, Pa, that's it, let's stumble along together this once: when we look up again we'll come face to face with ourselves. Do you know what? All I want from you is for you to see me as you see yourself, and that we love one another as we love ourselves, that's not asking for much.

I have always loved you, Konstant, unfortunately my love was locked up in my arms that had to carry us all, that's the only way I can express myself.

I understand you now for the first time, I see you for what you are. That's all, Pa, that's all. You and I will have to accept me as I am, Pa. It's no longer possible to deny that I am turning into a skeleton.

Are you sick, then, my child?

Unto death, Pa, and it forces both of us to see me as I am. I'm still fighting, Pa, I haven't given up yet, we Wassermans are fighters to the bitter end. Alas, I don't know anyone who's survived. Does Pa know how difficult, how incredibly difficult it is for me to say that I'm the only one I know who got the hell out of our country to go into the unknown to prepare for death? I'm not shying away from anything, such cowardly emotions I can't afford, I stand naked before you, now I am what I am.

Konstant, you may start getting ready now. Gordana's voice. Breathe in, gently, and then completely out. Gently in again, more fully out, press everything that's still in there out. Like that. Yes, that's good. Yes, gently now, out long, and gently empty first the left, then the right lung. Then your air passage, empty it as well. Excellent! Once more, in gently and out, long and gentle. You can open your eyes slowly. I'm just putting this light cover over you, here's a glass of water, right at your head. That's right, yes, you've done well, your time is over. I'll leave you alone for a while.

Dripping wet with sweat. My legs are lame after walking the long distance, out of breath over stones and driftwood. What was it then? And what was Jude doing there? At least I've done what I had to.

And now it's up and down, up and down like a Redskin reel, it gets the blood circulating and my legs ready for the walk back home. It's dark outside. Up and down all around Gordana's table, lame shoulders, sore shoulders, sour belly. Pummelled two cushions to smithereens. Can't believe it, honestly, two! Hold them up, Gordana, so I can see properly. White and pink and yellow sponge balls wherever you look. A little white one between my collar and neck as proof of my good work. What's done is done.

This time Gordana is silent, except to encourage me to stomp up and down fast. Everything has been said.

Thank you, Pa. It's done now, Pa doesn't have to look after me any more. From now on I'll celebrate my birthdays one after the other, and one of these day's I'll be old man enough myself to look after Pa.

White kapok falls: your
son becomes your father who
holds vigil and waits.

FOR A TIME THE cough becomes quieter. Even at night, when its hoarseness worries me most, I rarely use the spittoon Jude has put on a flat piece of driftwood next to my bed. What's more, I get the feeling that my blood, spurred on by the oxygen infusion, is flowing at an even pulse. Regular though never chronically essential blood transfusions also stabilise my blood platelet count.

So I make an appointment with a second naturopath. I want to test whether she is a woman of her word and I reveal nothing about my condition. She inspects my emaciated body with powerful hands, then examines my eyes, using iridology to diagnose me as splenetic.

It's a lovely day. She suggests we sit under the branches of her tree which is full of joyful birds. She steers my brittle body down the steps. Her sensitive gesture nurtures trust. We sit on a narrow wooden bench.

This time, I want to talk. So many alien things have recently taken possession of me I have been forced to learn about them from the latest medical bulletins and journals. Only now I'm able to describe my condition in words and phrases I have made my own. She listens attentively; I speak coherently. We conclude that it was an a posteriori matter, and that's how it should be approached: the cause of the blue spots must be traced back to blood platelet deficiency to haemopoesis to immune deficiency to a cooled-down spleen. Dead simple.

The naturopath speaks with compassion. The tree above reflects in her green eyes. She talks about a cold spleen being mirrored by a heavy spirit. The antidote to this condition is enthusiasm. I could generate it in my own kitchen. Braising calf liver with red adzuki beans and black sesame seeds will give off glorious warm aromas. Also, I could place my pressure cooker on an eager flame to stew root vegetables with wholesome bitter dandelion, chicory leaves, crisp endive, bitter melon, fresh radicchio ears, and also the tender tufts of white daikon, and young turnip.

Now, Konstant, listen carefully. After you have closed the kitchen doors and windows, lift the lids off your steaming pots and dish yourself generous portions. Chew well and eat slowly and don't let your thoughts wander, and so your body will become a receptacle for the powerful effects of these foods. When all is done, stand upright, your feet anchored to the floor. Remain attentive and visualise rising steam. Repeat the regime once a week, and you will achieve a warm spleen.

She accompanies me to the street and hugs me. I blink, become aware of a short, sharp pain above my increasingly dull-sighted left eye, recover, and catch the train home.

The eye starts bothering me even more, so I have to admit that the cytomegalo virus did not appear entirely out of the blue.

Still, it's a shock, Paul, I say, utterly devastated when he explains the diagnosis to me in his consulting room.

In a healthy body, the cytomegalo virus would not easily get a grip, but as your immune system is compromised, the door is wide open. Cyto is an opportunist.

It's what I feared most.

As before, I rely on immediate, honest information from Paul. And he in turn informs me about the indiscriminate destructiveness of the cytomegalo virus: in your case, it is unfortunately quite advanced – and the retina is coming loose from the chorion. The virus then also sends bacteria to attack the precious coli in the intestines, which causes chronic diarrhoea. In the worst-case scenario, it also affects the brain.

I don't want to hear any of this: God, don't let me go mad. At least allow me the chance to verbalise my body's decay to the very end. Not mad, please, don't let my brain ignite and my tongue spew forth the ash of demented words. Merciful God, don't allow my tongue's deft words to slip away.

Paul, I'm listening.

But show me some mercy, Paul - why do you seem so pale today?

There's a drug called azidothymadine that extends the life of infected people. However it can't be administered in conjunction with DHPG, the only drug to effectively counter the cytomegalo virus.

I immediately grasp what's being said here: it's a case of azidothymadine for my life, or DHPG for my eyes.

Paul continues: If you choose DHPG, you'll need a daily dose. I recommend you have a valve implanted under you skin. It's a minor procedure with only one risk: infection. Most cases I know of have been successful. A chest valve like this has two advantages: you don't have to find a new vein to be injected every day, which in your case is becoming increasingly difficult; secondly, it gives the DHPG direct access to the heart.

What are you saying, Paul, you're talking as if I've already made up my mind. Paul, don't you understand? This means that the combination of living and seeing is no longer granted me. Do you appreciate what that implies for me, Paul? Obviously you do, Paul. But you're not allowed to cry over dissipated lives and jaded eyes. Leave the pain to me. I know you know that I've expected absolute honesty from our first meeting. I never knew, could never have known, that so much would be expected of me. Cytomegalo,

I did not anticipate your arrival, you demand too much of me. My reserves are nearly depleted. You've overwhelmed me. You started gnawing at my right eye even before I could make my choice. Now I must choose. Now. Can't! Can't choose between lengthening my life and blindness, or a shorter life and the grace of sight. Also can't imagine where I picked it up. Looked after myself so carefully.

Let me articulate what I'm hardly able to say: I must choose between lifespan and clarity of vision. If I choose a longer life, I'll thrive, but go blind. If, on the other hand, I choose to see, I cast away my one and only life.

Before you go, Konstant, I'd like to suggest that you give urgent attention to your left eye. I can arrange a consultation for you at the eye clinic at Prince Alfred Hospital right away. To preserve the sight in your right eye I recommend that you receive DHPG immediately. The injection is done into the eye, and the course must be completed if you want to preserve your sight. Shall I phone Jude to fetch you; how did you get here? Unexpectedly demonstrative, he sits next to me, and comforts me with his arm around my shoulders.

Leave Jude out of it. Taxi, please, if I take the train, I'll go mad. Mustn't use that word so lightly any more. I hope and believe I won't lose my mind. Keep faith!

Take me straight to Shane. Hope this taxi driver doesn't want to make small talk. Don't have the strength. Shane or Jude may have advice for me, and they'll certainly give it. The final decision is mine. I've already decided. It's a terror of a pain: I didn't ask for it, did not ask to have to make such a choice. I looked after the temple of my soul so meticulously. How did the cytomegalo slip in? How? No one ever warned me. If only I had known, I could have prepared myself for it. Like hell.

Of course, Shane's not at home now, she said something about . . .

The taxi driver must turn around. *He's* still able to. Must take me home. I'll decide all on my lonesome ownsome. Haven't I decided already? What will Jude say? What more can he do to help me? My disease will finish him off too.

After the dinner of sweet potatoes, steamed butterfish and soft-boiled millet, I stay up with Jude and Shane. I sit on our only recliner without making any moves to go to bed, as if I don't want to let the last tasselled tail of my day slip out of my clenched hand.

Shane gets up after a while. Distraught by my news, and tired out by her day's work, she eventually has to leave. Jude, surprised that I am up so long – I'm usually an early country bumpkin of a sleeper, and here I'm all wide-eyed, life and soul of the party, despite my overburdened spirit – invites me to crawl into the double bed. I appreciate the gesture, though the practicalities of my bony body make sleeping together uncomfortable.

There is some good news, and a brave smile appears around my mouth: next week I move to the weatherboard house in Katoomba, and Albert is coming one of these days, not so, Jude?

Jude says something about Albert's arrival at the airport and I want to know exactly what he means, but I'm very tired.

Eventually I do get up. My teeth have been flossed and brushed. The music is turned down; I walk to my room and shut the door behind me. I undress slowly, put on my flannel pyjamas, crawl into bed, suspect that sleep will not come easily, and read – which, with my weakening eyes, I'm not really able to do.

Night can become a restless thing – that I know only too well. If I could, I'd get up now, take a taxi, and pop in at the sauna. All that liberating discharging in the steam makes you faint with tiredness. I missed many opportunities there.

What wispy feathers are these floating through my head? It's good the way it is. I'm glad I've got to this point the way I have and not by some other route. I'll leave the light on for a while, maybe open the window a little to hear the first train of the day. The carpet is nice and coarse under my feet. I'll lie on my bed like this, throw the eiderdown off, and keep the light woollen blanket on. The reading lamp attracts mosquitoes. Maybe sleep will come. What does it matter if I can't sleep tonight?

I've made my decision: it will be DHPG. I want to see until I die, I don't want to lose sight of the blue sky, or the red-winged rosellas in the Blue Mountains. I'll show Albert flocks of them in that garden. I'll see him again; I'll surely not deteriorate that quickly. DHPG keeps cyto in check. Tomorrow the valve must be implanted under my skin for a daily injection. And one in my eye too.

It's good to know that I'm able to face the night peacefully. After all, I'm well aware of the many traps that have ensnared me before: the sheets twisting tighter and tighter into a claustrophobic cocoon that eventually mummifies my head. If both the blinds and the curtains are closed, I smother inside the dark casing of the walls, with nothing but the cold chair and my silent clothes as witness, my pants with their empty legs and my sad shirtsleeves.

Everything must wait until tomorrow, and until then my room too will remain blind to my fate. I'm not afraid for what lies ahead. I could of course switch my reading lamp on. That's certainly a solution. I never do it – that's running away from what I know only too well by now.

The pressure to sleep weighs heavily. A good night's rest brings a healthy day's zest. All for the sake of the T-cells. How many in my body tonight? You were too weak, too few to keep the cytomegalo virus at bay. He slinks in, jumps up and kneels between my legs. Where are you now, my T-cells? You're blue with shock. He's here: come and get him! He arrives on a dark and moonless night: that's the megaloshe.

Don't you recognise him, my pale friends, my little blood-thirsties? You should be able to kick him off. Kick the megaloshe off – he wants to smother me: he pulls the blanket over my eyes. It's the old incubus. He wants to grab me. Can't understand why you don't see him for what he is. I recognise him immediately. He doesn't frighten me any more. Ironic, isn't it? My night fear becomes something of the past just when you have thinned out, my pathetic little cells. You forgot your own attack command! You should have shoved him off, my T-cell helpers. You should have given him the fist before he began advancing higher and higher to execute his megalomaniac plans. He wants to sit right on top of my head: he wants to destroy my last bit of sight. To incubate my eyeballs. And then what is there to be hatched? Rotten, blind old eggs. My T-cells: you could have helped me. After all, I did give you oxygen; I did eat calf liver to give you strength. How did you turn into such wimps?

Night is too far gone for you to be wrestling like this, Konstant. Herd them all together now, those weak cells. Down to the last one, or, rather, what is left of them. Herd each and every one into the kraal. May as well bring cyto closer too. Let incubus squat on the kraal wall. Observe the whole lot; count each one of the cells carefully, it's still possible. Cover cyto with a tarpaulin, and laugh at the stiff mannikin on the kraal wall. That's it, yes, have you had a good look at them all? Let them go now; open the gate so that the whole brood can scoot. Away with them, the bastards. And do you know? They accept the invitation. Just look! They're only too happy to piss off. All gone.

Empty, sweep out, scrape clean, clean up: now breathe in deeply, breath-of-life in through the nostrils and up through the head; in deeply, hold it there: clean up completely before you breathe out. Now blow it all out, all those musty things in the crop, all that blue-in-the-face smothering anxiety, breathe all the old blue air out, all out, and . . . hold it just there before you breathe in again. Hold it: clean up, clean up completely. And let pure white air in.

The days become shorter. Here in the Blue Mountains I go to sleep long before the first hen dozes off, scratching and scrubbing, in the neighbour's coop. Nothing more than a car wreck closed up with diamond-mesh fencing. Makes me think of Oupa Konstant who could never pass the crocky old cars of our town's teachers without: Heavens, what a chicken coop, that! I try to translate it for Shane when she drives the two and a half hours out from Sydney to Katoomba as usual for a weekend visit. She's learning to appreciate the tone of some expressions.

I'm deteriorating rapidly, become tired sooner, and sleepy sooner. Even when I listen to my favourite mediaeval plainsong, my head droops in the easy chair in the kitchen. It's chillier here in the Blue Mountains, and by dusk I make sure that the curtains Jude made are already drawn. Thick velvet with solid denim linings and a melancholic drag across the wooden floor to keep out the damp that seeps from the bush at night.

At night I sit before the fire with Jude, or Shane and Jude, or my neighbour, or often cosily alone without ever missing television. Old one-eye tires far too quickly for that. No, I much prefer the warmth of the bluegum flame. Although I do have to protect my eyes from the hearth, which I manage easily enough with the stiff front page of some or other magazine that I hide down the side of the easy chair at bedtime, ready to take out again tomorrow.

The diminishing circle of my life is filled, meaningfully, with such trivia. I now have to know where what is stored and where which piece of furniture is placed. Nothing may ever be moved after it has found its place. That implies a new turn in interior decorating for Jude, this time he appears to accept it.

For my sake, Jude spends a week setting up the house: tatami mats in my bedroom so I can step out of bed onto their straw cheeks; cushions that are stuffed into richly textured covers, I come upon them wherever my hand or buttocks wander. The music system is moved up from the city and positioned within my reach. I only use it occasionally. I prefer to listen to the humming of the wooden walls, the scarcely audible hymn that the old weatherboard lets fall on the well-worn carpets, the drapes of the curtains, the rich fabrics of the cushions and the extravagant throws on the chairs.

A load of wood is ordered, wheelbarrowed into the cellar and piled up to make an absorbent eucalyptus bed for the sounds of the house: the oiled creak of the floorboards, the toilet bowl that is flushed so often, the sudden yelps of pain when I bump into something despite Jude's cushion buffers. Jude has worked hard here so that I am able to live well one last time – and die well too.

Sometimes I feel sorry for him. I demand so much compassion. My body, becoming more vulnerable, consumes virtually his whole life. Which is why I'm glad when he returns from the city with hashish in the folds of his neck, or the yeast of my beloved cloudy beer on his breath.

I understand why I was forced to abstain from Jude sexually: it was to prepare me for this. Sometimes I recall the sensual pleasure of my erotic journeys, but I can just as easily pack those evocative postcards away, forget them, and say with conviction that I don't miss the over-ripe taste of Jude's sex. I have made peace with that. Don't even know when last I pleasured myself. These days my tongue tastes of pentamidine to remind me that I have already begun making my preparations. And I delight in the rowdy announcements the birds in the bush make about it.

Somewhere outside this house and this garden around the house, which has become the boundary of my life, a currawong or a puffed-up kookaburra continues to live exuberantly. If I'm lucky I am witness to the noble flight of a threesome of gang-gang cockatoos, with red-crested tiaras simmering like coal. High in the aromatic air above the eucalyptus crown they entertain me with their joyous flight. And before it gets too dark for me to see properly, the royal blue and rum-red rosellas visit our garden for a mixed snack of cracked mealies, oats and sunflower seeds. Specially put out for them in Jude's cleverly designed decoy bowl, an old wok on a thick stump. On the sharp promenade of the lip of the wok the parrots move foot by foot, round and round, whilst raucously cracking shells, grinding and spitting – then suddenly lift their varnished beaks to greet me, as an afterthought, where I'm standing motionless on the veranda. I clap my hands and they squawk back at me and fly up in an ostentatious blaze of colour to disappear in the bush that belongs to them.

Having arrived here in this bush, I can teach Pa how to grow old! And once more I want to confess that I am content. Sometimes I feel as if I could burst out in song. My happiness is like the kernel of a marble: rub it till it shines and soon its eye blinks, quite excitedly too. Sometimes, though, it can also become so pitiably dull if you mess with it in the dust.

The injection straight into my one last living eye is still my greatest agony. Long afterwards, after the anaesthetic drops have worn off and my eye is able to see again, it retains some of the dull pain. And sometimes in the middle of the night on the toilet, as life literally pours from me, I don't even hanker for a last bit of spit and polish. If Jude is sleeping over, he often comes to comfort me then. The swish of the toilet wakens light sleepers. He's up in no time and sits a while on the bed with me, ample Donegal tweed wrapped around his shoulders.

To me you are becoming more beautiful by the day, and more pure, every day we grow closer, Jude says softly.

Vulnerable in the belly of the night, and exhausted by the purging, I hold onto Jude's words, and become quiet under his fingers trailing through my thinning hair. I've always been such easy prey for the evils of the night, and allow myself to nurse old suspicions. Why is Jude so self-satisfied when such things are said?

The following morning, when the birds shake the cold from their feathers outside my east-facing window, I'm ashamed that I don't acknowledge Jude's effort. Caring for me has wrinkled his neck.

And I am not yet fully immune to sweaty wanderings through the many labyrinths of the night. Last night, or the night before, or the night before that, when I came back from the toilet, having shat myself cold, I lay half awake, obsessing about where I'd caught the cytomegalo virus.

There was the route of the infected saliva – or the many slipways of the blood transfusions. I wanted to investigate them all. For some or other reason that makes no sense any more, I wanted to get to the source of the opportunistic virus. Had it been bequeathed to me in someone's saliva? Highly unlikely. Beside Jude, no one kisses me open-mouthed any more. Or did I catch it during transfusions: at the ozone sangoma, or at the Prince Henry Hospital where I received blood to boost my platelet count?

Since cyto nabbed me, I've been surviving on the prescribed daily dose of DHPG. But the DHPG route is a toxic one. After a period of DHPG therapy they had to lower my dosage because of toxicity which created the danger that I might become haematopoeitic which meant that my blood platelets were diminishing which in turn meant that I would have to have another blood transfusion and thus run the risk of being re-infected with cyto and so I arrived back at DHPG which once again increased toxicity which led back to neutropenia which meant that I had become white blood-cell deficient which demanded a transfusion yet again.

All these routes become utterly inescapable during the night. I simply cannot understand it. I also fail to understand why I have to pass through this labyrinth of suffering. No one ever warned me, even the streets attack me.

Of course, I don't ever go to the city any more, except for my fortnightly eye injections. And the last time I returned from hospital alone with my all-seeing white walking stick, I took the familiar path from the station to Jude's house. I know it like the lines on my palm: the greengrocer on the corner where I never wanted to buy limp carrots, the fence that prevents toddlers from rolling onto the railway line. It's a path I'm able to follow blindly. On that particular day, in bright sunlight and supposedly safe, a thug nearly knocked me over: Your money or your life.

My life, of course, I mean my money, I blurted out.

You scumbag, can't you see I've made my choice? It's such a lovely day, go play somewhere else. You must be insane to want to rob me on my own turf. Besides, I don't have much left over.

His lizard eyes watch my every move and also for any possible sign of life around us or behind us. The next train could stop at any minute and spill a gaggle of commuters, someone could rush to my assistance any moment. A student could come walking along from university. At other times they irritated me, but on that day I called out for a Samaritan. How was it possible that there was nobody around? I was only four, five steps away from the front door. I must have appeared vulnerable: my calculated steps, veering to the right as my left eye is kaput, my shirt like a sack on my body. A year ago I'd have knocked the street-pirate out cold.

I just let everything pop out of my wallet. He fished my watch from my pocket where I carried it because of my emaciated wrists. That was enough for him. I escaped with my life, shakily opened our front door, and shakily I bolted it. After that narrow escape the cool dusky passage, the serenity of the minimal interior, refreshed me just like long ago. And I kowtowed to the good sense of Jude's decor, brewed rooibos tea with soya – like mother's milk – and phoned no one. I sat there with my hands full of tears and a warm jersey to quiet my shivers.

I hold myself tight. There's nothing like a night-time expedition to freeze me. Why this terrifying fear if I'm going to die, like all the living? No one ever warned me. What have I done to have to brave the thorny way barefooted? Could saliva from the mugger's membrane have got into my mouth? It was after I had begun the DHPG, wasn't it? Can you be re-infected? Was there perhaps a stray cyto in the ozone sangoma's sterile needle? What's the point of it all?

I eventually quieten down by breathing in deeply and taking another good look at myself, and become still calmer between the cosy flannel sheets as I breathe everything out, breathe every last thing out.

And so I start making peace with myself. In fact, I make peace with myself every day. Even the arrogance that once gave rise to dull looks, especially in the shop, I have transformed into humble expressions of self-validation. I very much want to be in control of my life to the end.

When the Mother Theresas of the Blue Mountains, the day nurses for home patients, visit me, I keep an eye on them. Sometimes they turn the tap of the DHPG serum too full. They enjoy my sense of accuracy, respect my survival instinct. They've also learnt that my boiled egg must be runny. Hardboiled flops are left abandoned on the kitchen table. Later, when they leave by the front door with a gush of assurances, I pick the egg up, and peel it bit by bit. It becomes an offering for the birds outside. I walk through the entrance hall - alert to the stairwell that leads to the cellar - and out again by the back door into the basking sun on the veranda. The sturdy balustrade comes in useful as I climb down and crumble the lukewarm egg for my mates who, beady-eyed, already know what's what.

I let my mother know to send a knee cushion with Albert. I need it at night. Joseph has been to visit, and on his recommendation I sleep mostly in the sleeping lion position. On my right side, right hand under the temple. Left hand on my left hip. That's when I need a wedge between my knees. Poor things, they've thinned down to bone on bone.

Can't wait for Albert to arrive, Albert with the little cushion under his arms and "Cook and Enjoy" as well, a special request. Ma's assured me over the phone that she's trained him in the kitchen to whip up all her old favourites. Long-distance calls suit me well. After the voice of the caller has died away, seconds elapse before you can reply. I use this lapse to breathe out. At the sound of Pa's voice I hold my breath, until it has said what it had to, and only then draw in fresh air. Not too long, now, my parents assure me, and they'll be coming as planned. They're waiting for the rain. The signs are promising. Tickets have already been booked.

My life is different now, Albert, a child's hand could enfold it. As you know, old men are children twice. Looking so forward to all the news from home. What do they say there, what do they hold back in letters and on the phone? What do they tell the townsfolk? The pestilential terror has thinned our son's face so that even the hand of a child can fit around it. The horror of his knees, fleshless bones that hurt if he lies down without a baby cushion between them. How could they know about stuff I even keep from the staff at the shop? Do they understand anything of what I'm going through? How could they? I've made peace with them: I don't spar with Pa in my dreams any more. There is still so much that I wanted to do, Albert, so much.

Shane brings news that Ava-Marie wants to visit, and Liz too, and Robert really wants to come and say hi, Deirdre Rosenbaum asks what's going on. There are many people, Shane reminds me, who can – and will – remain my friends unconditionally.

Don't let them come yet, I say to her, I need a bit more time.

There's a cricket plague in the city. The storeroom is crawling. Feelers peep out everywhere. Shane even found one in the miso barrel. When the shop opens for lunch they chirp from every corner. Some fundis say a flood's on the way. I hear what Shane is saying. But it doesn't touch me any more. No comment on this kind of news seems necessary to me any more.

Here's a snippet that *does* still touch me: there's an ointment for healing the terminally ill that is mixed in the Near East by an antique medicine man. Jude is first to hear about it, then Shane and me. In the corridors of the Prince Henry Hospital, hope in its healing power is expressed with healthy reservations. And even more indisputable strands are conveyed by word of mouth at the shop. One day on the beach, as I sit in the shade with a light blanket, a bather comes to me to bear witness to the miraculous results that have been obtained with the ointment on the West Coast of America.

I lend my ears to it, and why not? The way things are, I stand to lose nothing, only my life. My hope neither slumbers nor sleeps, ready to be resurrected. I light up. What's easier than raking up new hope – single-handedly, and anointed with a mysterious ointment? Deciding for or against is the most obvious choice I've ever had to make. For, of course, for-for-for, the crickets shrill in unison. They're a welcome sign to me. And the humble *for* word is embraced with such enthusiasm that even my lips close on its *f* at bedtime.

With his inclination towards organisation, Jude tracks down the supplier of the ointment via contacts of contacts at pub and club, and the same day an order is faxed to America. Shane, Jude and I don't hesitate to pay the full price for it. The three of us believe implicitly that our knowledge of the ointment, no matter how sparse, is adequate to the situation. I have the fullest right to test it out. And I will not tell doctor Paul about it, either. Trying out the ointment is ultimately my decision, and I do not want to allow his scepticism to spoil my hope.

The ointment soon arrives with prescription and all. It has a name printed on its container, which is: Cancell. When I unscrew the lid – a witches' brew of coal ash, dog piss and monkey liver – we all titter, the three of us gathered around the pot. Abruptly we stop. The spell of its foolishness has been cast. Silently, we all doubt the wisdom of allowing me to use something we know so precious little about.

My sound mind warns that I cannot invest much in such a quack-salve. In the end, though, despite reservations, I try it, willing servant that I am. I really *do* want to believe in a miracle. Twice a day I must rub the bitter ointment on my gums. If all goes according to prescription, a residue like beaten egg white will soon form in the mouth. The stuff is more bitter than aloe, and my teeth, still sparkling white thanks to the high calcium content of farm water, discolour to fungal black.

One morning in front of the mirror, when the first secretion stuck to tooth and cheek like masticated meringue, I was only too happy they had turned black and I called Jude excitedly. We both stared at the open crater of my mouth full of foam, I with only the remaining squint vision of my right eye.

Unexpectedly, I find myself in the midst of happy days. My runny stomach improves. As a result, my bum puts on a bit more cheek, and my wrists thicken so that my new watch almost stays on. If I measure my face with my hands, I can honestly say that it has filled out. It's simple: we are put together of courage and flesh. I still enjoy spleen strengthening congee of calf's liver, root vegetables and bitter leaves, and make sure that at night candles are lit as a sign of my newborn hope. During meditation I succeed in locating the source of my infection – the wandering plague cells in my blood – and manage to bundle it up and banish it from my body.

At night I lie awake with black balsamed gums, ma's big boy! Alert and full of plans. Maybe we should give up the house in Katoomba. As soon as I get my energy back I'll cook permanently at the shop again. Shane will be thrilled. I've already got a new sago pudding with citron and coconut milk in mind.

Will have to let Albert know he needn't bother any more. No; let him come. I'll buy new clothes. Also sleep with Liz if the chance arises, she so badly wants to. It will be safe: I grab all my chances, and take the right precautions. And talk to Shane about a second branch for me to manage. There's also the house in the city. Must discuss it with Jude. Now that I've been staying in Katoomba so long, I don't ever want to live in Jude's house again. Too close to the railway, the streets far too nasty. We must sell. Look for something else in the city, something small will do. And a weekender in the Blue Mountains. And when I'm really strong, I want to visit the farm. I'd like to hear the Karoo bustard cry out against the red sun one last time before night falls on the veld.

I use my new-found springiness to walk around everywhere with the long white stick from the blind society. The currawongs peer at me as I scatter their seed in the mornings. I decide not to tell Joseph and the gang what's the matter with me, ever – in reality there is nothing wrong with me, Konstant. They may as well think what they think anyway and be done with it.

After giving it some thought I call a taxi to Katoomba, to the furniture shop. The blankets on my bed are too heavy; a duvet will be both warm and light.

I wonder whether my eye will ever get better. The necrotic retina on the left eye has already loosened itself from the chorion: impulses no longer reach the brain. Opthalmologist Stephanie knows of cases where cyto has cleared up. A retina can even be transplanted and attached. Will send new impulses like lighting. Whose retina will I get? Elizabeth Taylor's, like hell! Azure eyes. My own mother won't recognise me. The taxi man probably thinks I'm crazy.

Here it is, thanks. People can't believe that I'm still able to stay on course. Able to outwit the darkness.

Money? He must take his fare from my wallet, won't rip me off. People have souls of gold. It always surprises me how deeply the traces of humanity lie in strangers, though few would believe me. This is where I have to get out.

Thanks a lot, mate. My voice remains strong, that's one thing.

Parking meter? Right here. My eye hurts today, what's the matter? How wide is the pavement? Here's the shop, here's the entrance. Smells middle-class inside, like newly-laid carpets. Bet you they stock a lot of ugly floral stuff here, don't know why they still design things like that. You'd swear everyone's blind. Double bed here. Must call an assistant. Why are they so slow today? Probably chatting somewhere at the back. Katoomba's a small place, here's somebody now.

You all right, mate?

Bloody hell, what kind of a question is that? I'll never get used to this lot. As Eybers said, it's precisely your own alienness that enables you to survive.

Goodday, yes, I need a good duvet, a hundred percent cotton, please. Without any synthetic fabric.

Nature's way for me, if ya know whad I mean. Hope they sell stuff like that here. Small towns have only plastic these days. Should rather have phoned, yet I felt so good. Tired now. Assistant probably guesses what I've got. She's walking too fast for me. Can't she think for herself, I don't know their shop as well as she does. Nice and soft, this one, feels warm.

Is it a queen size?

She's friendly, this old dear, wonder how long she's been selling duvets. She must know what my story is, even though my face has filled out again. One thing about the locals: they accept one and all.

I'll take this one, then.

Rather expensive, will have to check my bank balance. She'll have to call a taxi, please. I'm too tired now.

Thanks a million. Can you please . . .?

Oh, she's realised. Even carries the duvet to the taxi for me. People *are* kind. Must get to a toilet now, thought my diarrhoea was something of the past.

If the ointment hadn't worked, there would be no foam. There is foam, which means the ointment is working.

I latched onto the logic of the ointment unthinkingly, because I want to live, despite the fact that I have already begun making preparations for my departure. And yet, and yet. With the possibility of even the slightest bit of new hope, I let go of all the hard-won fruit of my preparations. Just like that. There's no redeeming salve for my lust for life. I still want to live, people, I really do. Joseph and Robert and Liz and Ava-Marie, do you now understand why I don't want to admit to the life-destroying pestilence that's taken hold of me? Please allow me to live in peace.

In time, I realise that it is no wonder-balm. Rather, it's a remedy that has healing powers, but exclusively for meditating Orientals, descended from generations of meditating ancestors from whom they have inherited the genes of patience, compassion and tolerance. They are initiates who can identify and pin down an intruder. Their bodies are perfectly mapped by the pricks of acupuncture needles. How could they possibly not register an intruder's footsteps? I, on the other hand, am a Westerner. I've taken antibiotics a few times in my life; right now I'm on DHPG. Animal fat clings to the walls of my guts. I hardly know where and what sort of thingies lurk about. My Western physician knows even less about this alien disease. And yet – see, hope never fades – did I not know that first tented night at the Wollondilly that an intruder had left a bloody trail too vile ever to regain my lost innocence? I will hope until my very last day, I will not betray hope.

I have to get up, something's wrong with my eye. Sticky egg-white foam. It's not supposed to bubble out like this. The prescription said nothing about foam in the eye. My left eye also began like this, every morning oozing a tiny bit more. I will definitely not use the ointment at the expense of the vision in my right eye. After all, that's a choice I've already made.

Must get to the mirror. Can hardly see a thing this morning, my eye is caked over like pink eye. Luckily I know the house, the doors. Here's the cupboard. Good thing Jude doesn't move the furniture around any more. My vision is returning a little. Where's Jude? I am not granted the peace that comes with being alive, but at least I am able to say it without bitterness. Stay where you are, Jude, I'll be okay. I'm not okay. Is my stomach upset again? It's just as bad as before. Did we eat something unsuitable yesterday? Apple sauce, it can't possibly be? Where's the ointment? On top of the fridge, its usual place. Won't use it again. It was a pipe-dream from the start. Must get the stuff out of the house. And rather continue my preparations. There's no going back now. I can't allow myself to be misled by life: that was the message of Cancell.

Rather prepare myself for Albert's arrival. Was it Shane or Jude who dropped some hurtful hint about me supposedly being too exhausted to collect my own brother at the airport? What exactly it was that made me choke on my tea, I can't recall. Once thing is certain though, both *are* well-meaning. Yet Jude can't control his planning mania, even when it comes to me and my family. Both he and Shane have, in their own ways, become sensitive to such remarks, and know they should leave me to make my own decisions about my own life. Not despite, but precisely *because* I can't even bath myself these days.

Albert will be in the arrivals hall within minutes. Will he know that he's the one who'll have to recognise me in this muggy cacophony of voices? Maybe this is what Shane or Jude were referring to. Thinking ahead, one of them realised that Albert's reunion would be a shock for him, no matter how it went. Now I understand a little of what was meant.

Here he is. The Wasserman voice. His fingertips touching my sleeve, my face. If I squint through my right eye, I can see he looks the same as ever. Fresh, farmboyish, shy. Does he still smell of youth? I smell my blood brother, my blood. Mine is mixed now. Maybe there're a few branches of curry bush in his pocket; maybe the baby cushion Ma's sent me will still smell of her hands.

Albert talks about her, about Pa, about his flight. It's the most obvious way to negotiate the stiffness after a long absence between loved ones.

So he holds me lightly on my arm, Jude at my blind side. Albert should be more excited than tired after the flight. I can feel he's strong from all the pure air, farm meat, he'll be able to handle the shock. How do I look to him? I so badly wanted to look my best. I'm wearing my best shirt, the one the colour of ripe wheat. I specially asked Shane to iron it two days ago. And to make sure everything goes well the day Albert arrives, I shaved the previous night. I undoubtedly leave beard stubble in the washbasin these days, just like Oupa Konstant in the olden days, he never rinsed the basin properly. My hair is nicely combed, my dry skin rubbed with sorbolene, teeth brushed, nails clean, I've done all I can.

That's how I prepared myself days in advance for the arrival of the envoy, the one sent to show the apple that's fallen off the family tree the compassion that is his due. My blood brother, Albert, privileges me with his visit. I'm glad that he experiences me as I am right away. Far gone, though at least not done for. Whether he saw me here or at the house in Katoomba, it's six of one and half a dozen of the other. That's lovely Liz's favourite expression. Albert may like her. I'm overjoyed that he has come, I suddenly feel cherished, and glad that I've prepared myself well by taking an extra Lomotil to hold my stomach back for the duration of the drive and the stay in the city.

Which reminds me, before we take the road to the Blue Mountains, I want to go to the deli in Oxford Street. Then we must collect my prescription of Lomotil, as well as the DHPG and the pentamidine. It should all have been put out together, ready to be loaded.

So here you are.

He nods, overwhelmed, answers without saying anything. We sit close to one another on the back seat of the car. My hand rests in his.

This way he'll feel the coldness that penetrates to the very bones of my hand. That may also shock, it's so unexpected. It might affect him even more than seeing my body that refuses to hold its food any more. I have become what he feels, there's not much of me left over.

You must open your suitcase and unpack all the stories of the farm, man. Did our old cat curl up in your case when you packed? I'll tell you a lot of my stories, not everything, I talk much less nowadays. I mostly occupy myself by living in my own body's space, that's the most comfortable. It's the designated place for me to yoke my thoughts and make them fit, two by two. That way they'll pull me forward without effort: strongly yet gently. Gently, Albert – if you know what I mean. They can't run wildly. I must forge on, straight ahead. If I can get it right in time, it will be a great help. Then my cold hands and my icy feet will be of no consequence.

This is where we stop.

Albert and I climb out of the car. Jude points out the Oxford Street deli to Albert. We're lucky to find parking nearby, seeing that it's so difficult for me to walk. The signs that days are coming to a close are as obvious as this.

It's lovely to walk on your arm in this street of grace where the physique of every pedestrian is weighed and measured with the most brutal of stares. This is the very pavement on which I also watched with sprung step and polished smile. And was watched. As a newcomer, you may notice nothing unusual here. And it's fitting to ask you whether you are ashamed of me. Your skinny brother on your arm. Two things are relevant here: firstly, that no one can blame you if you do feel embarrassed. And secondly, it is not unknown for pedestrians in this street to look upon people like me for what they are – without looking away.

I can smell we are close to the deli. My squint eye sees delicacies. Where is it? Here's the counter: a curve of glass, custom made, perfectly safe for the blind man's hand, like the Aga stove. She knows me, the old tannie. Will tell her this is my brother, fresh from my far-away country. She's a dear old accommodating tannie, unconditionally well-disposed towards me. Maybe there's a reason for it, it gets the till ringing. But I believe her heart is all sweetness. And her wrinkled hand smells of anchovy and of garlic remains under the nails.

What would we like?

All sorts of tasty treats so we can celebrate the coming of my brother to the weatherboard house in Katoomba. A jar of caviar, virgin olive oil from the first pressing, cheeses that run with ripeness, Belgian chocolate if you please, salami too, Filino, that's an especially good one. Everything of the best. Even though my constitution rejects all of these delights. I don't mind, I've already wintered the iciest nights.

Now we must move on to the Prince Henry Hospital in Little Bay. Under healthier circumstances, I'd have told you about the Bulgarian artist, Christo, who wrapped the coastal cliffs in fabric. Would've told you about it enthusiastically. Now I prefer to let it go. Let Shane or Jude tell you, if they can be bothered. I'm exhausted by the drive into the city and the excitement of your arrival, still, it feels good to lie against your shoulders in this warm car. The speed-bumps in the grounds of the Prince Henry used to annoy me, now they just cause me physical pain. Even though Jude tries to drive over them as carefully as possible.

In this brown-brick building ahead of us are people on beds in sterile rooms whom Jude sometimes sick-visits. Anecdotes, encouragements, pastries, and massages with diligent hand movements that make beads and bracelets tinkle, delight the deprived recipients. Jude has changed so much, Albert, I'll tell you about it. First we have to wait for Jude and Shane to sign for the small box of drugs dispatched on behalf of the life of Konstant Wasserman. That's what we are doing now. It took me so long to learn the art of waiting, I've perfected it. The difference is that now I know what I'm waiting for every time I wait.

We must get a move on, people, so we can be home before dark, otherwise it gets too late to warm me up. The fire in the kitchen must still be lit.

Jude will show Albert where the wood is kept and all that sort of thing. Albert is smart; he'll do a good job of helping to care for me. There's still something left over from last night's supper. We can warm it up.

Each day gives me enough time. When the day warms up and the bush's leafy carpet starts crackling, Albert carries my easy chair out onto the veranda. My feet, legs and hands drink in the warmth here, yet even so, they're getting too stiff for that too. Jude brings a blanket for my feet, or returns to the city to complete unfinished business. I don't ask about his comings and goings any more. It was only when he brought the results of my last blood test that my interest was aroused: my T-helper cells can't even be counted, they have thinned out so much. I hadn't expected it to happen as quickly as this. I'm sure they did their best.

There is something new to finish off every day. When my fingers discover hairy spider-legs on the bridge of my nose or in my ear holes, I let them be. For comfort, though, my skin must be massaged with sorbolene regularly. As Jude or Shane's hands work gently, I realise that the amnesia of the muscles of my calves and upper arms has set in. They no longer recognise their original functions. I make amends for it by way of an overview of my personal history. I've reached the languid days of my student years. I attempt to capture my life in a single succinct sentence so that I can savour it in the twinkling of an eye.

And only now do I discover that my father's outbursts of rage had another, second form, and this, too, I inherited from him. Destroying fire. Creative fire. It's the second kind that's relevant here:

I see Pa's lips as he kisses his daughters on the mouth, the curling of the fleshy inner lip on theirs. I see his strong forearm with its even growth of hair, so warm. And his open palm, roughened by labour on the farm. How it could fold and enclose, and how delicate its touch was too. I see his arm slip around my mother's waist and his hand touch the tanned skin of her back. I see too how Pa was able to prepare himself at night to ensure that he and Ma fitted into one another perfectly and with great joy. This I now see, so clearly: my own heat has been formed on Raster Wasserman's warm anvil. That's the way I was shod. I'm glad. I've done well with it.

It's always peaceful with Albert. He doesn't ask many questions. He gets nervous only when he has to see Jude and Shane off at the draughty front door. And doesn't yet realise his clumsiness in caring for my body. Instead, he fills my days well with his wood-chopping or bustling about in the kitchen. He prepares old-fashioned braised meat, or my mother's tomato stew, or milk noodles. And even malva pudding. For me to experience the taste, one last time. Jude tucks in along with us. But elsewhere in the house, where my vision no longer extends, he makes a rather scornful remark about my mother's meaty dishes in our vegetarian home. And: Konstant's become a little boy again. I hear what is not intended for me.

Jude experiences Albert's arrival as both a relief and a threat. So when he goes to the city, Albert takes the opportunity to show me photos of the farm. I look at them with my squint eye as he holds them up one by one.

His time for taking the photos was well chosen: in the Karoo, the light at sunset is sacred, and the drought less visible. And usually, at that time, you hear the bustards' last call: dokterrau, dokterrau, dokterrau.

There are Ma and Pa, before the camera on the lawn in front of the house, hands around one another's bodies. I peer at them intently. And in Jude's absence, I can freely say what I like: they look so sad, the two of them, each in their own way. Ma in the eyes, and Pa here, around his mouth. It would be good if they come to see me. I don't cry any more.

Jude returns from the city and rushes into the kitchen with a bunch of ericas, and, specially for me, a new choral piece dedicated to Romanian earthquake victims. Albert sits on the arm of my easy chair with his strong young arms around my shoulders. His body smells like that of my brother. There is also the warmth of the hearth and his lamb and green bean stew.

Still a little overheated by the car's heater, and now, encountering further heat, and with Albert so snug in the role of caregiver, Jude starts moaning that there's hardly any place for anyone else in the kitchen. But he soon modulates to his familiar, honey-smooth tones, and tells the day's tales. In one of the stories the name of K – whom by now I've virtually forgotten about – occurs. Clearly, Jude still has something of a life of his own. I'm glad about this. Later that night I ask whether he feels like massaging my feet, they need it badly. Albert leaves us to ourselves behind a closed door and enjoys a breather in front of the television.

Jude spreads a cloth on the floor, places the flask of oil next to it, and starts working on my feet. Muffled television voices seep through the chinks, and apart from this all I hear is the fire. The paper I hold up in my hand and my closed eyelids protect my eyes from the glare. I know Jude so well that I can even predict the sensation as his fingers move from one massage technique to the next. I don't need to see him any more. The day is done. It's been good. I have sat in the sun and eaten and soon I'll be asleep. Tomorrow I'll continue to gather in more of myself, until I fit neatly into a parcel, not to take anywhere, but to leave behind, with all its loose strings tied up.

My whole body is on edge. I'm due to go the city for the eye injection. Suddenly I'm unable to distinguish between my fear of the needle and my fear of the sting of death. I thought that I'd become accustomed to the dissonance of his voice, that it was something of the past even, but the prospect of bodily pain brings it back.

Albert accompanies me to the city, we agree beforehand that he won't be present during the administering of the injection. I sit next to him in the back of the car again. No one says anything during the journey. The road is rough on my sensitive body. Albert is amazed that I'm able to predict that we're almost there before we pull up under the covered parking at the Prince Alfred Hospital. As we stop, Shane is at my door. Jude must be somewhere else today.

It's stuffy here; the architect didn't have the vaguest idea of patients' needs. A waiting room needs windows, generous ones that open, even though most people here can't see very well any more. Everyone needs air. You'd also be able to smell the pine needles through open windows.

Poor Shane, she thinks she has to babble on to lessen my fear. Strange thing, fear. First I fear death, and now I can't devote a single moment to death worries. Now I'm afraid of the needle that has to go through my eye. And when that's done my first fear starts up again. It came so suddenly, I said to Albert, so strongly. I still wanted to do so much. How to explain the fear that eats away at me? I don't know. Surely it can't be a fear of the unknown, of what is going to happen to me, I've survived that so many times before. After Dr Stephanie has done with me today, and said goodbye, until the follow-up injection two weeks from now, I'll be as frightened again, this time by its familiarity.

The other thing that bothers me is the plastic chairs here. All too soon, your bottom becomes glued to them. Designers really don't have any idea. I wish Stephanie would call me now, she's such a special woman. Makes me think of Julie Andrews. The type Pa and Ma would like. Almost always wears red. Does she do it for the sake of her poor-sighted patients? People are surprised at what all I'm still able to see with old one-eye.

I just don't understand my fear. Shane reckons I shouldn't obsess about it: it's the same as my previous visits, I'm anxious I'll move my eye the moment Stephanie sticks the needle in. If that happens I lose my remaining squint vision. Must get myself ready now, it can't be much longer before I'm called. Shane's small hand, a hard old kitchen claw, on mine. Albert's on my knee. He's even more anxious than I am. Sorry, man, can't help you. You'll have to deal with it yourself. Too much of my own work to do. He's scared of my suffering, Shane says he says.

Must calm myself now: inhale that pure white air; take it through the shoulders, the clenched butt. The air in here is stale. Breathe out deeply, especially out. That's more important. Any anxiety could cause me to move my eye a fraction, just a fraction . . . All the nurses at this clinic are so good. Barbara and Barrie and that tiny old thing, Sweetiepie or whatever, the one who usually administers the drops to anaesthetise my eye against the pain. Must bring another chocolate cake for the three of them. Wasn't it Pa and Ma who always took benefactors a dozen green mealies or a piece of wet beef biltong wrapped in brown paper? How long will it still be? Surely my eye has sat it out long enough by now. There – Barbara is calling me.

Okay, here I go. Albert you wait here and be good. Poor thing, one moment dreaming away on the farm, and the next amongst the blind in the Prince Alfred. Don't have time for nervous wrecks. His sweaty hand made my knee sopping wet.

Here she is, now. Stephanie! Always calm. Her hair like a little girl's. I know Stephanie's theatre so well, once I'm lying on the operating table or whatever – why they call it a table, I'll never know – it's only that sharp overhead light, the heat of it, it's very uncomfortable.

Shane, hold my hand again, please. Shame, the first time my nails cut right into Shane's arm. Now I notice she only gives her hand. So everyone preserves himself. It's better that way. That's good, I'm ready.

The needle becomes a fishbone that pierces my flesh. Negative gearing, stop it, Konstant! Needlepoint. How many angels on it? Preserve me from the fine blade, the cleaving blade through the flesh of the eye, like oyster jelly, softest of all flesh. The flesh of my eye through which the needle *has* to go. The cornea and lens *must* be missed for it to reach behind to the hyaloid membrane. One fraction too low, or the minutest movement of the eye, and I lose my last bit of sight.

Okay, I'm ready. First elastoplast to keep my eyelids out of the way, then I freeze the apple of my eye, not my father's. Dead still, Billy Tell, if you blink, the arrow will pierce your eye. Believe like a child, stand firm like a mountain. All right, Stephanie: steady your specialist's hand. Don't shiver or shudder. Pierce accurately. You never dare show the stress of your profession. I'm ready, Stephanie. I believe my Lord and my God won't allow my eye to make the slightest tremble Shane grab me now it's coming flaming needle that comes it's coming have mercy on me seconds now seconds my eye lens can't move it's stone it stands like a mountain so firm my eye muscle sturdy as rock breathe gone heartstopsandstandsstiffasapokerrr

Sjoe, sjoe, Stephanie, it's done, another one down. A brave joke.

Can't see her now, my sight only returns in a little over an hour. I know that when everything is over her hand always lands warmly, never damply, on my forehead. Well done, loyal eye, slave of the syringe. Fight bravely to the end.

Dear Stephanie.

My dearest Konstant, she always says, her voice relieved and sherry mild after the moment of anxiety. You know I can only do it *with* you.

The yearning for life also present in her voice too. Her task is finished for now, her heart stays with me. Once again, her hart has escaped the hunt. Be off to pleasant pastures until fate brings you back to my table. How many injections are still to go?

There's a camaraderie between Stephanie and me. The success of the injections lies in the combination of her masterful technique and my control over the movement of my eye. Her self-assurance gives me faith; my desire to see amazes her.

I want to go, then realise Stephanie has something more to say to me. Is she crying?

Don't. What's up?

She sits next to me, her old self again, and starts explaining. She tells me that was my last injection. There's no need for me to come any more. It's not worth the trouble. The retina is coming loose. The cytomegalo virus can't be held in check any longer, it's progressed too far.

My dearest Konstant, I feel so much for you. She can't talk. No, there she comes again. She wants to add something.

You have fought so hard, Konstant. You have been an exceptional patient. You have inspired me with your rare spirit. Go well now, my dearest man, go well. She embraces me.

Stephanie, I say, Stephanie. I will never be ready. Stephanie, I say.

What does it feel like to be blind, Albert? You too saw like this once, don't you remember the membrane covering your eyes at birth, the blue veil over the eyes of a sleeping chick? Go to sleep, and when you wake up, open your eyes only slightly, then close the left one as tight as a possible and keep it like that while your right one remains ever so slightly open. Then with that screwed-up right eye, through the heavy fall of your eyelashes, look sharply to the right, and you'll see the way I see now: the edge of the kitchen table, the misty brown of the floorboards, the shadows of the walls, the dark exit of the kitchen, the darkness of the rooms further back.

Come and stand here in front of me, please, Albert. Let me hold onto your legs so that I don't even have to remember again what the colour was of the last flower I saw, so that I don't have to cry over the last words I've read. You're still so nice and warm, Albert. Do you remember how, one day, your eyes opened in your swollen baby head so that your life of looking and seeing and seeing again, amazed unto death, could begin? Without boundaries, so I also thought. From that first bright day of the beginning of my life and for all eternity I shall see, so I also thought. Why would the thought of blindness have cataracted my life then? I didn't even give the slightest thought to such a thing, I believed it could never happen to me.

I have to go to the toilet now, Albert.

Albert steers me so shyly, so delicately, by the arm. Afraid I'll break. My emaciated body. Sorry I can't talk to you about it more than I already do, Albert, I have so much I still want to do for myself before I die. I love you so much, my brother, you may as well put your arm strongly around my back. Remember how firmly Robert led me to the toilet the other day when he was here? How confidently I walked to the toilet in the crook of his arm?

What can still be tapped out of me? What do I still have to give back to the earth? Might have to get a commode when I'm no longer able to get up from bed. My bum, my bum, clapped out now: no more than skin, my two gluttonous cheeks – how you delighted under a caressing hand. My horny double cheeks, what chair could you not fill fully? What trouser seat, my billowing butt, could you not fill? Were you ever *not* stared at from behind, walking up a beach, my proud tail. You more than succeeded in your brief task. What's happened to you? Everything has been shitted out, my departed bum, your earthly remains await their final days on rusty chairs in the sewerage hall down below us in the garden, and if you show your face again it will be in my vegetable patch where you'll be dug into good soil to fertilise my fennel and basil, my pumpkins and green mint: two bums for a bushel of herbs.

I hear myself pouring out during the long sit, often in the day, sometimes also at night. Sitting is at least easier on this shiny-sat wooden plank. That's to say: if we were fated to sit on plastic, we'd have been delivered from our mothers complete with a plastic bag around the you-know-what. Born in plastic, despatched in plastic. Who was the clever dick who called that town Despatch?

No, I mustn't allow my brains to wander any more. White air, in deeply, hold it, hold tight, roll it up and despatch it, roll it into a bundle, let it go, far away, can't even see it any more. Breathe out, stale blue air out . . . Here I am. I escaped to this house in the Blue Mountains to laugh for the first time since cytomegalo got me, though it was never like before.

And it's not needed, my laugh has had its golden years. Always used it well, it helped me travel far, and everyone I met couldn't help but yield before it. I realise now that I had to come to this place where the people with open arms live, those who took me as I came. They are the ones for whom my laugh was intended.

All that keeps me here now is this wooden plank. I wish I could call it a day now.

When I'm done here, I'll sit on the back stoep. The birds can sing for me. There are so many of them, I don't really have to see them, they sing in colour. Not like the sparrows at the house in the city. I never felt at home there: the seagulls on the station platform made me feel too lonely. The Koori woman at the station entrance will not have to wonder about me any more. I won't go to the city again, my eye injections are done with.

When last did I produce a shapely brown banana, a feeling of contentment? Never forget it, you with the strong bodies who still unload yourselves by way of firm ones, it's not a right of the human body, but a peristaltic privilege. Consists mostly of water – I learnt that while still at school. Just water. Now I believe it. If only Ma could be here to hold me, to balance me on the potty, because it's hopeless, it is totally hopeless. My tears are running out of my behind. There's nothing left of me.

I won't be getting up from this bed again. This bed is a good place. I won't return to the kitchen or the veranda. The cushion on my easy chair will puff out soon enough. I hardly left a dent in it. I give the sun on the veranda back to the survivors. The merry birds won't miss me, I've said goodbye to them all.

Forward to my room that Jude has prepared for me. Soft the wooden walls, the straw-matted floor. My slippers patient for the last short journeys to the commode, tiny outhouse in the corner to the left. It fits perfectly there, without disturbing the symmetry. Shane has arranged everything on a cloth on my table, what material has she used? Let's feel it. That piece of mud-cloth, jute woven to imitate the rough soil of the earth. Pleasant to the touch. Now I'm able to stretch my hand out to all my last necessities. Not possessions. Here is the small stone hand-carved from slate, a touch object for the eyes of my fingers. Here's my bottle, straw stuck in its mouth so I won't spill. What's this? The holder with a fat candle.

I know where everything is. Now I see clearly that I need to grow old with a singular passion, one that will nurture me to my last day. It is the passion to prepare myself for death. That is what I've lived for.

Deloris phones. She says she's coming to Australia to say goodbye. She's flying out tonight and will be here tomorrow, in time. It's kind, but it's all the same to me.

A golden mist enters through the east window each glorious morning. I want Albert to bring me the telephone: I must give Pa and Ma a call. Where's he? That's right. Ring, Albert, ring, you'll know what the time is over there. I must tell them my room is made of wood, and it's good to be lying here. No more heavy blankets; I've got a duvet. I can feel the warm air through the window; I can hear the birds talking about this day. For the first time in my life, I'm not waiting any more. My time of waiting is finished: ahead the earth awaits, already turning its cold cheek. I must remember to tell Pa, so concerned about the good earth, that even I am returning, dust to dust, for him to pick up again. And Ma will be amazed at how quickly my body has aged. I'm old now. Never imagined I'd make such old bones before I die. That's it, yes, the call's gone through: it's a farm line.

Hi, Pa. Albert, move me up a bit, a cushion, yes, that's right, maybe another one. No, fine, Pa, just phoning to say goodbye, Pa. Ag, don't worry. Don't worry about coming over any more. Things are good as they are, everything's been said. It's over. I wish Pa could take me by the hand one more time to the field below the dam wall. That field with the freshly ploughed soil. If Pa could take me there at dusk, when the new dew is softening the sods. When the sky is getting darker, when the wild goose is calling his mate. I want to stand with Pa on the land and see how Pa bends down and scoops up some soil in Pa's hand and looks down at the rich black soil in

Pa's beautiful hand. I want to see how Pa grinds the clods finely and how Pa raises his hand and lets the dust fall from his fingers, and how Pa smells it. Will Pa hold me then so that I can also smell it? So that I can also smell the dust? Do I love Pa? I understand, Pa, I understand. I looked at myself in the mirror recently, when I could still see a little: does Pa know what I saw there? My skeleton looks just like Pa's. That's what I'll leave behind for Pa to inherit from me. Did you send biltong? Blesbok? Thanks, Pa, very . . . A prayer, Pa? Yes, that's fine. But don't pray around my skeleton, Pa. The pile of bones from Ma's womb won't be returning like this. Yes, Pa: pray to God for a blessing on my bleached bones, on what remains after my time of suffering. So that I'll never roam again to any foreign land, but will come to rest at last. My ashes will blow far from the Blue Mountains, Pa will see. I'll be everywhere, anywhere anyone wants to see me. My ashes will sift down onto the koppies for the dassies to nest in, for the dogs to roll in. That's how I'll return, Pa. Must say goodbye now, Pa, must still talk to Ma also. So goodbye, Pa, everything of the best, my Pa, everything of the very best.

Hello, Ma. No, stop, Ma, don't cry. Only makes it more difficult for Ma. I'm done, Ma, in my birthday suit and dead right. No, no, Ma, one can make a joke about anything. Ma's always been a bit of a joker. Yes, if Ma wants to, Ma can come and sit here, here on the riempie chair and hold my hand. My hand's cold. Yes, I know, Ma. Hey, does Ma think I don't know? No, Ma doesn't have to kiss me if Ma doesn't want to. Saliva is sterile, but it doesn't matter. I know Ma well enough. Just kiss me on the forehead. I can hear that Ma's grief over the first-born from her flesh is great. My dearest Ma. Ag no, what, don't cry like that. We'll all . . . again. It's okay. No, Albert made me some delicious stew. Ag, I don't eat any more, Ma. Just water, delicious cool water. If Ma wants to, yes, especially at night when I go to the toilet, then Ma can come and help. That's the worst for me. Now the commode's in my room, there's oil burning too. Ma knows: scented oil. Everyone is looking after me, my room is perfect, Ma, it's got an east window. Jude opens it every morning so the birds can come in. Feather blanket, yes, Ma. Nothing warms me any more. Albert is looking after me; he prepares the wood and keeps the fires going. Heater is on the whole day long. Hestertjie also wants to? Can't any more, Ma, I'm too tired now. No, don't worry: I know you all wanted to come. Everything has already been arranged, yes I appreciate it very much, Ma. No, that's really not necessary. Ma, mustn't feel bad about that now, and don't cry. Yes, my legs, yes, I remember how Ma always used to massage my legs. I can't any more, Ma, I'm too tired to talk to them. I remember Mirjampie and Tilla and Hestertjie. I won't be blind long enough to lose the memory of their pretty little faces. Ma, I'll die in time. Say goodbye now, Ma. Goodbye my Ma, my most beautiful Ma.

Albert, take the phone, I need, oh, here's the water. Want to be alone a while, please. I'm so tired now. No, it's okay; I've got enough pillows.

Miso soup?

Water, first some water. Wet my tongue, Shane, refresh me, your hand behind my head. Warm soup, not too hot. Won't eat again after this. Thanks, Shane. Enough, enough. All desire for food is gone. Shane, it's more important to touch you. That's how I want, that's how I will say goodbye to you. When I hold you, Shane, I smell that nutmeg scent of brown rice, cooked to a milky softness. You know of course how its lovely aromatic steam clears your nasal passages when you open the pressure cooker. Darling Shane, you knew I always watched your hand's handiwork, every carrot you cut so perfectly for me to look upon tastes of your walnut hands. I'll be gone soon, mate, you'll have to find a new friend. I know

you'll bump into him one day just as suddenly as the cry of the currawong breaks the silence. The child you want to give birth to will
inherit your own dark eyes. Perhaps you'll read something of me in
them, perhaps even taste a bit of me in our sago pudding with coconut and lemon. My sister you were. I've embraced you already.

Go now, Konstant, It's good for me that you go. I'll miss you;
I'll miss your food in the kitchen. You learnt so quickly, and then
you became more creative than me. I'm going to miss you for years
to come. You became my brother, I'm letting you go now. I set
you free because you want to go. It's your choice. After all's said
and done, it was still you who made the choice, not so, Konstant.
You never let anyone else choose for you. Do you still remember,
Konstant, do you still remember what you said to me: I'll hit you
so hard that your granny will mistake you for a duck. I'm getting
up from my seat here next to you, Konstant. I'm going now. I don't
want to cry in front of you, you are ready. Your face is beautiful to
me, your eyes kind, like candlelight. Goodnight, Konstant. Well
done, my mate, see ya, see ya.

Come in, Albert. Come, you're hesitating. Are you crying?
Hey, man, don't. You've become so beautiful to me, Albert. Have I
told you I now know that my family were like people I met in the
marketplace: greeted, chatted with for a while, enjoyed, suffered
pain with a little time - and then I had to move on, Albert. You'll go
back and tell, and you'll tolerate one another, all of you, everyone
just as he is.

Help me get onto the commode now, Albert. Faithful slippers.
That's right, thanks, Albert. Water too, bottle's there, you know
how. Water, I . . . I

. . . can't get my hand down any more Albert, take the bottle
the bot it's finished now, you may as well say, Albert. That way it
will become easier for you too. Finish off now. Tell me you're also

ready to leave me. Albert, man, I'm so glad you got here in time. Don't walk around with such a long face like a Greek widow any more. Be kind to yourself too, man, you've done everything well here. As best you could. It's over, give me a kiss, Albert, dearest little brother.

Now Jude. This is my last candle, the one next to my bed, it's your work, isn't it? You didn't want me to lie in the dark, looked after me like your own child. The care that you've given me has scooped so much life essence out of you too. I'm glad you wanted it so. After this you can rest sweetly, my Jude; you can fold your hands, rest your good head against something soft, let your hair down: there's nothing more to organise. My life's been packed away; the fired urn is ready for my ashes, placed in its niche. I don't want any music, no human voice, no stale words, you know, we've spoken about everything. I trust you, now. Everything will go okay. Everything is in its appointed place. You've done well; after this your burden will be feather-light, a milk-bush plume. I won't be there to miss you any more, you'll scarcely feel me. A puff of dust. Your feet can wander peacefully wherever you wish. I've finished calling. You never need to prick up your ears again, Jude, your finely shaped ears. I still smell your gorgeous body; its burnt olive oil was also given to me to enjoy for a while. I'm glad I could caress it once. Follow a fine path through the bush to your favourite tree, clasp your arms around its trunk, which listens, which wants to listen to you as you always listened to me. You know, Jude, you learnt from the trees how to listen. I was the creation of your brown hands for only a short time, and I know now that it was good for me too. The riddle unfolds only when, old and spent, we guess its answer. Go now, go. I know you won't cry. We said goodbye long ago. Go off to your trees. They're old, they're strong, they'll serve you with vigour. But before you go,

Jude, turn me onto my back. I can't stay in crouching lion position any longer. On my back, then, that's how I'll go, thanks, Jude.

Be gentle on yourself, Konstant. Gently now. Just like you breathed your first breath of life, so let your last living breath go. Gently now, gentle on yourself. It's over. Just gently, dearest, dearest Konstant.

I know, I can see my arrival now. My heart's still warm: only a little wandering around left here. Go now Jude, Jude, you were my loveliest Judy, go gently, go sweetly, my Jude.

Just your outline, just your . . . not talk any more, tongue swollen. Verbs don't fit my *I* any more, *I* am not to be found any more. More voices outside. The dog, wind? Comes in through the window, he's everywhere, windows everywhere. Who's that, what's talking? Ears go everything up deaf just Sha still left just shadowy around bed still, where bottle, where water? Heavy now. Gone, always gone. Must hand to forehead . . . Scratch, too heavy, fingers stumps. Can't even to cheeks, hollow now. Gone. Deeper down, heaviest of all. Feather blanket. Must get Ma to take it away, too heavy. Feathers so so full lead apples don't swing can't hand too heavy. Somebody extra here too, somebody? More people figures, too many here, too many outlines. People bodies weigh too heavy . . . a trembling image. It's a big body, hand. Somebody takes my hand. Voice in inside head. From far away, she. Hear her with inner ear. She she's so full, my hand in hers.

I see you, Deloris, I see you.

Sowhycomesofarsofardeljustoseemesleep.

Turn around. Okay like this, no, on side, turn around . . . on side plea on side . . . lef no right I more cushions one too many more or less sweeter sleep the sweet wind blows everything away, away inne dust trembling after after more after the dust there he is, there the mirage.

Nose running. Water. Out. It's not tears. Eyes don't just cry. Fluids will be last. Don't need again . . . to soil you, last pants-shit this. Hands whose? Is she still here? Whose hands? Careful, you lot, body shivering still, can't smell anything. Last thing had no smell. I just water, only water. Trembling now, mouth dry throat leathery. There's no more water lips suck up all wet gone. Terribly thirsty now, must drink more. Why doesn't anyone give water? Everyone so slow, where's water? Right here, me. Can nobody see dry tongue? Too worried about smell, drying up quickly, the smell dissipates, the smell nice here come to pool, arrived here, glow over peaceful waters where little boys play in sunny pools of golden glass, but quickly passed, away, everything washes away again, chosen the foggy way . . . So much mistiness here. There they are, little puffs of smoke, there they are in the mist, weak little breaths.

Going off now, last bit of warmth in toe in foot, away. All warm clapping little hands cold creeps up, running hard up running to heart, there's nothing more just cold fire at nose cold breath who are you? Cold breath, ice on my tongue iced everything, Pa's name? Gone everything unknown. See sounds. Take away the water, weaned. Hear faces. Whose are you, whose? Everything up in flames, everything together now small pile may as well set alight, whole life collected together: just a pile of sticks. Flames now, it's good like this. See them, hear them. Red sparks atop holy fire.

Breath short-short, rasp raaasp, ghuuu thereisntnothing nothing here nothing more all for naught blow out big breath out see him it's Oupa Konstant smells like white bread his hands so beautiful white what wind brings blow big wind, hey, oupa wind around my heart . . . last little bit last bi . . . warmth there lamp of the heart . . . oupa comes with glowing lamp red and right in just a tiny, tiny breath long out . . . blue breath out, everything out . . . all suff blown out, all suffering for ever. That's it! . . . there it is now . . . eye of the lamp is . . . is white light is white I see around . . . it's around, it surrounds me everywhere pure white

I

GLOSSARY

aai – exclamation of surprise, dismay, etc.

Al die veld is vrolik – reference to an Afrikaans song: the fields are all jolly, and by implication to the friendly way in which missionary work is conducted

amanzi – water (isiXhosa)

atjar – fruity chutney

* * *

baas – boss

baie – many or much

bakkie – pick-up truck

blesbok – a white-faced southern African antelope, often hunted for its meat

bobotie – traditional baked spicy mince-meat dish, topped with scrambled egg yolk, and bay leaves

boer – farmer, usually Afrikaans-speaking, sometimes derogatory

boertjie – diminutive of 'boer'; can be used derogatorily or in a friendly, familiar way

boeremeisie – farm girl

boerewors – traditional farmer's sausage made with beef and coriander bokkie – a small buck, also used as a pet name for a child or a lover

braai/ braaiing – barbecue(ing)

* * *

Clocktower ointment – a traditional ointment used for the treatment of skin diseases

congee – a type of rice soup or porridge

* * *

dagga – marijuana

dassie – a rock hyrax

Despatch – a small town in the Eastern Cape

dominee – minister, e.g. of the Dutch Reformed Church

dorp – town

* * *

Ek sal jou slaan dat jou ouma jou vir 'n eendvoël aansien – Afrikaans idiom meaning: to make someone see stars

Eybers –Elizabeth Eybers, an Afrikaans poet

* * *

FAK – Federation of Afrikaans Culture

frikkadel – a traditional baked meatball

* * *

gemsbok – oryx, a large antelope found in southern and east Africa

* * *

Hemel-en-Aarde – Heaven-and-Earth, a wine

hensoppers – from the English 'hands-uppers', originally used by the boers during the Anglo-Boer War to describe those who surrendered to the British

Hoe ry die Boere sit-sit-so – an Afrikaans song meaning: how jolly the farmers ride along

* * *

ja-nee – sure; indeed; oh, well!

japie – a yokel or simpleton

Jou Martie, jou liefie, die son sak weg – reference to an Afrikaans song: "my hartjie, my liefie, die son sak weg"/my darling my love the sun's goin' down

* * *

kardoes – paper bag

katel – old-fashioned steel bed

kleinbaas – little boss

kombu – (Japanese) edible kelp or
seaweed

Koori – Aboriginal person of
Australia

koppie – a hillock

kretek – Indonesian clove cigarette

* * *

"Let the candles burn" – English title
of an Afrikaans drama: "Laat die
kerse brand," by Gerhard Beukes

* * *

malva pudding – baked pudding over
which a sauce is poured

mastag – God almighty (exclamation)

mealie – corn

megaloshe – conflation of
"cytomegalo" virus and
"tokoloshe"

meid – young black woman
(derogatory)

mies(ies) – missus

muggies – small flying insects

* * *

olka bolka riebie stolka - a children's
rhyme recited when one has to
be picked from the group

omie – diminutive of oom, uncle

onnagata – (Japanese) female role
played by a man

Ontevrede – discontented (name of
farm)

oom – uncle, also used as a
respectful form of address for any
older man

Oom Sarel – a colloquial name for an
old-fashioned type of yellow cling
peach

oupa – grandfather

* * *

padkos – food to be eaten when on a
journey

papaya – paw-paw

pasella – a small bonus, a gift (isiZulu)

piesangs – bananas

Pula – rain (Setswana), also the
monetary unit of Botswana

* * *

riempie – long, thin piece of treated
leather

rondawel – a round thatched-roofed house

* * *

Saamstaan – Stand together (name of farm)

sangoma – witchdoctor (Nguni)

shek – a rolled cigarette

skollie – thug, gang member

skyf – a joint or zol

stoep – veranda

strooise - round thatched-roof houses in rural areas

* * *

tannie – aunt. Also used as a respectful form of address for any older woman.

tiekie – a coin (worth 2½ c) used during the time of the Union of South Africa

tjali – a shawl, often crocheted

tokoloshe – in African folklore, a mischievous and lascivious goblin or sprite

tjap – stamp

* * *

Valbazen – a brand of sheep's medicine

Valskop – False hill (name of a farm)

velskoen – hand-made leather shoe

Ver oor die diep blou see – Afrikaans song: far, far away, across the deep blue sea

voertsek – scram, a command used for dogs

Voortrekkers – Afrikaner youth movement, similar to the Boy Scouts

* * *

witblits – home-brewed brandy, literally 'white lightning'

zol – spliff